The Village Christmas Party

BOOKS BY SUE ROBERTS

SUE ROBERTS

The Village Christmas Party

bookouture

Published by Bookouture in 2024

An imprint of Storyfire Ltd.
Carmelite House
50 Victoria Embankment
London EC4Y 0DZ

www.bookouture.com

Storyfire Ltd's authorised representative in the EEA is Hachette Ireland
8 Castlecourt Centre
Castleknock Road
Castleknock
Dublin 15 D15 YF6A
Ireland

ISBN: 978-1-83525-352-6
eBook ISBN: 978-1-83525-351-9

For all of my readers who love the magic of Christmas.

PROLOGUE

I've always loved Christmas. It's such a magical time of year and I love everything about it, from cosy nights in front of the fire, to seeing family and friends. And, of course, it is the season of giving.

This year, as usual, I will be busy arranging the Christmas bash for the pensioners at the local community centre in the village. I have been ticking off my endless list and checking it twice, leaving nothing to chance, so I know that this year's party will be another huge success. The other wonderful volunteers and I will make sure of that, as we all hate the thought of anyone spending Christmas time alone.

This time of year always makes me think of my grandparents, fondly remembering the happy times I spent with them – it's one of the reasons I started volunteering after they passed.

One evening, I had sat with my grandmother on the window seat in her red-bricked Victorian house and looked at the white moon in the navy sky. The sky was studded with shimmering stars that evening and the dark streets illuminated softly by street lamps.

'Is that the North Star?' I asked my gran, pointing to the brightest star in the sky.

'Actually, Lauren, no it isn't,' she had told me. 'Many people think it is, but in fact the brightest star in the sky is called Sirius.'

'So is that the one the Wise Men followed to see the baby Jesus?' I asked her.

'It is.' She smiled.

I was six years old and had been practising for our school nativity, so I'd learned all about the Three Kings and baby Jesus.

'I wonder if baby Jesus liked his presents?' I asked.

'I'm sure he did.' She had smiled again. 'Everyone likes to receive presents, don't they?'

'Yes. What are frankincense and myrrh?' I'd asked.

My mum told me that from an early age I liked to ask a lot of questions.

'They were scented oils that people used as perfumes,' Gran explained. 'The giving of gifts at Christmas has carried on ever since, to celebrate and remember the birth of Jesus.'

'Those kings were very kind, weren't they? Walking all that way to bring the baby Jesus a special gift,' I said thoughtfully.

'They were, although he was a very important child. Probably the most important thing in life is to be kind and giving.' She had smiled down at me.

'Just like you, Grandma.'

I slid off the window seat and followed the scent of vanilla coming from the Christmas biscuits that were baking in the oven. Later, I had helped Gran to decorate the Christmas tree, hanging a snowman I had made in school, along with some foil snowflakes and a robin made from felt.

Of course, I was too young to remember the exact details of the conversation I had that evening, but my mother was to recount it to me twenty years later, when we were clearing out my grandmother's house after she had sadly passed away. I'd glanced out at the stars on a winter's evening from the very same window seat and Mum had told me tales that made the memories come flooding back.

Grandma Lily had taught me lots of things throughout her life, including how to make Christmas cookies, but what I will always remember her for is telling me that we should always be kind to people, especially those who don't have as much as we do.

It's something that has stayed with me throughout my life.

Kindness can go a long way.

ONE

'Here.' I slip some perfume and face cream samples into a bag for the elderly customer at the cosmetic counter at Bentham's Department Store.

'Don't tell the boss I have given you more than one sample,' I whisper, nodding towards a colleague who is standing a few feet away. We are frequently told not to give out too many free make-up samples, unless customers specifically request them, which I always think is a bit unfair. Especially as there are often loads left over after the Christmas rush that are usually pocketed by the staff.

'Ooh, thank you.' The pensioner in the grey woollen coat with a maroon scarf tucked inside looks delighted. 'I needed a little something extra for my daughter's present, these samples will go down a treat. Merry Christmas, love.'

'Merry Christmas,' I tell the lady, who, having forked out forty pounds on a face cream, I'd say deserves those freebies.

It's ten days before Christmas and the shoppers are out in force, many of them taking advantage of the Christmas wrapping service, which although it takes a little time, we have plenty of part-time staff over the holidays, mainly college students, assigned to such tasks.

It might not have been my lifelong ambition to work in a department store, but the look on customers' faces, especially at Christmas time for a service well done, always gives me a feeling of job satisfaction. Especially when I give them a makeover. I trained as a beauty therapist and still enjoy the buzz of working on the make-up counter in a large store, rather than a small salon.

Bentham's is what you might call an upmarket store, selling designer goods and luxury items, especially at this time of year when indulgent food hampers adorn the food hall that is always busy with shoppers looking for that extra special gift. The two upper floors accessed by a thick red carpeted staircase and solid dark-wood curved bannister gives the store an air of opulence and the staff – both male and female – wear black skirts or trousers and crisp white shirts. I wear my long, glossy brown hair in a tight bun and favour immaculate – though natural looking – make-up on my face but with a slash of red lipstick.

'Two hours until closing.' My colleague and friend Gemma glances at her watch. 'I don't think the first drink will touch the sides. Are you coming to the pub?'

She heads to a nearby counter, and coats her finger in a berry-coloured lipstick sample before sliding it across her lips.

'I might skip it, I've got too much to do,' I tell her, thinking about my never-ending to-do list.

'Aw, just one drink? It's the last Friday before Christmas, we always go to the pub,' she pleads.

I remind Gemma that we have in fact already had a Christmas night out the previous weekend, which she said she would rather not talk about. I'm not surprised really, as she drunkenly flirted with Mr Bentham's married son and somehow lost one of her shoes on the way home, before vomiting into a dustbin. It was a fun night though, dancing the night away at a local hotel, despite Gemma saying she doesn't recall much of it.

'I think a few of the others are going to the pub, I'm sure you won't miss me.' I smile. 'I've still got lots of wrapping to do and I'm busy tomorrow,' I tell her.

I also need to defrost the freezer to make space for a mountain of festive food. I need to make and freeze the mince pies for the pensioners' party when I have a spare minute too.

'You know your trouble, Lauren,' says Gemma, picking up her bag and sliding it across her shoulder. 'You've forgotten how to have fun. All work and no play make for a very dull girl.' She wags her finger at me.

I look at Gemma with her ready smile, always up for new and spontaneous experiences and sometimes wonder how we manage to be friends, as I love a schedule. I would be a ball of anxiety if I didn't know what was coming next.

'Well have a drink for me.' I smile but as she leaves I ask myself, have I really forgotten how to have fun? Maybe I will join the work gang for a drink. Surely one gin and tonic can't do any harm, can it? It is Christmas, after all.

I'm not sure if the shrieking sound is the noise from my alarm, or the ringing inside my head. I open one eye and slam the alarm on my phone so violently, it slides off the bedside table. Why didn't I just come home after work last night, instead of letting Gemma talk me into going to the pub, merely to prove to myself that I haven't forgotten how to have fun? I have so much to do that I can't believe I actually went out last night instead of sorting out my kitchen cupboards.

It was nice to feel the season's cheer though – the Greyhound pub was filled with Christmas revellers last night, the roaring log fire with the Christmas garland placed across the hearth giving it a cosy, festive feel that felt so welcoming. There was such a jovial atmosphere that one drink quickly turned into a few. Definitely the atmosphere I want for the pensioners' lunch – but maybe with less drinking!

I can't deny I had a good time, and a bloke who looked a bit like Ryan Gosling in a certain light smiled at me from across the bar but I don't have the time for romance, my life is busy enough.

I can't believe how irresponsible I was, knowing I must go to work today. I ease my way out of bed and into a cool shower, before glugging down a strong coffee. Caffeinated today, rather than my usual decaff or herbal. I need the stuff.

Finishing my coffee and a bowl of porridge with blueberries, I look at my list of chores on the fridge, annoyed that last night's present wrapping and mince pie making never took place. Not to mention writing and posting cards to the neighbours in the little cul-de-sac where I live.

I know it isn't fashionable to send Christmas cards, but a lot of my neighbours are elderly and I know that they appreciate them. Plus, they are always cards that support a charity and are made from recycled paper. I'm cross that the mince pie making session has gone out of the window though.

Gemma laughs at me for making my own pies when the supermarket ones are so good these days, but it's a little bit of a tradition, and something that reminds me of my childhood, making them with my gran. The spicy smell of the pies baking transports me right back to those days.

And they go down so well at the Christmas lunch at the local community centre that I really look forward to planning and preparing for. I take comfort in the fact that even if the pensioners spend the actual day without company, they will at least enjoy a lovely meal and a gift on Christmas Eve, which I know they truly appreciate.

I have half an hour before I need to leave for work, so I sit at my smart grey marble-topped dining table – not real marble, but you would never know – and write out cards to the neighbours. Some of the younger residents in the street don't bother with Christmas cards, but I like to include them all the same. It's hard for me to imagine this time of year without a string of cards displayed along a wall in a warm and cosy lounge.

My parents moved into this house, that was once my grand-parents', having always loved the house with the high ceilings and stained-glass windows. After their divorce – Dad lives with someone else now, and Mum is in a ground floor apartment and has made lots of new friends – I now live here alone. Both my parents have great pensions, so live in locations that suit them both, Mum preferring to be in the town centre. My parents told me that the house would be my inheritance anyway, so why not have it sooner rather than later? The spare rooms are always made up if they want to stay though, which works well for all of us.

Initially, with my parents' blessing, I thought of selling the house and buying a brand-new build a mile away close to the river, but decided against it. This is a beautiful house that simply needed some modernising, although I have been careful to keep its original features, that include cast-iron fireplaces and the stained-glass windows.

I can still picture the green artificial tree from my childhood threaded with multicoloured lights and chocolates in shim-mering purple foil hanging from the branches. Mum was good about letting my friends stay over, and we would sit and watch television, munching chocolates before going to bed and sneaking teenage magazines upstairs to read by torchlight. We used to giggle at the problem pages, and I remember spending weeks wondering whether Mary from Macclesfield ever did sleep with her boyfriend, even though the agony aunt advised her not to.

I occasionally wonder whether I will ever have a child of my own to make Christmas memories with, but I am coming up for thirty-three and I still haven't met the one. And truthfully? I'm not sure it matters. I won't settle for anyone less than my soul-mate, so if that means spending the rest of my life alone, so be it. Whatever happens, Christmas will always be my favourite season and I will never forget the first year I got involved with the pensioners' Christmas party. It showed me the true meaning of Christmas.

I grab the little boxes of handmade shortbread I made a few days earlier and drop them off at the elderly neighbours', along with the cards, before I head off to work, and they are thrilled with them as they always are. Last year I made vanilla fudge and my neighbour Eileen shed a tear when I handed it over, as it was the first year without her husband. She told me he would be mad that he had missed out as fudge was his absolute favourite. Eileen is really looking forward to Christmas dinner at the centre this year, and was thrilled to be asked to attend.

I'm about to climb into my car when I receive a text message from one of the other volunteers at the centre, asking if we need any more decorations for the Christmas lunch. I tap out a reply, suggesting maybe some balloons as we still have the table deco-rations and Merry Christmas banners from last year. She sends a thumbs up emoji and I tell her I will call her tomorrow.

Sue began volunteering after taking early retirement, although she admitted that retirement wasn't all that it was cracked up to be. She had been on three cruises with her husband, Barry, and travelled to Australia, before trying golf and yoga. At sixty-three, Sue said she wasn't ready for daytime television and crosswords, so took up Zumba classes and began volunteering at the centre, and enjoys every minute. Her husband found his thing in golf and plays regularly, but still joins Sue in volunteering at the centre occasionally, especially around Christmas time.

Heading into the town centre, a steady drizzle falls from the sky, but the lights from the shops lift the greyness, the shimmering tree at the centre of the town square standing proud. Gold foil angels playing trumpets are threaded across the main street, along with red and silver trees and a large inflatable Santa is suspended from the rooftop of the council office. A grotto across the square, complete with reindeer, has a steady line of excited children, despite the rain.

One thing the council in the village of Fellview in the Lake District never scrimps on is Christmas – even though the residents frequently complain of potholes in the roads and untended trees that spread their roots into their gardens. Christmas has always been a joyous time in Fellview though, where hostilities between residents and council officials seem to stall during the season of goodwill.

Last year, a well-known boy band from the late nineties switched on the Christmas lights and danced around a stage that had been erected especially. Most of the teenagers in the crowd had no idea who they were, which made me feel ancient. So did watching my teen hero hide his balding head beneath a cap as he sang one of their massive hits from over two decades ago. It was a stark reminder of how quickly the years pass by, but I try not to dwell on it. This year, a bloke from *Only Fools and Horses* is doing the honours of switching the lights on, so at least the older population will be happy.

Arriving home after work, I kick off my shoes and give my feet a little rub, before pouring myself a glass of red wine. I only ever have one glass during the week, a little treat at the end of the day, sometimes in a scented bubble bath, sometimes with my dinner.

'We wish you a merry Christmas.' The strains of children's voices singing a Christmas carol on the doorstep rings through the air, so I head to a tin where I keep some coins. Two rosy-cheeked children, accompanied by their parents, smile as I push a pound coin into the palms of each of their hands. I wonder briefly whether carol singers will soon become a thing of the past in an ever-growing cashless society, unless they start carrying card readers around with them, with householders tapping their cards against them. What an alarming thought.

'Would you like some home-made shortbread?' I ask the parents, the two kids and Mum wearing matching red bobble hats, thinking of how much I have left, and they eagerly accept.

'Ooh, yes, please, that will go down well later with a hot chocolate,' says the guy, rubbing his hands together, his cold breath in the air. 'Thanks very much.'

After the carol singers have left, I open the fridge and glance at the two meals in boxes, one bearing a sticker telling me it contains a chicken curry, the other a veggie lasagne, both home-made. I enjoy cooking and swore I would never live off takeaways when I became single, so on my days off I batch cook, or make enough of an evening meal to freeze an extra portion.

My ex would have been happy to exist on takeaways and, when he left, I binned all the menus from the kitchen drawer. He would eat, drink, and spend money on just about anything other than our future. When he spent over a thousand pounds on a mountain bike that barely saw the light of day and just sat in the shed, I thought maybe our priorities were a little different. He was so handsome and funny that I probably stayed with him far longer than I should have done really. I still smile when I think of some of his witty one-liners, but I guess good looks and wit were never going to be enough if he wasn't prepared to commit to our future. I've been single for eighteen months now, and doing just fine.

I change into sweatpants and curl up on the sofa, sipping my red wine, when I hear the sound of the cat flap opening.

'Hi, Tony.' Tony leaps up onto the sofa beside me, purring loudly, bringing the scent of the crisp winter evening with him.

'What have you been up to today then?' I stroke him as he

climbs onto my knee, almost knocking my wine from my hand. He miaows then and settles down next to me when I show him to his place, a square of sofa covered with a fleecy blanket. At least he hasn't brought me a present in the form of a mouse or a bird this evening. I almost passed out the first time he brought a bird through the flap, and dropped the poor thing, that I thought was dead, at my feet. The bird, clearly only stunned, then proceeded to flap its wings and cause mayhem in my lounge, with Tony in hot pursuit, before I captured it. I did wonder whether Tony – named after Tony the Tiger on the Frosties cereal box, as he's a stripy tabby – realised how much he'd upset me, as he has never brought anything alive through the cat flap again, thank goodness.

I catch up on a couple of episodes of *Bake Off*, and add ingredients for the red velvet cake that was made on the show to the list on my phone before I head to bed. It looks amazing and I really must give it a go.

Although having missed the mince pie baking, I'm running a little behind on my schedule. Very unusual for me, but I'm sure it will all be fine.

TWO

The store is busy once more the following morning, especially the beauty hall. A group of young women are browsing brightly coloured eyeshadows, some with extra sparkle, probably in anticipation of Christmas parties. A free sample of a moisturising cream on special offer is also helping sales along nicely.

'What's so good about this cream then?' A woman turns a jar over, and examines the contents. 'And what exactly is hyaluronic acid? Surely that can't be right, putting acid on your face.' She grimaces.

'I'm sure it's perfectly safe,' I say with a beaming smile, even though I'm not exactly sure myself. 'It's supposed to plump out lines, and give the skin a more youthful appearance,' I add, sounding more confident than I am.

'Hmm,' says the woman looking doubtful, before placing the cream back down. 'My mum is coming up for eighty and she has the most beautiful skin, and she used a cheap cold cream from the chemist for decades,' she tells me. 'She was gutted when they discontinued it, so I thought I'd buy her a new one. Never mind, maybe I will buy her a new dressing gown instead,' she says, but not before dipping her fingers into the sample jar and rubbing it into her hands. She wanders off towards the clothes department then, leaving me googling hyaluronic acid which it turns out is perfectly safe.

I'm thinking about the Christmas party at the community centre, and wondering if I ought to add a little extra gift for the pensioners? There are drawers full of scent and make-up samples, so I'm sure the store manager won't mind. And how lovely it would be for them, alongside the box of fancy chocolates they usually get inside a little goodie bag. I can't wait to see their happy faces when we serve them lunch and hand out presents.

'I'll text you,' I hear a good-looking bloke in gym gear say as he hands Gemma her phone back, before heading towards the door. I also notice his wedding ring as he does so. I vaguely recognise him from the pub, but I can't be certain as everything was a bit of a blur after the third gin. Gemma slides her phone back into her pocket before serving a young man holding some tartan slippers in a box, probably a present for his dad.

I don't have time to dwell on the married bloke though as a mum and daughter head to my counter, the mum asking for some advice about a foundation. I direct her to a chair at a make-up station to try out some samples.

'I never used to be this pale,' says the mum. 'Everything fades when you get older.' She sighs.

'Nonsense, you have lovely eyes,' I tell her and mean it. They are a rich brown. 'And great eyelids. Not hooded at all, which is unusual as you get older.'

'Oh, thanks.' She smiles.

'And don't worry, we can look at fixing any paleness you're unhappy with using the correct colour foundation,' I tell her.

'Oh lovely, I can't wait to see you work your magic,' she says excitedly. 'But don't worry, I'm not expecting miracles.'

Having selected a suitable shade of foundation and applying it to her face, she selects a bronze-coloured eyeshadow.

After a swirl of mascara and a slick of caramel lip gloss, I pass her the mirror and she is delighted with the results.

'How lovely, is that really me?' She smiles, clearly pleased. 'I should come here every week.'

'Well, these products suit your colouring. I'm sure you will do just fine applying them yourself, with a little practice,' I reassure her.

'Thank you so much.' She can't resist taking another look at herself in the mirror and smiling.

'That was just the tonic,' the daughter whispers to me. 'Mum's been a bit down in the dumps lately, since her brother passed away. We're off to the theatre now. Mum looks fantastic, I can't thank you enough.'

'Happy to help.' As the daughter hands over her card and pays for the make-up items I slip a couple of free samples into her bag.

Watching the daughter thread her arm through her mum's and head off, the mum still smiling broadly, I think of my relationship with my own mum.

Mum has never been one for the girlie shopping and lunch thing, preferring to catch up at the green café for an oatmeal decaff, or at the local food bank where she volunteers. Occasionally, we will take a beach walk to look for driftwood that she fashions into all manner of things and sometimes sells to shops. I must admit it would be lovely to have a spa day together, lounging around and chatting in between some beauty treatments and sipping a glass of something, but that isn't really Mum's thing. Still, we are very close, and I have happy memories as a child, doing lots of family stuff, before she and Dad broke up.

Mum almost has a heart attack every time she calls in to Bentham's to say hi, wondering how people can spend money on such luxuries, including some fancy Christmas crackers with an eye-watering hundred-pound price tag.

'What's inside?' she had asked last time she was in the shop as she examined the box. 'Gold jewellery?'

'No, but there is a very expensive bottle opener. Oh, and a pair of nice cufflinks. None of your plastic frogs in there.'

'I think I can live without those,' she had said, placing them down and shaking her head. 'And who would I give the cufflinks to? Maybe I will have a go at making my own crackers this year.'

'You don't need to do that, Mum. I'll buy some good crackers, although maybe not quite so expensive,' I reassure her.

Mum and Dad separated six years ago and, if I'm honest, I think towards the end of the marriage Dad got a bit fed up with getting a lecture every time he bought a new shirt instead of buying one from a charity shop. Not to mention being dragged to protests about the destruction of the planet. When Mum glanced through the window of a local restaurant and caught him furtively eating steak and chips, you would have thought poor Dad was single-handedly responsible for the hole in the ozone layer. He told her he was sick of lentil stew and sleeping in recycled fabric bed sheets that felt like sleeping on a kitchen scourer and brought him out in a rash.

Looking back, I think the public row was the beginning of the end for them. Apparently, the poor waitress stood open-mouthed, unsure what to do with the impressive-looking ice cream sundae she was about to deposit at Dad's table, that he told Mum was made with 'proper milk and not that soya shite'.

Thankfully, I enjoy a pretty good relationship with both of my parents, and even though they can be in the same room together, I can't imagine they will ever really see eye to eye, a fact they have come to accept.

Saying goodnight to everyone at the end of my shift, I head to the local Sainsbury's to buy the ingredients I need for the red velvet cake from *Bake Off*. I do sometimes like to bake a traditional Christmas cake, but with Christmas puddings already sorted, I do like to have an option for people who don't want an alcohol-soaked dessert, so might decorate the red velvet cake with Christmas cake toppers instead.

I fall into step with Gemma as we leave the store and into the twinkling lights of the high street. Gemma keeps glancing at her watch, I can't help noticing.

'Do you have to be somewhere?' I ask her.

'What? Oh yes, I'm meeting someone in the pub at eight,' she says, not giving much away.

Gemma is a good friend and we have no secrets. Usually.

'Who are you meeting?' I ask as we walk.

'Some bloke I met. I wasn't going to say anything until I know how the date goes,' she says casually.

'It wouldn't by any chance be the bloke you were talking to at the shop, would it?'

We have stopped outside Sainsbury's.

'Yes, as it happens.' She smooths down her hair, something she always does when she's nervous.

'The one wearing the wedding ring?' I raise an eyebrow.

'Oh, Lauren, don't judge me, please.' She sighs. 'He just seems nice. It's a long time since I've been attracted to anyone.' She looks down at the pavement.

'Wait, you think I'm judging you?' I tell her. 'That's not it at all. How about I'm a little concerned about you, that's all. Is he at least separated?'

'He says so, yes, although only recently. I've served him a few times now, and he seems genuine enough,' she says, meeting my eyes.

'Right.'

'Right what?' asks Gemma.

'I was just wondering why he still wears his wedding ring if he is separated?' I press.

I know she doesn't want to hear it, but she's my best friend and I do not want her getting hurt, or messed around by anyone.

'I don't know! Anyway, the truth is I'm getting a bit fed up staying in on a Saturday evening alone,' she huffs. 'I know that we go out sometimes' – she holds her hands up – 'so no offence, but I just want to have a little fun, that's all.'

'This is the second time you have told me I'm boring.' I stick my nose in the air.

'What? When have I ever said that?' She looks aghast.

'When you dragged me out for drinks after work yesterday. It messed up my baking session, not to mention my ice-cold shower. Oh gosh, that does sound really boring, doesn't it?'

We both burst out laughing.

'Yes. Do you tell people you can't go out because you are washing your hair? And as for a cold shower, in this weather, really?' She gives a little shiver.

'The scientific benefits are well proven. Cold water therapy releases hundreds of endorphins that can set you up for the day,' I inform her.

'So can a bacon sandwich and a mug of tea and I know what I would rather have.'

I hope I haven't become boring lately, although I did turn down a date from a guy I met at a pub recently, as I wanted to spend the evening cleaning the oven after a cake mix had spilled over. I simply could not leave it any longer, the fact I hadn't had time to do it before heading to work had already stressed me out. I find ironing quite therapeutic too. And, let's be honest, who doesn't love a list that can be ticked off with satisfaction once a task has been completed?

I don't turn down dates with female friends though, so maybe I just can't be bothered with men. At this point in my life, at least.

'Each to their own, I guess. I really am just concerned about you, that's all,' I tell Gemma softly. 'What kind of a friend would I be if I wasn't? Let's hope it's a real separation and he doesn't go back to his wife.'

'I promise to be careful. I'll be off like a shot if he's lying about his marital status, don't you worry,' she assures me.

'Good, because I don't want you to be implicated in someone's divorce proceedings.'

'I know, and I am grateful for your concern, really I am.' She touches me lightly on the arm as we head towards the supermarket. 'Anyway, what are you buying from here?' she asks, changing the subject as we step through the sliding doors at the entrance.

'Ingredients for a red velvet cake. You?'

'A bottle of gin.'

We look at each other and burst out laughing again.

'I think my evening may just be a little more exciting than yours,' she teases.

'You may be right... Just be careful.' I sigh once more.

'I will,' she reassures me, but I get a feeling she will not heed a single word I say.

I love Gemma, but we are so different. I couldn't be involved with someone in such a complicated situation.

THREE

There are Christmas carols playing on Alexa as I fold and beat the cake, the tempting chocolate aroma filling my nostrils.

Later having decorated it with a rich cream cheese frosting, I am tempted to cut into it and enjoy a huge slice, but of course I don't. This one is a trial run for the pensioners' party, which will be offered along with the usual mince pies that will take me no time to rustle up. The staff at work can enjoy this one.

I sing along to the Christmas songs, my voice filling the air, when I hear a tap on the front door. It's Eileen, my neighbour.

'Was that you singing?' she asks as I invite her inside.

'What? No, the radio I think, although I was singing along to it.'

I'd been singing along to 'By the Rivers of Babylon' by Boney M., one of my favourite songs.

'I think it was definitely you I heard; you have a lovely voice,' she says kindly.

'Thanks. I do enjoy singing, but usually when I think no one is listening,' I tell her.

'I'd be singing everywhere if I had a good voice, there would be no stopping me.' She grins. 'You shouldn't hide your light under a bushel. Anyway, I only popped in to ask if you fancy coming for tea tomorrow? I've made a beef casserole that will be even nicer by tomorrow, and there is far too much for me. I'll pop some dumplings on before I serve it up.'

Eileen, pretty and with clear grey eyes, waits patiently for an answer as I mentally go through all the things I have planned for tomorrow. I've volunteered to work an extra hour to revamp a Christmas display at work, before visiting one of the older ladies from the centre who has recently had a fall, and taking her some flowers. Later, I will be heading into Grizedale Forest for a moon bathing experience with a group of women.

'Oh, Eileen, that does sound tempting, and it's years since I've eaten dumplings, but I have a lot on tomorrow evening, and won't be home until after nine, I'm afraid.'

Eileen's face falls for a second, before she musters a smile.

'Oh, don't worry, love, I just thought I would offer. I can freeze the casserole. Unless I give half to you, and you can have it another time?' she offers.

'Thanks, Eileen, I really appreciate it. Would you like a cup of tea?' I suggest, feeling bad about not taking her up on her invite.

'I won't actually, love, there's a crime drama about to start that I've been following. Right, I'll be off then.'

'Okay, see you soon. Enjoy your programme.'

A couple of hours later, I consider knocking with a slice of cake or a mince pie for Eileen, but think it may be a little late, so I will offer her something tomorrow.

I settle down with a glass of wine and think about Gemma's date. I hope her evening is going well, and that the newly separated guy from the shop is the real deal. She deserves to be treated well and have a bit of a good time, as she's had a tough time of it lately, after losing her dad, who she was really close to. It made me think of my own dad, and having to face the fact that our parents won't be around forever, which is a harsh reality to face.

Glancing out of the window, the lamp from the lounge is illuminating the front lawn, and I gasp when Tony leaps onto the window ledge and stares in. The frosty air bites as I open the patio door and let him inside.

'Not staying out tonight then?' I ask and he mews as he heads straight for the log burner, his basket lined with a thick tartan blanket.

'Although I can't say I blame you,' I say and he responds with purrs, before he curls up in front of the fire.

Sitting here alone, I briefly think of something that has been bothering me, before taking a sip of my wine and pushing it to the back of my mind. Besides, I only noticed it last week, or was it the week before? It's hard to keep track at this time of year as the days seem to merge into one. Anyway, it's Christmas Day in just over a week, so I will get things checked out in January with the doctor. Right now, there are far too many things that need doing. First on the list is booking in an appointment to have my curtains steam cleaned before Christmas.

In the kitchen, I reach for a tall latte glass and notice a nearby champagne flute that looks as though it could do with another polish. I add the task to my list, as I want all the glasses sparkling before the party season arrives.

'So how was your date?'

We're sipping coffee on a break at work, in the staffroom, a beige rectangle of a room that has none of the opulence of the rest of the store.

'Okay,' says Gemma, not giving much away.

'Only okay?'

'Yeah. It's strange that Joe, that's his name, is always nice in the shop, funny too.' She cups her drink and stares ahead.

'And?'

'So I thought he would be like that on the date, but he hardly said two words.' She takes a sip of her coffee and tells me off for bringing the red velvet cake in to work, asking me how on earth she is supposed to resist. 'In fact,' she continues, giving in and cutting herself a small slice, 'he seemed more interested in going back to my place than having any sort of a conversation.' She sighs. 'Which was a complete turn-off.'

'Oh, Gem, I'm sorry it wasn't the evening you expected it to be.'

I'm fuming with the selfish sod, who clearly had nothing more on his mind than a one-night stand.

'And I think you're right about him not being as separated as he claimed he was,' she continues. 'In fact, I know you are right.'

She takes a bite of the cake and makes an appreciative noise.

'And you know that for a fact?' I ask her, dreading what is coming next.

'Unfortunately, yes,' she says, licking cream cheese frosting from her fingers.

'So, what happened?' I ask.

'Well, we drove to this country pub, in the middle of nowhere,' she says, wiping her fingers with a napkin. 'And there we were sat in front of a gorgeous roaring fire enjoying a drink, him taking quite an interest in my flat, and suggesting we go there.'

'The cheek.'

'I know. I thought we would at least chat about something, his job, plans for Christmas, the cost of living, anything, but no. I was going to bail out and send you a text asking you to call me.'

'Go on.' I can't believe the nerve of the man.

'Well, we were just chatting when all of a sudden he looked like he'd seen a ghost.' She reins herself in from having another slice of cake. 'He literally covered his face with a menu, as he swiftly made his way outside.' She shakes her head.

'You're joking, what was that all about?' I ask, shocked.

'I stormed outside and asked him what the hell was going on, and he told me his wife's friend had just walked into the pub.' She sighs. 'I asked him why that was a problem if he was separated? He stammered a bit when he finally replied. I think his exact words were, "Well, we're not officially, but there's nothing between us anymore." Even then, he only owned up after I threatened to go inside and ask his wife's friend.'

'So, what did you do?' I ask, still mad on my friend's behalf.

'I told him to get stuffed, went back inside, and ordered myself another drink before ordering a taxi home.'

'Oh, Gemma, I'm so sorry. It was good that you found out early on though,' I try to reassure her.

'Yep, I agree. It's a shame but as you said, there's no way I'm going to be the other woman in a marriage break-up.' She wipes crumbs from her mouth. 'Don't worry, I'm fine.'

She reminds me then about the gingerbread house decorating competition the day after tomorrow, and how she is looking forward to it.

'Oh, me too, I can't wait.'

Every year, in the Fellview Community Centre across town, a competition takes place that involves decorating gingerbread houses, having a chat and drinking mulled wine to the strains of Christmas songs in the background.

It started off with half a dozen of us, hosted by a lady from the local bakery, and is now a bookable event, with over fifty people attending last year. We meet people from the village and beyond and have a brilliant evening, filled with fun and laughter, especially at the sight of some of the gingerbread houses, but it is all in good spirit. There is an overall winner who wins a baking masterclass and lots of smaller raffle prizes up for grabs.

'I wouldn't miss it. It always puts me in the mood for Christmas.' I smile even thinking about it, the Christmas carols in the background, the sound of laughter ringing around the room, the fizz of bubbles hitting my tongue.

'It's a shame it's mainly women though,' moans Gemma. 'Apart from that old guy at the next table last year.'

'Which one? I think there were at least two blokes.'

'The one with the very red face and the white beard, who looked a bit like Santa,' Gemma reminds me.

'Oh yes, I remember him.' I smile. 'Well you never know who will turn up this year, the event gets bigger every Christmas. And maybe it was the real Santa.' I wink.

Gemma has never been good with her own company and hates not having a boyfriend, but it's not so easy to meet someone in a small village, which is why she often meets blokes in the pubs in our closest town, or in work. She was with someone from high school but when he headed off for university in Newcastle, they went their separate ways. I've told her multiple times that it's better to be alone than with the wrong person, but I guess we are all different. I'm quite happy with Tony the Tiger in my life. For now, at least. Life is so much simpler this way.

FOUR

'Someone got arrested?' I ask in shock, unable to believe what I am hearing.

'Yes, banged up with a one-inch mattress that was no better than my yoga mat by all accounts,' Mum tells me. 'It's a good job it was one of the younger protestors, as I am not sure my back could take that. Maybe that's why the young policeman didn't pick on me,' she reasons.

'Oh, Mum, I do worry about you. And I'm not sure how much these protests actually achieve.' I sigh. 'Have you thought about maybe posting some leaflets through doors, or something similar? Maybe I could help you put something together?'

'Hmm. Worth a thought, maybe. Anyway, the real reason I'm calling is to ask if I can come over for a shower? Mine is on the blink at the flat. A plumber is coming out tomorrow morning,' she informs me.

'Of course, Mum. But I'll be leaving for work in exactly twenty minutes,' I say, glancing at my watch. 'So you may need to call a cab,' I tell her, feeling a little torn. 'I'll pay for your taxi though.'

'I'm not short of money, love, but thanks anyway,' says Mum. Never one to take a freebie from anyone, even me.

I truly hope this protesting doesn't get out of hand. She's already expressed her disgust at the amount of money the council have spent on the town centre Christmas decorations, especially the tree, when 'that money could have gone straight to the homeless shelter or the women's refuge'. I have visions of the tree being daubed in orange paint or hacked into a dozen pieces and thrown into a skip.

'So there we were, peacefully protesting with placards about the proposed bypass through some ancient woodland not twenty miles from here. There's a nature reserve in that area too,' Mum explains. 'Some people we spoke to knew nothing about it which is what they want.' She takes a slurp of her tea. 'And only an inch of coverage in the local newspaper that no one would even notice.'

We are sat in my kitchen and Mum is hungrily munching on some toast and drinking a second cup of tea.

'We did consider chaining ourselves to the council office railings, it was good enough for the suffragettes back in the day, which, okay, was at the House of Commons, but you get my drift,' she says.

'Oh, Mum.' I gently shake my head.

'Anyway,' she continues. 'This policeman tells us to move on, which of course we refused to do,' she says defiantly. 'Mind you, it probably didn't help when he said he understood our plight, and that he really loved trees himself, then someone went and asked him if he was from Special Branch. He said he could do without any smart-arse comments, and that he was missing out on a family birthday to be here.'

'I can see his point, to be fair. Anyway, why would he ask

you to move on if you were protesting peacefully?' I ask puzzled.

'Well, maybe he didn't think sitting in the middle of the road stopping traffic was peaceful enough,' she admits. 'And the lady who was arrested shook her fist at him, which is apparently classed as threatening behaviour.'

I look at Mum, still pretty in her mid-sixties, her long dark hair in plaits. She is wearing a khaki parka with a fake pink fur-trimmed hood, a black jumper, and jeans all purchased from Vinted. I'm not sure exactly when she became an eco-warrior, but I recall her being nothing of the sort when I was growing up. In fact, I recall my parents being rather wasteful, especially with food, loads of which Mum would chuck in the bin from the fridge when her and Dad returned home with the weekly shop.

I think she had some sort of epiphany when she befriended a lady at her yoga class who was living off-grid in a forest some-where and introduced her to an alternative lifestyle. Thinking about the arguments though, I guess her and Dad were having marriage problems anyway at the time. I think Mum's new life-style choice just gave them a solid reason to separate.

'Oh, Mum, really? I don't believe you should ever stop traf-fic, someone might be heading to an emergency.' I frown.

'It makes the news, and that's the point. Although, I wouldn't stop someone if it was a matter of life or death,' she says quietly. 'I'm not sure about some of the others though,' she adds as she sips her tea. 'One or two have actually considered supergluing their hands to the floor. I read about someone who did just that, and part of the road around them had to be removed.'

'That really is taking things too far. Promise me you will never do anything like that, Mum.'

'Of course I wouldn't. I worry about the destruction of the forests, and the state of the world in general, but I would not do anything like that. Right, that's me off for a shower before I head down to the food bank,' she says as she rinses her cup in the sink. 'Have a good day at work, love.'

I know Mum means well, and we need people to fight the good fight, but I worry she might get into trouble or find herself in a sticky situation, quite literally if she considers gluing herself to something. I guess I must believe her when she says she wouldn't take things too far.

'Okay, I'm late for work. Try and stay out of trouble,' I tell her, feeling a bit like a mother admonishing a child.

'Don't worry, I'm heading home after my stint at the food bank to upcycle a mirror using some driftwood for the frame.'

'That sounds nice,' I tell her. Feeling relieved she is settling for a quiet day at home.

Mum has always been energetic and I'm glad she still is, but she isn't exactly a young person and I hate the thought of her being involved in anything dangerous at these demonstrations. I've suggested her work at the food bank should be enough, and of course she is always happy to help at the community centre.

Mum can also be relied upon to help in any situation, and also enjoys helping out at the pensioners' Christmas lunch, but I worry that she seems to be getting more involved in demonstrations of late. At least she lives close enough for me to keep an eye on her, I think to myself as I leave the house.

FIVE

The sky is that strange grey, suffused with orange, that casts an almost ethereal glow in the streets, indicating snow. I had hoped it might snow on Christmas Day, imagining me, Mum and Tony ensconced in the cosy lounge watching old movies and feasting on Quality Street – just me and Mum, obviously – but I guess the one thing I can't plan is the weather.

I've just pulled into the car park when Sue calls.

'Hi, hun, I was just wondering, do you think the pensioners would appreciate a six-foot dancing snowman at the party?' she asks cheerfully.

'Ermm. Because you just happened to have one hanging about?'

I close the car door and head into the town centre, the solar lights from the car park welcoming me up the stone path to the shopping centre.

'Something like that. Actually, it belonged to my next-door neighbour. The husband who erected it in his garden every year has sadly passed away,' she explains as I take the short walk to the store. 'His wife always hated it, apparently, but endured it.' She laughs loudly. 'She found it clearing out the loft with her son, who didn't want it either. He said it would give his little kids nightmares, although the kids around here always thought it was hilarious.'

'A dancing snowman would give them nightmares?' I ask, puzzled as I shrug off my coat.

'Well, it does have rather angry-looking eyebrows.' She laughs her big, contagious laugh once more, and I can't help laughing too. 'It looks a bit like Denis Healey, but you're too young to remember him.'

'Are you sure you don't want to keep it in your street? It sounds like the local kids might be expecting it.'

'No, my neighbour says it would remind her of her husband too much. So it's the charity shop or somewhere that can make use of it.'

'If it sings and dances, then why not? I think the pensioners would love that.'

'Okay, hun, speak to you soon,' says Sue, before hanging up.

In work, I hang my coat up then google a picture of Denis Healey, and can't help laughing. He was once a Labour MP, apparently known for his bushy eyebrows. I really can't wait to see this snowman and I'm so looking forward to the pensioners' Christmas party!

Gemma and I head to the Blue Teapot for lunch and order steaming bowls of bacon and lentil soup, with sourdough bread.

'Are you looking forward to your walk this evening?' asks Gemma, as she half-turns around to look at a good-looking bloke heading for the exit.

'I am actually. It might relax me a bit, and not leave time for me to do any chores that I don't need to.'

You could eat your food off my kitchen floor, it has been scrubbed so many times lately.

'I'm going to the cinema with someone from my yoga class to watch *Barbie*.'

'How old are you exactly?' I laugh.

'I know, but apparently there is a lot of stuff for adults in it too, and you know I have always had a soft spot for Ryan Gosling.'

'Now we're getting to the real reason.'

I think of the guy in the pub the other evening, who had a look of him. But then Gemma never mentioned it, so maybe it really was the gin.

'It makes a change, doesn't it? We don't exactly have a lot of choices of things to do in Fellview.'

'That's true enough. Have you ever thought about moving somewhere a bit livelier?'

'I did consider to moving to Carlisle once, but, well, I kind of love it here. In the summer months I can't think of anywhere more beautiful,' she says, taking a sip of her latte. 'And my best friend lives here, so I think I would miss her a little too much.' She winks.

Gemma, being a bit of a social butterfly, has many people she can do things with, but is a bit like me in that she only has one or two that you might call real friends. The type you could land on their doorstep any time of the day or night if you needed to.

'Right, that's lunch over.' I glance at my watch. 'Back to work then, let's see what the afternoon brings.'

I still feel a little guilty about turning Eileen's dinner invitation down, so fill a little velvet pouch with some samples from work that include a mini lavender pillow spray and some bath foam. I knock on her door when I arrive home.

'Lauren, good timing. I've popped the kettle on.' She smiles broadly as she opens the front door.

'Much as I would like to, I can't really stop as I have an evening out planned,' I remind her. 'I just came to give you these.'

'Oh gosh, of course, you did tell me you were busy this evening, what am I like?' She rolls her eyes and laughs.

She invites me inside for a minute as she opens the purple velour pouch.

'Oh, how lovely, Lauren, you shouldn't have!' she says as she examines the contents. 'Sleep spray, hey? That might be a good thing as I haven't slept properly since Geoff died,' she tells me, her eyes filling with tears.

'I'm sorry to hear that,' I say gently. 'Actually, do you have a mobile phone?' I ask.

'I do, although I don't get many calls. Why do you ask?'

'There's a sleep app I can download for you, if you like. It always helps me to drift off if I'm overtired or if my mind won't switch off.'

'Along with the pillow spray? You might have to knock and wake me up in the morning,' she jokes.

Sod it. Maybe I don't have to change my bedding before I head out for the evening.

'Go on, I'll have that cuppa.' I smile as Eileen invites me to the lounge.

The room is neat as a pin with a pink sofa and matching curtains. The main wall is covered with photos of her family, who she doesn't see too often as they live down south.

An artificial tree stands in the corner decorated with multi-coloured fairy lights and reminds me so much of the one in the house when Gran was alive, it brings a lump to my throat.

She soon returns from the kitchen and sets down a tray with a pot of tea, two cups, and a plate of shortbread. I sip the tea, but politely decline the shortbread, as I have baked a cake to enjoy later with the walking group. With a naturally sweet tooth I do have to watch my sugar intake, which is why I tend to bake cakes for other people to enjoy.

We chat for fifteen minutes, as she asks me about my day, and I ask her about what she has been up to.

'Not much. I had a stroll to the shops this morning, then I had a video chat with my grandchildren. They are teenagers now, so they will no doubt be wanting money or some electronic gadget or other for Christmas,' she tells me. 'I imagine you're mad busy at this time of year in the shop.'

'You're not wrong. I love the buzz at Christmas time though.'

I enjoy the hustle and bustle, the faces of the excited children and the scent of the crisp, outside air every time the doors open. I don't even mind the queues. Everyone seems in good spirits at this time of year. At least most people anyway.

'Oh, it's such a beautiful store. My husband used to love the café there on the second floor. I was surprised when they closed it down,' says Eileen, taking a bite of shortbread.

The space was used to extend the floor that sells children's clothing and toys, due to demand.

'I know, it was a shame, although I think they had a lot of the competition from the Blue Teapot café next door.'

'Probably. I must admit, I miss my working days sometimes,' says Eileen with a faraway look in her eyes.

'What did you do before you retired?' I ask, realising I know nothing about Eileen's previous life, only the person she is now, and even that is not on any deep, personal level.

'Geoff and I ran a café in Kendal near the river,' she tells me, a smile spreading across her face. 'Christmas was magical. We had a huge tree outside and served up hot chocolate with all the trimmings and my lemon biscuits. Families would call in after a long walk,' she recalls. 'They were happy times.'

'That sounds wonderful. I love working in the shop, but I could also imagine myself behind a counter serving hot drinks on freezing days to walkers. Maybe I could even bake some of the cakes.'

'I do miss the days in the café sometimes,' Eileen tells me. 'I didn't really want to retire but, to be honest, we were both worn out by the time we sold up. Growing old is such a nuisance,' she says, and I imagine how hard it must be for those who still have an active mind, but grow tired. 'And you could definitely serve your own cakes if you had a café, they're wonderful,' she says kindly.

We're having such a pleasant conversation I have to tear myself away, and even consider not attending the walk, but I am the one that has organised it. Besides, it is always nice to make new friends. I don't really have many, apart from Gemma, and a friend from my school days that I stay in touch with, but only meet up with occasionally since she moved out of the area. Eileen could most definitely become a friend, age being no barrier to friendships once you allow yourself to consider the possibility. I guess there are opportunities for friendships all around if we actually look for them.

'Ooh, before I forget, I'll get that casserole for you,' says Eileen, getting to her feet.

She heads into the kitchen, before returning and presenting me with the food in a red earthenware dish.

'Thank you, Eileen. I will enjoy that.'

'No, thank you for stopping for a chat. And for the lovely gift, it was thoughtful of you.' She smiles as she escorts me to the front door.

'And I have your number now, so I'll give you a little text in the morning and tell you how I slept,' she says, holding her phone tightly in her hand.

'Great. Thanks again, Eileen. Sweet dreams.'

SIX

The moon walking experience last night would have been better in the spring I realise, although it wasn't a complete disaster. There was one particularly nervous young lady though, who I must admit I felt a little concerned about, and even thought about this morning when I woke up.

I received a text from Eileen this morning, telling me she slept like a log and I send her a thumbs up emoji, feeling happy that some good came from my staying and having a brew with her.

'So how was the walk in the forest? What did you say it was called, moon bathing?' Gemma raises an eyebrow.

'Not quite what I imagined,' I tell her, which is a bit of an understatement to say the least. 'It was absolutely freezing for a start.'

'What do you expect in December.' She laughs. 'You wouldn't catch me out there in the middle of December, that's for sure.' She gives a little shiver as she reaches for her coffee, placed under the counter at work in a travel cup. It's lovely having this time in the morning, before the main doors open and the customers drift in.

'True enough. Anyway, the path through the forest was so dark we could barely see in front of us. I was annoyed that the flashlights I supplied weren't very bright,' I tell her. 'I could actually kick myself about that, but luckily the group were fine about it and used the flashlights on their phones.'

'Not the best start then.'

'Not really. It was really slippy, and the sound of nocturnal animals was a bit disconcerting, to be honest,' I tell her, recalling the sound of a screech owl and what sounded like a gunshot that had us all gasping. 'It was only a firework from someone having a Christmas party somewhere, but in the darkness of the forest...'

'Your imagination runs away with you?'

'Exactly.'

She pulls a face. 'It doesn't sound that relaxing, although I don't know exactly what you were expecting.'

'Neither do I really. I guess I imagined a calm, mindful experience. I had even asked a lady from the community centre along, who is a trained counsellor. She was happy to volunteer her services, maybe in the hope of picking up some business, as she runs forest retreats. Anyway, we eventually reached a clearing where we set up our chairs and I managed to get a campfire started.'

'That sounds nice though?' says Gemma, restocking a drawer with some gift bags.

'Yes, it was nice and very warming, briefly anyway. After that, we were asked by the counsellor lady to tell the group three things we were grateful for.'

'I hope I was one of them,' says Gemma, giving me a nudge.

'Naturally.' I smile. 'Anyway, after that, she wafted a sage stick and played some relaxing music for us to meditate to, which on a warm summer's day would be really lovely.'

'But not in a dark forest in winter?'

'Not really, no. The fire had gone out by then because it was so damp, and I had feet like blocks of ice,' I recall. 'Thankfully I had the flasks of tea, and, of course, the home-made cake, so that cheered us all up a bit.'

'Thank goodness for that.' Gemma laughs. 'Your cake could cheer anyone up.'

'Thanks. Anyway, just as we were beginning to relax a bit and enjoy a nice chat with each other, the screech owl we had heard earlier came swooping down and almost lifted the beanie hat from a particularly nervous member of the group. I think it had been attracted by the fur bobble.'

'Oh no, what happened?' asks Gemma, her eyes widening.

'All hell broke loose. She started crying and saying she wished she had stayed at home and that it had been her mum's idea for her to go and do something relaxing, as she had been suffering with anxiety after losing her beloved dog. I felt so sorry for her.'

'Oh, my goodness!' Gemma covers her mouth with her hand. 'The poor girl. Did you get her name? Maybe we should ask her to the gingerbread evening, if there are any places left.'

'Yes, her name is Audrey, and you know, that's a great idea! I also know she works in Boots on the high street. I was going to call in at some point, and see if she is okay. I will text Jo now, see if there are any places left.'

The group assured me at the end of the evening that they had enjoyed themselves, especially the sitting around and chatting, but I can't help thinking that it could have been better. There was no charge though, just a suggestion to contribute to the community centre Christmas fund, which everyone did. Oh, and the counsellor lady took three bookings for a weekend forest retreat in March.

I tap out a text to Jo, the local bakery lady who judges the gingerbread house competition, and unbelievably she has had a cancellation, so I book Audrey in. I can always cancel after I have spoken to her, if she isn't free.

The juddering of the exterior metal shutters being lifted signals the start of opening time as a security guy heads to the glass doors to open them. There are already a few people standing outside, ready to have a browse through some of our special Christmas offers.

An hour later, the store is as busy as ever, and traditional Christmas carols are playing over the Tannoy once more, rather than the Mariah Carey ear-splitting type tunes.

A young child buys a gift set for her mum and counts her money out at my counter, which I automatically add a sample face mask to. She races over to her dad, and shows him the bag excitedly, and he nods in my direction with a smile on his face.

'I've got my eye on a bag over there,' says Gemma, pointing to a bag and scarf display when there is a rare lull in sales. 'I really hope it goes into the January sale. I could never afford it at its current price. Oh, and did you see that hot guy?' she asks.

'Don't start.' I smile, shaking my head at my friend.

'I was about to say, I think he was checking *you* out.'

'What guy, where?' I glance around.

'Oh, you're interested now.' She laughs as a lady approaches the counter with a woollen scarf and gloves set in a box.

'The guy with the little girl,' she tells me when the customer has departed.

'The little girl?'

'Duh, the one who counted out her money and bought the gift set for her mum.' She laughs.

'Oh right, that guy. Yeah he was okay, I suppose.' I shrug.

The man in question was actually very attractive. Dark, slightly curly hair, wearing a brown casual leather jacket with a scarf tucked inside. Nice smile too, I remember that much.

'Although, I don't think he was checking me out,' I tell her.

'He was simply acknowledging the little extra gift I popped into the bag.'

'If you say so.' She grins.

'And actually, why would he be looking at me if his daughter was buying a gift for her mum, surely that means he's married?'

'Not necessarily, he could be separated,' she suggests.

'Like the guy you went out with?' I raise an eyebrow.

'Point taken, but not everyone is like him.' She rolls her eyes. 'And why wouldn't that guy be looking at you, you're gorgeous,' she says kindly. 'He was definitely eyeing you up,' she whispers as another customer approaches the counter.

The afternoon passes in a flash, as discounted knitwear, gift sets and perfumes fly off the shelves as people pop in for last-minute gifts. Gemma is still eyeing the bag stall, hoping the bag she has her eye on won't sell and might go into the January sale.

I think about the cute little girl with pigtails, wearing the white quilted coat, and how she counted out twenty pounds, that included a five-pound note and fifteen pounds' worth of coins, to purchase a pair of pyjamas in a box tied with a gift bow. Some of the assistants pull a face when children produce cash and wonder why their carers can't pay by card. I like to remind them that Christmas is for everyone and not just those who can press a card against a reader. The joy on the face of a child who has saved up their money and bought someone a gift is absolutely priceless.

'Any plans for this evening?' I ask Gemma as we step outside into the frosty air, when the store finally closes.

'No, I'm shattered. It's a Netflix series and a hot chocolate for me,' she says, already yawning.

'Sounds good to me.'

'How about you?'

'Something pretty similar, I'm pooped today.'

We go our separate ways, Gemma's place is in a modern

block of apartments a short walk away, my house a five-minute drive away. I make my way to Boots before heading off, to see if Audrey might be on shift. If she isn't maybe a staff member can advise me when she will be.

Pushing through the door, I have a quick look at the special offers, and end up heading for the checkout with a designer beauty bag filled with goodies that has a fifty per cent price reduction. It's the kind of bag you might take to a hotel on a weekend away, and it occurs to me that I can't remember the last time I did anything like that. My ex did splash out on an overnight stay at a luxury hotel once that cost as nearly as much as a week away in the UK, or at least a long weekend abroad, which kind of spoilt it a little, if I'm honest. I'm all for a bit of luxury occasionally, but sheer overindulgence leaves me cold. I might ask Gemma if she fancies booking something after Christmas to rejuvenate us a little after the Christmas rush.

As I approach the checkouts, I notice Audrey on the till closest to the door, chatting to the lady on the next till.

'Hi.' I place my basket down, that contains the weekender bag and a bottle of conditioner. I'm a bit obsessive over good quality conditioner, but it does keep my long dark hair shiny and in tip-top condition.

'Hi.' She smiles. I don't think she recognises me as she wordlessly scans my items, although to be fair the last time we met I was muffled up with a heavy coat, a scarf pulled up to my chin and a hat. Plus it was dark.

'We met last night on the moonlight walk,' I remind her as I pay for my items.

She scrutinises me for a moment.

'Oh gosh, yes, hi, it's Lauren, isn't it?' she asks, her skin colouring a little.

'It is. You're Audrey, right?'

'Yes. I'm sorry about my little outburst last night,' she says in a low voice. 'I made a right show of myself.'

'You didn't at all,' I tell her. 'We all have our moments, we are only human.'

'Thanks,' she says, placing my items into a bag.

'Listen. Do you fancy grabbing a coffee?' I ask. 'You're closing soon, aren't you?'

'In eight minutes,' she says, glancing at her watch. 'And, yes, I'd like that.' She smiles.

We arrange to meet at the Blue Teapot in the village square.

SEVEN

'I hope I didn't spoil the evening for everyone,' Audrey says as she sips a gingerbread latte topped with cream and sprinkles of gingerbread cake.

We are sitting in the Blue Teapot on the square, the independent café that serves the most delicious coffees and cakes, and no doubt led to the demise of the café at Bentham's, which isn't surprising really as for a high-end store the café sold bought-in cakes and unimaginative sandwiches.

We've managed to get a window table though with a view of the street outside and as I glance out over the square at the streetlights and Christmas decorations, I feel all warm and toasty.

'Not at all.' I smile. 'And with hindsight, perhaps it would have been better in the autumn,' I tell her. 'I imagined this soothing moonlit experience gazing at the stars, and connecting with nature but it was freezing and muddy.' I pull a face.

'And so overcast you couldn't even see the stars,' Audrey reminds me, and we both laugh.

'My mum kind of suggested it as she'd read online about local events,' explains Audrey. 'She thinks I need to make more friends.' She scoops up some cream from her coffee and spoons it into her mouth. 'And I did enjoy it really, everyone was so lovely, but that owl just freaked me out.'

Audrey, with her long dark hair and pale skin, has a beautiful, fragile look about her. Her nose stud and dark eyeliner against her paleness give her a vaguely gothic look, although the rest of her attire is quite modern. Today she is wearing black jeans and a blue mohair jumper the colour of her eyes.

'Do *you* think you need more friends?' I ask, sipping my own decaff cappuccino with hazelnut syrup.

'Dunno.' She shrugs. 'I did have a best friend but she moved down south for uni. We stayed in touch for a while but she met a bloke there and decided to stay.'

'Does she never come home?' My tummy gives a little rumble, and I debate having a delicious-looking chocolate brownie I spied at the counter on the way in.

'Only occasionally. She never did get along with her parents so doesn't make the effort to come back too often. I kind of thought she might have come to see me but...' Her voice trails off and I can see the hurt in her eyes. 'I got the train down there a couple of times to see her,' she says in a quiet voice as she stirs her latte.

'People change,' I say gently. 'It's probably nothing to do with you, she's probably just caught up with the romance of her new boyfriend,' I tell her. 'Believe me, so many girls ditch their friends, especially in the first flush of romance. Even me, I'm ashamed to say, but we live and learn.'

'Suppose so. I've never really had a boyfriend, so I wouldn't know,' she tells me honestly. 'I mean, I've had boys as friends, but not what you might call a real boyfriend.'

'I remember my first boyfriend at the age of sixteen and how I wanted to spend every spare second with him,' I tell Audrey. 'That is, until my friends told me that they missed me hanging out with them.' I take a sip of my coffee. 'I took it to heart and tried to balance things a bit. In the end my boyfriend dumped me anyway, when I refused to sleep with him.'

'That's awful.' Audrey shakes her head.

'I know but looking back we were never really suited.' A fact I acknowledged when I realised we had nothing in common and I only fancied him because he reminded me of Justin Timberlake. 'So are you friends with anyone at the shop?' I ask.

'Not really. Don't get me wrong, the younger staff have tried to include me in their nights out, but loud bars and cocktails aren't really my thing.' She smiles. 'And there is a nice lady who is retiring soon, but I don't think we have any shared interests.'

'I guess so, although older people can surprise you,' I say, thinking of the interesting chat I had with Eileen, and some of the pensioners at the community centre. 'I do think your mum is right about you joining groups, but maybe the moonlight walk wasn't quite the right thing.'

'Maybe not.' She grimaces. 'And I really do hope I didn't put a dampener on things.'

'I wouldn't worry about that,' I reassure her, smiling. 'I'm the one who arranged it, as I'm in a similar spot – it can be hard to meet new people at our age. It was so lovely to meet you and the other ladies. Everyone was so friendly and warm, even in the cold.'

'You're right, they were. Thanks, Lauren, I feel better talking to you. I'm glad you asked me to come and have a coffee.'

'My pleasure. Oh, and I'm so sorry to hear about your dog,' I say, remembering her mini meltdown on the moon walk.

'Thanks. I loved Milo. Here he is, look.' She turns her phone to show me her screensaver featuring a gorgeous black Labrador.

'Ah, he looks wonderful.' I smile at the photo of Audrey with her arms draped around her beloved dog. 'He's a proper dog, as my dad would say, who isn't a fan of these smaller cross-breeds.'

We had a German Shepherd called Duke when I was growing up and I remember feeling heartbroken when he finally passed away.

'Anyway, as you obviously like gingerbread,' I say, nodding to her ginger latte, 'I was wondering if you fancied the gingerbread decorating evening at the community centre on Friday? I remembered you saying you worked in Boots, so was glad I caught you there today.'

'You came in especially to see me?' She looks surprised.

'Yes, although I did need some more conditioner, and that beauty bag was too good to miss.' I wink.

'I did think about the gingerbread evening,' says Audrey. 'But I have no one to go with.' She tucks a strand of hair behind her ear. 'No one at the shop seemed interested when I kind of mentioned it.'

'Well, me and my friend Gemma are going, so you can sit with us.'

'Really?' Her pretty face breaks into a broad smile. 'But don't you have to book a place?'

'Already done. If you weren't available, I would have cancelled it. It's a fun evening, you get chatting to lots of people you don't know, so it's a great way to make more friends,' I tell her, thinking of the fun we had last year. I remind myself to take it easy on the Prosecco this year though.

'You're so kind.' Audrey's eyes mist over a little. 'I would never have walked in there on my own.'

'You came to the moon walk alone, didn't you?' I remind her.

'Yes, but I was almost hyperventilating all day just thinking about it. And I know it sounds stupid, but it was dark, and that kind of helped.'

'I know what you mean. Sometimes it's easier to be in the shadows.'

'Yes! Maybe that's it.' She nods. 'I've never been very good at being in the spotlight.'

'Then you have done very well working in a shop. Dealing with the public isn't always the easiest thing, so you should congratulate yourself on that.'

It's a strange irony in life that the best people often lack confidence whereas those distinctly average types can be full of it.

'You must let me buy you another coffee, if you have the time,' says Audrey. 'You have been so lovely.'

'I do actually.'

'Great. Do you fancy a mince pie?' she asks.

'Sure why not. I'll get that though.'

'No, you won't, it's my treat,' she insists, before striding towards the counter.

We finish our coffees and delicious mince pies, and I discover that Audrey lives a couple of miles away, so I drop her off rather than her waiting for her bus in the cold evening air.

As I watch her walk up the path with flower borders of the neat semi-detached house in the cul-de-sac, she turns and waves, and I get a warm feeling inside. The thrill of helping others never fails to make me feel good.

EIGHT

'Oh, Mum, really? Do you have to? It's freezing outside at this time of year.'

'You have to take a stand for what's right, love, and if local shops are on board it's a good start.'

Mum is telling me that she and a group of friends are staging a protest outside the Co-op tomorrow, as they have refused to ban products containing palm oil.

'You could just stop buying things that contain palm oil?' I suggest as I put a wash on, but she insists on being part of protests that will make the local news.

'Well, of course I already do that. It isn't necessary to use it while there are so many alternatives,' she insists. 'Those poor orangutans are losing their habitat at an alarming rate.'

She takes a bite of a chocolate chip biscuit, of which she never checked the ingredients, it could be full of all sorts of planet-destroying chemicals, let alone dairy. It isn't, it's Sainsbury's organic range, but she doesn't know that.

I spotted Mum walking towards my place as I drove home and stopped to give her a lift. We are now sitting in the lounge, Mum enjoying a herbal tea and a biscuit.

'You have made it lovely here, you have a real eye for design,' says Mum as she glances around. 'I can still remember my parents' tree in that corner,' she says, nodding towards mine that wouldn't look out of place in a Bentham's window display.

The lounge walls are painted a soft grey and I have lots of plants and black-and-white prints on the walls.

'I do love this house and I always enjoy it when you come and stay,' I remind Mum. 'You know that, don't you?'

In some ways I wish she would move in. I would love to look after my mum when she gets a little older, just as I recall her looking after my gran and grandad.

'I know, love, but I'm perfectly happy in the flat, you know I prefer the location.'

'Well, you should at least come and have a sleepover soon. You know, have a girlie night, a movie and so on.'

'Would you really like that?' She seems surprised by my invitation. 'I thought you preferred your friends for that sort of thing. Not your old mum.'

'You're not old. And, oh, Mum, of course I would! I miss you sometimes,' I find myself saying, which isn't really like me to say out loud, and feel a lump in my throat. 'I mean, we see each other regularly for a brew and a chat, but I would love us to spend more quality time together, watching old movies and laughing at something silly.'

'I'd like that too.' Mum smiles.

'Great. Maybe we could look through some old photo albums and have a glass of wine too,' I suggest.

I worry then that looking at photos might dredge up bitter-sweet memories for Mum, of her life together with Dad, but we all have a past I suppose.

'That sounds nice.' She smiles. 'And it's good to know you enjoy spending some time with me, as I did with my mum. I guess I must have done something right then.' She smiles again and I reassure her that she did.

'I remember Christmas with Gran. It was so cosy, wasn't it? I remember how Grandad loved Gran's baking.'

I loved making biscuits with Gran as Grandad, after his lunchtime sandwich and mug of tea, would soon be snoozing gently in his chair. As soon as the biscuits were baked he would try to eat them, and I remember Gran slapping his hand away and telling him to at least wait until they were iced.

'He certainly did.' Mum chuckles. 'One year she made a Christmas cake, and made the mistake of leaving it in a tin on the kitchen counter. He scoffed a giant piece one evening when Mum had gone to bed, before she'd even had a chance to ice it. She never spoke to him for days,' Mum recalls.

'They were happy though, weren't they?'

'Oh yes, they loved the bones of each other,' she says, pushing the biscuit tin away. 'Mum was never the same after Dad died. I wasn't surprised she joined him the following year,' she says wistfully. 'I wish me and your dad could have had that kind of enduring love.' She gazes off somewhere in the distance.

'Do you?' I'm a little surprised by this, as I assumed neither of them had any regrets.

'Well, of course I do.' She reaches over and takes my hand. 'I wanted you to feel the same love and security I felt as a child, but we failed you.' Her voice catches in her throat. 'Although I guess you were older when we separated.'

'I was an adult,' I remind her. 'Oh, Mum, where has this come from?' I ask as I squeeze her hand. 'You most certainly haven't failed me; I had a lovely childhood.'

I truly did enjoy my childhood, enjoying picnics at the beach in the summer, and spending winter evenings at home, warm and cosy, watching family films together. They must have been sick to death of watching *The Santa Clause* movies for the umpteenth time at Christmas, but they never complained.

'You did? Oh, I don't know, ignore me. I always get a bit sentimental around this time of year.' She musters up a smile.

'It's just, you know, I imagined me and your dad sitting around a Christmas table with you for dinner, not us all doing our own thing.' She takes a tissue from her bag and blows her nose.

I wonder for a minute if I could make that happen? But then, I don't suppose his new partner would take too kindly to the idea.

'Do you regret splitting with Dad?' I think of him with his new partner, Rose, who he seems to get along with well enough, but I don't think is the love of his life.

'In some ways,' she admits. 'Although, don't get me wrong, we weren't right for each other deep down. I just miss the family thing I suppose. I told you, 'tis the season to be sentimental.' She rolls her eyes.

'Aw, Mum, we will have a nice day at the community centre lunch though, won't we?'

'Oh yes, I always enjoy that.' She smiles.

'And we will have that girlie evening very soon.'

Tony jumps up onto her lap then, purring loudly, as if sensing she needs a little comfort and she strokes him.

Last year, as in previous years, Mum and I have dined here after a busy Christmas Eve at the centre, lounging around after lunch watching Christmas films, sipping Baileys and trying, unsuccessfully, to stop ourselves from dipping into the chocolate tin.

We had a lovely time, and later played chess until late in the evening. My dad taught me to play chess years ago and I wished he could have joined us but all the same, watching the lights twinkle on the tree, as we enjoyed a nightcap for bed, I felt truly blessed.

'Well as long as you're okay,' I say gently. I've never known my mum to be sentimental at this time of year before. Maybe it's because she's getting a little bit older and reflecting more on her life.

'You know me, I'm fine,' she says. 'Anyway, I must get going as me and a couple of the girls from the food bank are going for a talk at the community centre about making your own eco-friendly detergent, from conkers would you believe.'

'Conkers. Really?'

'Apparently so. Worth a try I think, although there won't be any around at this time of year. It's something to bear in mind for next autumn.'

She prises a reluctant Tony from her knee and heads into the hallway to retrieve her hefty, navy duffel coat.

'Make sure you get home safely,' I tell her as I wrap her in a hug.

'I will be getting a lift, don't worry. Night, love.'

'Night, Mum.'

As I close the door, I wonder when the roles became reversed, and I worry about my mum getting home safely. I also wonder whether she is truly happy, but I guess our personal happiness is something we all must figure out for ourselves.

NINE

The room is decked out with every Christmas decoration you can think of, including a huge tree at the entrance of the hall, hung with striped candy canes and gingerbread men. Tables are set out with slabs of gingerbread for the houses, alongside an assortment of decoration pens and sweets. At the far end of the hall a table is laden with mince pies and nibbles, along with mini bottles of Prosecco and non-alcohol versions.

Audrey, Gemma, and I take a seat at a long table, and say hi to the other people, all women. We seem to be the last to arrive, and a second later Jo makes the introductions with a microphone.

'Good evening, everyone, and thank you all for coming. I hope you have brought your purses, oh and wallets' – she smiles towards a table with two older guys sitting with ladies of a similar age –'as I will be walking around with raffle tickets shortly,' she announces, waving a book of pink tickets.

She gestures to several hampers on the wooden stage behind her that include a toy hamper as well as smaller prizes of chocolates and toiletries. 'So have fun and I will be announcing the winner in a couple of hours' time.'

I glance around the room, and on a table a few yards away I notice a familiar face, but not before Gemma does.

'Oh my goodness, it's the guy from the shop,' she says, nudging me. 'Three o'clock from us, don't look now.'

'I've already noticed,' I tell her as I snap off the tip of a green icing pen, ready to channel my inner van Gogh.

It's hard not to notice him really, over six feet tall, that dark slightly curly hair, dark-green eyes, and effortlessly sexy style. Dammit, do I really think that?

'I wonder who he's with?' Gemma says, scanning the table that has an empty seat next to him. Suddenly, a little girl appears from under the table waving an icing pen triumphantly, as her father smiles.

'Ah, he's brought his daughter here, how sweet,' Gemma says. 'I wonder if one of those women is his wife?' she asks, looking over.

'I'm sure I don't know,' I tell her, but can't help wondering if he has brought his daughter along for the evening alone. Not that that means anything. He might have brought his daughter out so her mum can wrap some presents. In fact, why do I even care?

Eyeing the selection of sweet accessories in front of us, I soon set to work creating my storybook house, in between taking slurps of drinks and chatting to the other women. Christmas songs are playing making me feel so Christmassy as I deftly create some green windows with an icing pen, before moving on to the roof, carefully using a red pen to give it a brick effect. Adorning it with jellies and mini candy canes, I'm rather proud of my effort so far, although it seems I am surrounded by a lot of very talented ladies, as compared to their efforts my house looks pretty basic. I don't mind though, this evening is all about getting in the festive spirit and I am happily singing along to the festive tunes and really enjoying myself.

'I'm going to grab a snack,' I say, getting to my feet and heading for the buffet table.

'I'll join you,' says Audrey, who has already begun creating the neatest, most beautiful roof of her house.

'I just wanted to thank you for asking me to join you,' she says as she piles some pretzels, and a slice of Christmas cake onto her plate. 'I'm really enjoying it here, everyone is so friendly, and the lady sat next to me actually lives in the next street. I'd never even noticed her before.'

'Really? Well there you go, you have made a new friend already.' I smile.

I grab a non-alcohol glass of Freixenet, and as I turn around, not looking where I am going, I literally bump into the hot shop guy, and my full glass of Prosecco lands all over his trousers.

'Oh, my goodness, I am so sorry.' I cover my hand with my mouth as I hear a giggle from his daughter.

I quickly grab some napkins from the buffet table and hand them to him.

'Don't worry about it,' he says, in a delicious Irish lilt. 'Although it's a good job it didn't go over my jumper or I might have been electrocuted.' He raises an eyebrow.

'Electrocuted?' I ask, puzzled, as he dabs at his trousers.

'Daddy's jumper lights up. Look.'

The cute little girl wearing a white fluffy jumper, black leggings, and shiny black boots, presses the button on his jumper, and an array of coloured fairy lights flash across a Christmas tree.

'That's quite something,' I say, listening to the little girl's adorable laughter. 'And I really am sorry. I must get back,' I say, before returning to my table feeling completely mortified.

'Did I see you chatting to hot shop guy?' asks Gemma open-mouthed when I return, plonking the plate of snacks down.

'Assaulting him more like.' I tell her about dousing him in Prosecco and she bursts out laughing.

'And of all the places. He looked like he had wet himself.' I cover my face with my hands.

'Oh, Lauren, it was an accident. I'm sure he isn't bothered,' says Gemma, giggling.

'I'm not so sure, he never exactly laughed about it,' I say, recalling his serious expression, despite him telling me not to worry about it. Then again, he was happy to show me the flashing lights on his jumper, I guess, so he can't have been too mad after all.

I glance over at a lady chatting to him at the buffet table and handing him another napkin, and I wonder if it's his wife?

I put all thoughts of him away as I get on with the task of finishing my gingerbread house. I don't mind that mine isn't really in the same league as one or two others, especially Audrey's, if I'm honest. I wonder if they have all been practising.

'The lady at the buffet table isn't sitting on the same table as hot shop guy,' Gemma tells me as we put the finishing touches to our houses. 'She must have just been a Good Samaritan, passing him some more napkins. Oh, and he's been looking over, you know.'

'Gemma, I'm sure he hasn't,' I tell her, appraising my handi-work I'm not sure green was the right colour for the window frames after all, but there's nothing I can do about that now. 'And I don't really care if he has,' I add.

'Sure, you don't.' She smirks, adding a final jellybean to her impressive looking roof.

'Has he really been looking over?' I ask, despite myself.

'Ha. And you tell me you don't care. Yes, he has, at least twice. I can't help noticing him as he is straight in my line of vision.'

'Well, whatever. He's probably just looking over and silently cursing me for soaking him,' I say, although I wonder whether he has really been checking me out? Or perhaps it's someone else at the table.

'That must be it then,' she says. 'He's plotting ways to get his own back. I wouldn't walk past his table if I were you, he might throw something on the floor for you to slip on.' She grins.

A few minutes later, I can't resist glancing over and he and his daughter are concentrating on putting their finishing touches to their house. I can't deny it's an adorable scene watching them both.

Soon enough, the decorated houses are standing proudly on tables as Jo prepares to judge them, clipboard and pen ready in her hand.

The evening has been interspersed with the raffle, and the little girl with the guy from the shop – I wonder what his real name is? – squealed with delight when she waved her pink ticket and received the toy hamper, filled with colouring books, a cuddly toy, and a chocolate Santa.

A lady from our table won a foot spa and an older bloke, who was accompanying his wife, was delighted to win a bottle of whisky.

'And now,' says Jo, clapping her hands together. 'The main prize of a cookery lesson at the bakery in January. Along with the trophy, of course.' She lifts a golden gingerbread man trophy. 'I've been really bowled over by the talent in the room this year,' she says kindly. 'But having had a good look around at some of your very impressive houses, I am thrilled to say I have selected a winner,' she announces as murmurs can be heard around the room.

She strides towards our table, and people glance at each other in anticipation. I know the winner won't be me, but there is already one clear winner in my mind. And it seems that Jo agrees.

'This is the most beautifully decorated gingerbread house I have seen in a long time,' says Jo, pointing at the masterpiece in front of her. 'It's immaculate and pretty, and looks just like the house from "Hansel and Gretel", even prettier if that is possible. So huge congratulations go to...?'

'It's Audrey,' says our winner, blushing slightly and grinning from ear to ear.

'Well done, Audrey. An outright winner if ever I saw one,' says Jo as the crowd bursts into thunderous applause.

She hands Audrey the golden trophy. 'I'll get your details to book you in for the bakery lesson,' she tells a delighted Audrey. 'Well done.'

'Wow, I can't believe it,' Audrey says, placing her hand on her chest. 'I'm in complete shock. I never win anything.' She is genuinely thrilled.

'You deserve it, love,' says a woman at the end of the table. 'Mine looks like it's been in an explosion.' She roars with laughter as she points at the house, its roof dripping with icing, and the left wall threatening to cave in. 'I've had a blast though. And the house looks like it has too.' She giggles, and we all laugh along with her.

Audrey asks if I mind her going home with the lady from her street, who has driven here, and I tell her of course I don't, thrilled that she has made a new friend.

'So do you fancy the pub then? Finish the evening off with a nightcap?' asks Gemma as she links arms with me and we step outside into the crisp night air.

'Nice idea, but I must get home and take a wash out of the machine and into my tumble dryer, or the clothes will smell if I leave them overnight.'

'Surely not? Leaving them for a day or more I can understand, but not what, eight hours?'

'Um, well maybe not, but I can't take the chance. I swear my bedding smelt weird last time I left it until the next morning, so

I had to wash it all again. And I don't want to leave the tumble dryer on when I go to work as it's a fire hazard.'

'If you say so.' Gemma rolls her eyes at me, but she's laughing. 'I should probably get back too, come to think of it. I'm pretty sure my skirting boards need cleaning.' She frowns.

'Are you taking the mickey?' I pull a face.

'Me, really?' She looks up and whistles. 'You know I'm only teasing. And maybe it is best if we call it a night as we have work in the morning.'

'I think so. No doubt there will some overindulgences in the days to come anyway.'

'Probably.' She grins. 'You know, I really enjoyed this evening, Lauren, and I'm thrilled for Audrey. It was a nice thing you did going into the shop and inviting her along.'

'As I recall, it was your idea,' I remind her.

'It was, wasn't it? Well, I'm glad she came, she seems really lovely,' says Gemma.

'She does, doesn't she? And she deserved to win, she has real talent. Jump in then, I'll give you a lift. I've been on the non-alcohol stuff.'

The community centre is on a country road slightly out of town, so I drop Gemma off outside her flat.

'See you in the morning for another busy day. Some of those pre-Christmas promotions start tomorrow,' I remind her.

'I know. See you tomorrow then.' She blows me a kiss as I drive off.

When I eventually arrive home, Tony is waiting at the front door, miaowing loudly.

'Hi there, buddy. Have you been waiting for me?' I ask as he threads himself through my legs miaowing even more loudly, and I wonder what's up with him as he is never normally so vocal, especially outside. He normally just waits on the step, or lets himself in via the cat flap in the kitchen door. In fact, he seems a little bit agitated.

'Too lazy to go around and use the cat flap at the back door, are you?' I ask him as I press my key into the front door while he continues making loud noises.

My senses are heightened, as something immediately feels off. I walk towards the kitchen with trepidation, having pulled my phone from my bag, fingers poised.

Feeling a chilly blast as I edge the kitchen door open, I hope I had just opened a kitchen window to let some air in, although I never normally do that in December.

My heart beating loudly, I push the door open further and gasp as I notice the shards of glass on the kitchen work surface beneath the broken window above.

I take in the scene and my heart sinks. My flat screen TV has gone from the wall, and more frustratingly, my laptop from the kitchen counter. It has my diary and planning notes for the party on it, not to mention all of my photographs organised in folders. I breathe deeply, while trying not to panic. Why on earth did I leave my laptop out in full view? I usually hide it away somewhere, just in case, but this morning I was in a hurry.

This cannot be happening. I choke back a tear as I must face the awful truth that I have been burgled.

TEN

I can barely take it in, and find myself wandering from room to room, checking everything is in its place, and maybe desperately hoping my laptop will magically turn up in a different room but, of course, it doesn't. I think of the photos on my laptop and my heart sinks, although thankfully I had the foresight to have most of them printed out and delivered by post, via an app. Mostly family photos that I treasure, especially as Mum and Dad are no longer together. I also keep a notebook, thankfully, reminding me of things that need to be done before the party.

I try to tell myself that worse things happen, and I am about to call the police when I hear banging on the front door and my heart thumps. Surely the burglars wouldn't return. And they would hardly knock at the door, would they? Peeking through the frosted glass, I think I can make out the couple next door. I really ought to get one of those Ring doorbells with a camera. In fact, I will order one tomorrow in light of what has happened.

'I think this belongs to you.'

Standing on the doorstep is my giant of a neighbour from a few doors down, Martin, holding my TV in front of him.

'And this.' His diminutive wife, June, is clutching my laptop.

'My things! But how? I don't understand.' I almost cry at the relief of seeing my possessions, especially the laptop that I use to organise my life.

'Well it was Tony that alerted us,' Martin tells me as I guide him and June inside, feeling overwhelmed and suddenly a bit shaken.

'Tony?' I ask shocked as Martin places down the TV and strokes Tony under his chin, whose head looks tiny next to Martin's giant hands and muscled tattooed arms.

'Yes, he jumped onto our window ledge. In fact, he launched himself at the window like a missile, didn't you, fella?' says Martin to a purring Tony. 'He nearly gave us a heart attack. When I went outside, he was miaowing like crazy and pacing around,' Martin continues. 'Then he raced around the back of the house, with us in hot pursuit.'

'I said something was wrong, didn't I, love?' says tiny blonde June, dressed in her grey tracksuit with pink stripes down the legs.

'You did. We followed him through the back gate, and saw the thieving bugger on the road, hurriedly loading your TV into his car, so I grabbed it back,' says Martin, sounding affronted. 'I mean, I didn't know it was your stuff at first, but then I saw your back gate wide open and put two and two together. And with Tony acting the way he did...'

'Oh, Martin, thank you, are you okay?' I ask, concerned, as Martin is well into his sixties, although thinking about it he keeps himself very fit. He has also told me on many occasions that he used to do a bit of boxing back in the day.

'Of course I am, he was no more than a kid,' he reassures me. 'Probably just some little opportunist thief who noticed the house in darkness. You must be careful at this time of year, love,' he advises. 'You should leave a light on in these dark evenings.'

'Gosh, yes, I normally do leave a lamp on,' I tell him, feeling annoyed with myself that I hadn't done so before I went out.

'It did unsettle me a bit,' says June. 'I hope it was a one-off, as we have never had anything like that around here in the past, have we?'

'No, that's true. Hopefully Martin is right about it being opportunist thieves at this time of year. Honestly, I really can't thank you both enough.'

'I can board your broken window up for now, but you will need a glazier. And the police,' advises Martin. 'Although I suppose it's good that at least the thief never managed to get away with your things in the end.'

'I know, thanks to you. If there is anything I can get you?' I ask, already thinking I will buy them a nice bottle of wine or something.

'Well, if there is ever any more of that fudge going begging, I wouldn't say no,' Martin says with a wink.

June nudges him then, and says he is supposed to be watching his sugar intake.

I'm half tempted not to bother with the police as it's true I have my things back after all, but I guess there will be a thief out there ready to pounce on another unsuspecting victim and I don't want that on my conscience.

An hour later, the police have taken a statement and Dad is coming around first thing in the morning to sort the window out, bringing his friend who can source a cheap window for me.

As they leave, I notice Eileen outside chatting to June. I don't want her worrying about thieves in the neighbourhood, but it seems June has already filled her in as I approach them.

'That's awful,' says Eileen, twisting her gold cross necklace. 'I'd been thinking about getting an alarm fitted, I might just do that now.' She frowns.

When Martin and June leave, Eileen asks me if I would like

to spend the evening in her spare room. 'Just until your window is fixed tomorrow.'

'Thank you, Eileen. I think I'd like that.' I smile. 'And I will order us both one of those security doorbells if you like.'

I have no doubt Dad will tell Mum about the break-in, unless I ask him not to as I don't want her worrying. Then again, I wonder if my parents even share news about me with each other anymore.

'Yes, please order one for me, Lauren. And it will be nice, you staying over. We can have a large brandy. For the shock.' She winks.

Eileen's guest room is as neat as the rest of her house, and the bed comfortable, but I toss and turn as I go over the events of the evening. My first thought was to go to Mum's but I didn't want her worrying about me. Besides, she's meant to be on the demonstration outside the Co-op tonight. I texted her earlier from the gingerbread evening, and she told me the protest was cut a bit short due to the freezing weather, and that she was on her way to the protest organiser's flat for coffee. At least there were no police involved this time.

My thoughts turn to the burglary and I fume with anger when I think of the audacity of the thief. Imagine if I had a child and their presents were set out under the tree? Christmas would be ruined for the family if the presents were stolen.

I suspect Martin was right though thinking it an opportunist thief who noticed a house in darkness and took a chance. He obviously hadn't banked on Martin, or indeed the neighbourhood watch in the form of Tony the cat. Who knew a cat could be as good as a dog in protecting property?

Sleep doesn't come easily, the pleasantness of the evening I had been enjoying earlier at the gingerbread evening now soured. And despite my anger I can't help feeling a little vulnerable, which is a feeling I really don't like at all. I also think of

Tony, out for the evening. I kind of wish he was here right now, curled up at the foot of my bed as he sometimes is when he chooses not to go out all night. But then I can't really expect that if I am in Eileen's house. I will buy him his favourite tinned salmon tomorrow as an extra special treat.

ELEVEN

'Hello, love, are you okay?' Dad kisses me on the cheek.

'I'm fine, Dad.' He follows me into the kitchen where I pop the kettle on.

It's the next morning and Dad has turned up with his friend in tow carrying a pane of glass. In no time at all, my window has been replaced and I breathe a sigh of relief.

'That's a bother with the burglary, there are some right toerags around these days, are you sure you're alright, love?' Dad asks, a concerned look on his face as he sips a cup of tea. 'Maybe you should ask your mother to come and stay for a bit,' he suggests.

'I wouldn't want her to do that, although of course it would be lovely, but she has her own life. And Dad, I'd prefer it if you didn't say anything to Mum about the break-in.'

'Don't worry, we don't really speak socially,' he tells me. 'Not that we've fallen out, but our paths don't really cross.' He shrugs. 'I won't say anything if you don't want me to, love, but if there was anything serious to report, then I'm afraid I would,' he says decisively. 'We are still your parents after all.'

I look at Dad, his complexion ruddy from his gardening

career and with a thick head of grey hair. He still tends to several gardens a week, retirement not being for him, as he was still so active when he was old enough to claim his state pension. Thinking about Sue and her husband, maybe there are a lot of retirees that feel that way. Especially as people seem to be living longer these days.

'Of course, Dad, I get that. I wouldn't ask you to keep anything secret that was serious.'

'I'd maybe think about getting an alarm,' says Dad. 'Or a big dog.'

'I don't think Tony would be too impressed by that.' I laugh. 'I have actually ordered one of those camera doorbells though, I've ordered one for Eileen next door too, as she's on her own.'

'Well that's a good start, although maybe an alarm is a good idea too. I can sort that out for you.'

'Okay, thanks, Dad, if it's not too much trouble.'

'Nothing is too much trouble for my only daughter. And I know someone who can give me a good price,' he says.

'I thought you might.' I giggle as Dad seems to know a lot of people who can supply just about anything 'for a good price'. He got to know a lot of people in his gardening days, chatting to householders who were often tradesmen who could help him out if he ever needed anything, which has come in very handy over the years.

As my dad and his friend sip a mug of tea before they head off, I think of the forthcoming party. Checking my list, I realise we don't have any Christmas crackers. I also think of Mum's face when she saw the price tag on the ones we stock in Bentham's, so they will be from a discount shop, unless I can persuade the manager to donate some. He did last year, but things have been a bit tight this year, with sales targets not always being reached. Let's hope the pre-Christmas sales will boost things a little. The town needs a store like Bentham's.

. . .

After Dad and his friend leave, I apply my make-up for work and my finger glides over the tiny lump on my cheek. I'm a bit old for teenage spots, which I thought it was initially, but it isn't, and doesn't appear to be going away. I'd read an article recently in a magazine about skin cancer, which concerned me enough to get it checked out which I will do, of course, but I've just been so busy at work, especially in the run up to Christmas. I'm probably worrying over nothing, although I will see a doctor after Christmas.

'Oh my goodness, why didn't you call me?' asks Gemma as we replenish some lipsticks on a make-up display and I tell her all about last night's burglary. 'That must have been awful walking into the house and seeing it like that.'

'It was a little. I'm sorry I didn't call, but it was getting late. Eileen next door gave me a brandy and the use of her guest room for the night,' I explain.

'That's good. Although I would have come over and stayed the night if you'd called, you know that.'

'I know you would.' I lean over and give her a hug. 'You're a good friend.'

'So are you.' She smiles at me.

I'm sat in the staffroom at lunchtime when I receive a call from Sue.

'Hiya, honey, are you okay to talk?' she asks brightly.

'I am. I'm on my lunch break, so good timing,' I tell her.

'Great. I was just calling to see if you wanted any more decorations for the centre. There was more stuff in the loft where the giant snowman came from apparently. They are a bit old-fashioned, crêpe lanterns and that sort of thing, but hey, it's a pensioners' party I guess, so it might be to their taste.'

You would never think to listen to her that Sue is actually a pensioner herself, albeit still in her sixties.

'I think that would be wonderful! And, yes, I'm sure they would love them and they might bring back lots of memories,' I say, suddenly thinking of the chat I had with my mum. I also recall making those paper chains in red and green with Gran, and a snowman I'd made at school, made from a kitchen roll and covered in cotton wool. It stood proudly on the fireplace at Christmas time. I heard recently that kids aren't allowed to bring toilet roll tubes in to school now, something to do with health and safety I think, which is baffling, especially as they're allowed to play in mud in outdoor areas that are known to be teeming with germs and bacteria.

I've thought about Mum a few times recently, wondering if she is happy living alone, although I'm sure she would tell me if that wasn't the case. Or would she? She's always protected me from worrying about her and Dad, believing that parents shouldn't burden their children. I guess that's what parents do.

'Old decorations do make you feel a bit nostalgic,' agrees Sue. 'Oh, and there is also some of those three-dimensional plastic reindeer and rosy-cheeked Santas that can be displayed on windows. We could really go to town with the decorations this year,' she says excitedly.

'Can you imagine what the council would have to say about us climbing ladders and hanging things from ceilings if they knew. They would probably insist we do a risk assessment first,' I say, laughing, but thinking that they most definitely would.

'I won't tell if you don't.' She laughs. 'Right. I'm off to have my lunchtime Slim Shake now. They taste like pond slime, but I need to shift a few pounds before Christmas.' She chuckles again.

'I'm sure you don't need to worry about your weight,' I say.

'I don't usually, it's just I bought a dress in the sales a size smaller than I am. It was too much of a bargain to resist so I am determined to get into it. It's hard work though, and your mince pies at the Christmas party won't help. I simply can't resist them.'

Sue, still raven haired with regular trips to the hairdresser to keep the grey at bay, has a shapely figure. I could imagine her being one of those young women with a really tiny waist.

'Right, I'll keep the decorations,' says Sue as we are about to wrap up the call. 'Oh, by the way, who won the gingerbread house competition?' she asks. 'I couldn't make it last night.'

'It was a young lady called Audrey. Her house was out of this world, it looked really professional,' I tell her, recalling how perfect Audrey's house had been and wouldn't look out of place in a confectioner's window.

'Oh, lovely. I'm glad there is a bit more competition now. Do you remember when the old postmistress won it year after year, before it turned into such a big event?' asks Sue.

'That was maybe a little bit before my time, but I did hear about it, yes,' I reply.

Before Jo opened the bakery in town and offered a master-class for the winner, the prize was simply a silver trophy, which was displayed on a shelf behind the post office counter for all to see. My mum often told me stories of the formidable post-mistress who won the competition annually, back in the day.

'She was crushed the first time she didn't win the competition, but I won't lie, I was secretly chuffed,' confesses Sue. 'Do you know, I once saw her turn the door sign to closed on a lady with a parcel in the rain, because it was one minute to closing time,' she tells me, and I can imagine her shaking her head. 'And carol singers at her door were given short shrift too, she was like bloody Ebenezer Scrooge. Anyway, I'm off, speak soon.'

'Bye, Sue.' I hang up with a smile on my face, as I always do after I've had a chat with her.

It's a busy afternoon, and a promotion on half price Christmas candles is pushing sales along nicely. At this time of year we all pull together and take varied items at all the tills, rather than our specialised ones as the manager doesn't want people waiting in queues. The staff from the lighting department upstairs are suddenly rushed off their feet. 'And earning their money, instead of standing around with their thumb up their arse,' according to Gemma. Maybe she has a point, as every time I've popped upstairs the staff are rearranging displays and chatting. Christmas time definitely keeps them on their toes.

'Have you got any plans for this evening?' asks Gemma when there's a rare lull in sales.

'Actually, no,' I say, watching a young woman practically give herself a free makeover with the cosmetic samples on display. As it's Christmas time I don't want to approach her with the hard sell, so I leave her to it. She's probably on her way out to a Christmas party. And to be fair, some of the products are pretty expensive in here.

'What, no jobs to tick off the list this evening? Ironing the tea towels, maybe?' she teases.

The young woman makes eye contact with me before smiling and darting out of the shop. I hope she has a good evening.

'I'm not that bad.' I laugh. 'Am I? And actually, I was just going to watch a film. Maybe try out a cocktail in the cocktail shaker I got in the Secret Santa. What are you up to?'

'Coming to yours for a screaming orgasm, if you have the recipe,' she says, and has me laughing out loud.

'Of course I do, the cocktail shaker had a little recipe book. I have all the ingredients, apart from amaretto for that particular cocktail.'

'I'll grab a bottle on the way,' she says, and I am more than happy to have my friend's company this evening.

'Great, it's a date, then. I've got some chilli in the freezer I can defrost for dinner, if you like?'

'Sod that, let's order a takeaway. How about Indian?' says

Gemma. 'Not something I'm likely to have much of over Christmas.'

'Me neither, I suppose.'

I think of my ex, rifling through the kitchen drawer and shouting the takeaway options through to me in the lounge, and I wonder whether I should have tried harder with him? Don't sweat the small stuff, and all that, although I quickly remind myself that it wasn't in fact small stuff. He could easily squander hundreds of pounds a month on gadgets and take-aways. It wasn't as though we even had to save for a mortgage as I own the house, but he might have shown some interest in at least saving up for a wedding. I'd been wearing his engagement ring for two and a half years, having been together for four. I realise it's been over a year since I treated myself to a takeaway, the thought of it triggering painful memories. Maybe it's time to grasp the nettle and get on with things. And I do miss the occasional takeaway, truth be told.

'You're on. A curry with all the trimmings sounds just perfect,' I say as we grab our bags from the cloakroom.

'Great, see you at seven,' says Gemma. 'I'll bring the menu from A Passage to India.'

'Oh my goodness, I'd forgotten how good this tastes.'

I devour some of the delicious lamb curry before taking a long sip of Indian beer. The banquet is spread out on the kitchen table, with pakoras, bhajis and dips all vying for space and some nineties music playing in the background.

'Do you want me to stay over tonight?' asks Gemma as she dips some naan bread into a dip.

'I don't mind. Do you want to?'

'I wouldn't mind.' She shrugs. 'I just thought you might like some company.'

'Do you mean after the break-in?' I ask.

'Yeah, suppose. Although with it being Sunday tomorrow, I thought we could have a late night and sit up chatting like we used to. I can download some Take That to listen to.'

'Gosh, remember listening to them?' I say, recalling being at a disco where everyone was raising their arms in the air and singing 'Never Forget' at the top of their voices.

I think of my plans for tomorrow then as the day of the community centre party draws closer. There are sausage rolls to make and freeze, as well as a Christmas toy drop-off at the children's refuge. And someone is coming tomorrow afternoon to steam clean the curtains in the lounge.

'I mean, I won't if you don't want me to,' says Gemma, noting my hesitation as I think of my plans for tomorrow and I feel like a bad friend. 'I just thought it might be nice, that's all.' She shrugs.

'Of course it would be nice. In fact, not just nice, it would be lovely. I do have a few things to do tomorrow, but we can still enjoy this evening together.'

'Great!' Gemma clicks her beer bottle next to mine, before she leans in close and glances at me.

'Is everything okay, Lauren?'

'Yes, fine why?' I ask, backing away slightly.

'I just... I've noticed you being a bit preoccupied lately. I've known you long enough to notice that. I hope there isn't anything you aren't telling me. I have noticed you stroking your cheek a lot too lately.'

'Well, I thought it was nothing at first, just a spot but it won't go away.' I sigh. 'I haven't had spots since I was a teenager, even then it was rare that I got one. But it isn't a spot, it's a clear bump. I'm sure it's nothing though.'

Gemma is quiet for a moment before she speaks.

'Look, I don't want to frighten you, but you ought to get that checked out,' she says gently. 'Moles and lumps shouldn't just appear out of nowhere.' She frowns.

'Yes, I've thought about that too. I've just been so busy with everything lately. I'll make sure I get it checked out after Christmas.'

'You will not.' She places her beer bottle down firmly on the coffee table. 'You will make a doctor's appointment on Monday.'

'It's literally just over a week until the new year. Besides, I wouldn't get any results until after Christmas, so let's just enjoy the holidays.'

'Okay, but promise me you will get it checked. I am sure it's absolutely nothing but, well, you were a bit of a sunbed fanatic when we were young, as I recall,' she reminds me, as if I hadn't already thought about that myself.

'I know.' I sigh. 'Okay, I promise I will get it checked, let's not put a downer on the evening and fire up some more tunes.'

I reassure myself that there is no history of skin cancer in the family and there is probably nothing to worry about.

As I listen to the music, Gemma's comment makes me think of a holiday to Spain, headphones plugged into my Sony Walkman, soaking up the sun on a beach on the Costa del Sol wearing the lowest factor of sunscreen. I was determined to impress my friends with a tan when I got back, instead of heading to the local sunbed shop, which was essentially a room at the back of a general store. It was called Golden Days, which, thinking about it, would probably have been a more suitable name for an old folks' home. The shopkeeper would hand us a bottle of lotion and take our money, never restricting our visits. It was big business then, and there was always a queue of girls, desperate for a tan before they donned their glad rags, ready for night out on the town. If anything, I'm surprised I don't have any more sinister moles.

We chat about the old days as we always do when we play our favourite nineties songs, and as midnight approaches, my eyes feel heavy with tiredness.

'Time for bed then, is it?' asks Gemma, who I get the feeling would be happy to sit up all night chatting.

'Gosh, I think it is, yes, I can't take the pace anymore.' I smile as I collect our plates to take to the dishwasher.

'I wish I could feel sleepy at bedtime, but it takes me hours to get to sleep,' reveals Gemma.

'Does it?' I ask, surprised.

'Yeah, the minute my head touches the pillow my brain goes into overdrive,' she admits. 'It's so annoying. The other night, I found myself googling Jennifer Aniston films at one in the morning. Why on earth would I do that?'

'You never said you were having trouble sleeping. Is something bothering you?' I ask.

'Not especially. I just don't like being in the flat on my own sometimes. Only lately, that is. And maybe you having a break-in has made me a bit nervous, even though I didn't think it had,' she admits.

Which probably explains why she offered to stay here tonight, and, of course, the other night, thinking about it. It never occurred to me that she might be the one who is feeling anxious.

'Aw, I'm sure you're perfectly safe, especially being on the second floor,' I reassure her. 'And you have secure entry downstairs. Unless you imagine someone shinning up the drainpipe.'

'Well, I hadn't thought of that, but I am now, thanks.' She widens her eyes at me.

'That's hardly likely it, is it? Just keep your windows locked though.'

'I do anyway.' She laughs. 'I don't like the thought of spiders getting in.'

'You should put some lavender along your windowsill. That will keep them out apparently.'

We head to bed, and I remind Gemma there is a TV in the guest room, if she can't quite get to sleep.

'I'll probably sleep better with you in the next room,' she

says, and I wrap her in a hug. 'Although I might just stick it on for the drone in the background as that usually sends me off.'

'Okay. Night then.'

'Night, Lauren.'

Despite Gemma's assurance that everything is okay, I can't help wondering if I am not the only one with something playing on their mind. I guess I will find out when she is ready to talk. We always do in the end.

TWELVE

'What exactly is vegan honey?'

After breakfast at a local café, a treat from Gemma, I'm at a green Christmas fayre with Mum. It's early afternoon on Sunday and I've made the sausage rolls and frozen them, as well as changed the beds, and nipped to my neighbour Martin's with a batch of freshy made fudge for recovering my stolen goods from the burglar. I have also installed mine and Eileen's security doorbells. I've left the guy steaming the curtains in the lounge and, as he is another acquaintance of Dad's, I feel quite comfortable doing so.

I half apologised to June with her mentioning Martin's sugar intake, but he laughed and said he would share it with her. After that, I dropped a box of toys, courtesy of Bentham's, at the women's refuge and they were over the moon. It breaks my heart to think that children could be without gifts at Christmas time.

'It is apple based,' says the stallholder.

'Interesting,' I reply, although I can't quite understand why it's cruel to use bees, it's what they do, isn't it? Chatting to the stallholder further though, she tells me it's a good alternative which I kind of understand and some of the beekeepers use antibiotics so they are not always as organic as we think apparently. She suggested I ask about the hives when purchasing honey, which I think is good advice.

Mum is admiring a pretty fake leather bracelet at a stall, with tassels and studded with coloured beads.

Moving on, I come across items made from sustainable wood that include lamps, framed mirrors and a particularly attractive pair of earrings made from oak and painted with a swirly pattern. Mum admires then at the same time, so when she nips to the loo, I buy them for her as part of her Christmas present.

Having perused the rest of the stalls and bought some jams and essential bath oils, we are sitting in a café area sipping an oat milk coffee, which, although I am not vegan, is really quite delicious.

'What are you up to later?' Mum asks and I think of how I might get a scented bath and an early night. Last night was way later than I'm used to these days, but it was fun spending the night with Gemma and playing the music of our youth. Music does that, doesn't it? A place, an event, a time in our life can all come flooding back to us when we hear a particular song.

'Not a lot, you?' I sip my coffee.

'I'm going to the cinema,' says Mum, stirring her drink.

'Oh, that's nice. Who are you going with?'

'Someone from the food bank. His name is Terry and we are strictly friends, before you ask,' she says firmly.

'If you say so.' I grin.

'I do, and I must say I'm really looking forward to it. The film, I mean,' she adds. 'I can't think of anything worse than getting romantically involved with someone at my age.' She pulls a face. 'Any males I meet will stay strictly in the friend zone, as you young ones say. It would take someone very special to change my mind.' She grins. 'Anyway, speaking of dates, when was the last time you went on one?' Mum says, but not unkindly.

'A while.' I shrug. 'But I'm okay with it. If I meet someone, I meet someone. If not that's okay too. Anyway, I should probably make a move now,' I say, draining my coffee. 'Enjoy your film.'

'Thanks, love.'

I think about Mum's comment, realising it has indeed been a while since I've been out on a date, and enjoyed that tingle of excitement: getting dressed up and ready to be whisked off somewhere. For some reason, when I think of this, the image of a certain someone pops into my head.

Driving home later, I can't believe that I actually spot hot shop guy. I inwardly cringe when I think of how I doused him in Prosecco the other evening. Even if it was the non-alcoholic type!

Stopping at the traffic lights, I watch him leaving a local restaurant with his little girl, holding her hand as they approach the busy road. She looks so sweet, a pair of white fluffy earmuffs over her dark hair. He looks effortlessly sexy in dark jeans and a brown leather jacket. I almost want to wave out of the window, but then, why would I? I don't even know his name, after all, and I'm not sure he wants to see the woman who was responsible for making him sit in damp jeans all evening.

All the same, I can't help noticing that it's Sunday afternoon and there is no sign of a wife or girlfriend, but just the two of them once more. Not that it's any of my business. I glance at them in my rear-view mirror as the lights change to green and I drive on.

THIRTEEN

I had a chat with Mum on the phone this morning, following her cinema trip, and she told me she had a nice evening, once again dismissing any thoughts of romance.

'Well, I for one think it's nice that you are at least having evenings out with friends that don't involve chaining yourself to a lamp post, or similar, for a good cause.'

'I don't think I would go that far, but I take your point,' she agrees. 'It was really nice being in a toasty cinema watching a good movie.'

Maybe she is beginning to realise that being outdoors isn't such a great idea during the winter months. At least, I hope so.

'Anyway, I'm off to work now, Mum. Speak to you soon.'

'Bye, love. Have a good day.'

I head to Sue's place on my way in, as she has invited me round to show me the six-foot Santa, along with the boxes of Christmas decorations.

'And I see what you mean about it being scary.' I laugh as it stares at me with a smile showing giant teeth and thick, brown eyebrows. Surely someone designed this thing as a joke.

We rummage through all of the other stuff, and the lengths

of twisted crêpe paper decorations and home-made paper chains have the memories flooding back.

One year, my grandad allowed me to paint the inside of the lounge windows with a beautiful scene from *The Snowman* movie, where the snowman is flying over the mountains with the little boy. Dad had found the box of paints in the cupboard, not realising they were Gran's acrylic glass paints from her crafting box. It took days and lots of hard work after Christmas to get the windows back to normal, although Gran couldn't help but be impressed with our handiwork.

'I'm so looking forward to the pensioners' Christmas lunch,' says Sue, lifting some red shiny tree baubles from a box. 'It makes you really feel good being involved in something charitable, especially at this time of year,' she muses. 'Sometimes I think I ought to do a little bit more though.'

'Oh, it does,' I agree. 'And I know what you mean about volunteering more, although life can get very busy, I suppose. It's important we all look after each other at Christmas though.'

'Definitely. A friend of mine, who lives in London, volunteers at a soup kitchen on Christmas Day and says it hands down beats Christmas at her house,' Sue continues. 'Then again, her family are a bunch of crackpots and all they do is fight, especially after a few drinks.' She laughs. 'Last year, her grandad ended up in the garden half naked after taking a dip in the hot tub, then locking himself out. Apparently the music was so loud inside no one heard him knocking on the kitchen door that someone had locked.' She guffaws. 'That poor man.'

'Oh, Sue, you do make me laugh.' I shake my head, imagining the poor old man freezing in the garden whilst his family partied on.

'Ooh and did I tell you, I've got a record player?' Sue tells me excitedly. 'A friend of Barry's works in antiques, well, junk mainly, but he has a load of vinyl. I thought the pensioners might like some golden oldies if I took it along to the party.'

'That's a great idea! I've been thinking about purchasing one myself, some of them look quite stylish.'

I'd spotted a black and cream one that would fill a space against my grey wall in the lounge.

After spending all day on my feet, I head home just after six, ready for a hot bath and to wrap Mum's earrings, when I receive a text from my dad's partner, asking if it is convenient to call me, which leaves me mildly concerned as Rose never usually contacts me. Apart from the one occasion when she called and asked me if I knew where Dad was. It seems he had bumped into an old friend and popped into a local pub for a pint, that turned into several, and his dinner was ruined.

I tap out a reply to the text and a few minutes later, Rose calls and my heart thuds as she tells me Dad has been taken to the hospital by ambulance with a suspected heart attack.

'What? When? Is he okay?' I manage to get the words out.

'A couple of hours ago. Yes, he's okay, well, when I say okay he's conscious and everything, so don't worry. The doctors are running some tests,' says Rose, sounding flustered.

'Tell him I will be there in half an hour,' I say, hanging up and praying he will be well when I get to the hospital.

All the way there I worry about what I might find. The thought of losing Dad is almost too much to bear. He's always been so strong, and fit for his age. And he's hardly ever been ill, as I recall. Even when he was, he would shrug it off and recover quickly, although a recent health check at the GP suggested he ought to watch his cholesterol as it was creeping higher. Perhaps he hadn't heeded the advice, although I would be surprised by that.

My head spins as I drive, willing myself to get there quickly but as safely as possible. Why are traffic lights always on red when you are in a hurry? I tap my hands on the steering wheel impatiently as I wait for the lights to change to green.

A grey-haired man walks past on the pavement, accompanied by a woman young enough to be his daughter. He throws his head back and laughs at something she has just said and I swallow down a lump in my throat at the thought of never being able to do that again with Dad. I say a silent prayer that he will be alright as the lights finally turn to green.

FOURTEEN

'Oh, Dad, thank goodness you're okay.' I sigh with relief.

A tired-looking Dad, who is hooked up to a blood pressure monitor and has pads all over his chest, manages a smile. A nurse in a blue uniform bustles about checking things, before bringing me a chair.

'I'm alright, love, don't you worry.' Dad takes hold of my hand trying to reassure me, but looks as though he has aged several years overnight. I think of some of the older people who have lost their partners, and how they told me the community centre Christmas party really lifts their spirits at this time of year. I hope this year's bash will be the best one ever. Dad being here in hospital reminds me that we don't have our parents forever.

Rose is sat on a chair next to him at the other side of the bed, red eyed and twisting her handkerchief.

'So what happened?' I ask gently.

'I had this crushing pain in my chest,' Dad explains. 'I thought it was indigestion at first, what with diving into that Christmas pudding before Christmas. I've learned my lesson now though as it gave me a right scare.' He exhales slowly.

I take a sideways glance at Rose, who knows Dad should not really be eating such things. He has had a heart scare before, and his cholesterol is higher than it ought to be, which I know she is well aware of.

'Well, yes, maybe you should have waited until Christmas,' I say, trying not to sound like I am scolding him.

'He didn't have much,' says Rose, avoiding my eyes.

'He shouldn't really be having anything like that at all,' I say evenly, determined not to cause a scene. 'Christmas Day, I understand a little treat, yes, but we are not there yet,' I remind her.

'Yes, I know, we probably shouldn't have opened that pudding,' concedes Rose. 'I like getting Christmas treats in early, as the shops are so busy at Christmas that I avoid them. Last year they had sold out of some of the things we like. Maybe I should hide the not so healthy things though.' She frowns.

'Hmm,' I say just as a doctor arrives.

I bombard him with questions, before being told that Dad has a blocked artery and will need surgery.

'When?' asks Rose anxiously.

'Sooner rather than later. We will take you to have a stent fitted for the time being.' He turns to Dad. 'You are okay for now, but you have a blocked heart valve so will need valve replacement surgery in the new year. You will be discharged with some medication in the meantime, but it would be wise not to overindulge over the festive period, as difficult as that might be.' He glances between me and Rose and I nod.

I know it's ultimately down to Dad to look after his own health, but can't help thinking that Rose shouldn't encourage him. He's always been a lover of rich foods and red wine though, which is no doubt why he is counting the cost now. Christmas at our house growing up would have Dad rubbing his hands together at the sight of mine and Mum's home-made bakes, and polishing off a cheeseboard in the evenings as we played board games. Remembering those evenings brings a lump to my throat. If only I could turn back time to enjoy one of those family evenings once more.

'You might have to give all those mince pies away,' Dad says to Rose with a sigh.

'Or I could take them to the food bank?' I suggest.

'Maybe we could keep one box,' says Rose and I throw her a look. What does she not understand about the fact that Dad has just had a heart attack?

'Or maybe not, gosh, what am I thinking?' she says apologetically.

'I'm not stopping you from enjoying yourself,' says Dad to Rose good-naturedly. 'Maybe just eat things in secret, hey.' He winks. 'Keep temptation away from me.'

'Oh, Dad,' I say, taking him by the hand. 'I'm so glad you are going to be alright. My heart sank when Rose phoned and I couldn't help fearing the worst.' I swallow down a lump in my throat. 'And I'm sure after your surgery you will be as good as new.'

'I'm alright.' He smiles. 'And maybe I ought to have looked after myself a bit more. I never was one for fruit and vegetables,' he muses. 'Perhaps there is something to be said for the plant-based diet your mother has.'

'Everything in moderation, I say,' sniffs Rose, clearly not pleased that Dad has brought Mum's name into the conversation.

'Well, yes, Dad, I guess it is your responsibility.' I smile at Rose, feeling a little guilty that I may have blamed her a bit. 'But we all need to be on board. We want you to stick around for a while yet, Dad.'

I squeeze his hand.

'You know, maybe you ought to consider coming to the party at the community centre this year,' I suggest, glancing from Dad to Rose. 'It might be nice to have someone cook for you, what with you still working, Rose.'

'Hmm, well maybe, although I always thought it was for people much older than us, or those who have lost partners,' she says, unconvinced.

'The majority are, I suppose. You know you are also both welcome to join Mum and me on Christmas Day,' I offer, deciding to bite the bullet.

'At your house? I'm not sure about that,' says Rose, smoothing down her skirt before Dad has a chance to answer.

'Well, the offer is there.' I smile.

'Thank you. I think we'll be okay though,' she says a little tightly.

'Of course.' I smile again. 'But be sure to ask me if you need help with anything.'

I might be mistaken, but looking at Dad's expression I get the feeling he would love for us all to spend Christmas Day together.

I grab some coffees and stay for a while chatting, feeling relieved that, hopefully, Dad is going to be okay.

'Bye, Dad,' I say, giving him a kiss on the cheek before I eventually leave. 'Bye, Rose, and remember give me a call if you need anything.'

'Of course, thanks, Lauren,' she says, but I don't believe for a second that she will.

FIFTEEN

The day before the party, Sue and I take the boxes of decorations to the community centre. Mum has arrived to help and tells me she has just been to see Dad at the hospital.

'Really?' I ask, surprised. 'What did Rose think about that?'

'She was at work,' says Mum, plonking a box down onto a table.

Rose works part-time at a health food shop in town, an irony not lost on either of us.

'Did he seem okay? Was he expecting you?' I ask as I unravel a set of tree lights that has seen better days from a box.

'Well, he seemed in good spirits, and, yes, he was expecting me. I texted him when you told me about the heart attack,' she tells me as she unpacks a foil ceiling star and smiles. 'We talked about the only other time he had been in hospital, which was when he fell off a ladder and broke his leg. You were only about six years old, so I don't suppose you remember it,' says Mum as she now pulls a rather tired-looking angel from a box.

I vaguely recall the incident, although I think I remember it more because the story was retold so many times. Dad had climbed a rotten wooden ladder unbeknown to him, and a rung gave way and he fell onto the patio. Thankfully not from too great a height, but enough to break a leg.

'He said the hospital food hadn't improved much. I took him a slice of sugar free chocolate beetroot cake, and he said it was lovely. There's hope for him yet.' She giggles.

As it's two days before Christmas, the usual keep fit classes and slimming clubs have finished until the new year, so we spend the evening decorating the tree and hanging the nostalgic foil decorations from the ceiling.

The giant Santa has been inflated and plugged in near the entrance, and when it starts singing 'Frosty the Snowman', we roar with laughter. It has a deep voice that matches the scary appearance, and I wonder who on earth designed it? Or maybe it is just malfunctioning. Either way, it's hysterical.

'Do you know, me and Barry were sat last night all cosy watching a drama and having a little drink, and I started thinking about people on their own at this time of year,' says Sue as she places a string of paper lanterns across a window. 'It feels so good to bring them together at Christmas, even if it's only for one day, although I know it's more than a day, which is down to your thoughtfulness,' she says kindly.

A couple of years ago us volunteers also took details of anyone who would like a visit through the week from one of us, or put them in touch with Age UK, who arranged little outings. One lady was very reticent at first, shy by nature, but ended up enjoying trips to Blackpool and Lytham St Annes. It was the highlight of her trip when she ran into a one-time TV comedian outside Blackpool Tower, who duly posed for a selfie with her.

I'm sure Sue was thinking about the older people at Christmas, but it can be lonely for younger people too. Even when surrounded by family you can still feel lonely, something I know only too well, especially being an only child. Or maybe it's a feeling of being alone rather than lonely, as after the big day everyone goes back to their busy lives, don't they? Which was why I was determined to help some of the older people make connections all year round.

'No one should be alone at Christmas, love, including yourself, so if the situation ever arises that you are, you know where we are, the more the merrier I say, and you too, of course,' she says to my mum.

Sue always has a crowd around her Christmas table, and I know she means every word.

'Thanks, Sue,' I tell her genuinely. 'But I can't lie, after the busy Christmas Eve I quite like a quiet one on the day itself. I don't know where you get your energy from.'

'Me too,' says Mum. 'I always look forward to a Christmas movie in the evening.' She smiles warmly at me. 'With a Baileys or two.'

'I've always thrived on being busy,' says Sue. 'I never know what to do with myself when I have some spare time.'

'She usually drags me out somewhere, which generally involves spending money,' says Barry good-naturedly and Sue tuts and tells him that you can't take it with you when you go.

'You should take some time to relax though, or doing too much can catch up with you,' I tell Sue, thinking of Dad and his heart problems.

'Talking of taking a break, I'll go and pop the kettle on and make us all a brew,' says Mum.

'Oh, don't get me wrong, even though I like being on the go, I do know how to relax,' Sue tells me. 'Especially later in the day. I can spend hours in the bath reading. Ask Barry, he's forever banging on the door telling me to hurry up.' She chuckles. 'We really do need to get a second loo downstairs.'

'Maybe we would have the money to do that if we stop going out for lunch,' he says and she scrunches up a paper napkin and throws it at him.

I stand back and look at the festooned hall that is beginning to look a bit like a grotto. I hope we haven't gone overboard, but then, can you ever have too many decorations at Christmas?

'Will your dad be home for Christmas?' asks Sue as she straightens a slightly wonky-looking Christmas Santa on the window.

'Yes, he's being discharged this afternoon, with an operation scheduled for after Christmas. I did ask him and Rose to join me and Mum for Christmas lunch. At least that way I could keep an eye on him,' I confide to Sue.

'Did you? That was a nice idea. What did he say?' asks Mum, returning from the kitchen carrying a tray with mugs of tea.

'He turned me down, or, more accurately, Rose did. Dad never actually said anything,' I tell her, recalling his resigned expression.

'Well, it was nice of you to ask. Maybe you just put them on the spot, and they will come round to the idea.'

'Maybe,' I say doubtfully.

Sue opens her bag and pulls out a box of After Eight mints and offers me one. 'Dark chocolate is actually proven to be very good for you.' She winks, before popping one into her mouth.

'Go on then, if you say so,' I say, taking one, unable to resist my favourite dark chocolate.

Thinking of the pensioners who are alone at Christmas makes me think of the Christmas I spent by myself, when Mum and Dad decided to go on a cruise. That was before Mum became interested in saving the planet, of course. She would never go on a diesel guzzling ship these days. They had tried to persuade me to go along too as I'd just split with my boyfriend but, in all honesty, I just wanted to binge-watch TV and eat too much food. I painted on my brightest smile and convinced my parents I would spend the day with Gemma, who was actually going to Prague with her boyfriend.

The reality was, I hit the gin and cried through Christmas

Day and ended up asking a colleague to do a shift swap, meaning I was back at work for the Boxing Day sales. I told my parents that I'd had a fine old time, and swore Gemma to secrecy about me spending the day alone.

'Well, I think that's as much as we can do for now,' I say and Barry says he will come around Christmas Eve morning and get the tables and chairs out.

'I'll be here. We can all give a hand,' I say, before taking the cups into the kitchen and washing them.

There's a dark sky looming when we leave the centre at four o'clock, and a stillness in the air. I wouldn't be surprised to see some snow later.

My grandad taught me how to smell the weather. A fresh, almost earthy scent, means rain, and an unseasonal mildness, while a warm coloured sky often means snow. I always get a headache just before a thunderstorm too.

'I think it might snow,' I say, looking up at the grey, slightly orange-streaked sky.

'Do you? But Christmas is two days away. If it snows today, it will all be mush by Christmas Day,' says Mum as we walk towards the car.

'Unless it's really thick and it sticks. We might get snowed in, like we did years ago,' I say, recalling the sleigh rides down the nearby hills and cosy nights around the fire sipping mulled wine after a heavy snowfall that hit almost the entire country.

'Oh, I remember that. 2011, wasn't it? I dropped my front door keys in the snow, which was almost a foot high,' Mum says, laughing. 'It took your dad ages to find them, digging around with a spade, which was baffling as I'd dropped them straight down in front of me.'

That was the last Christmas we spent together as a family, before my parents went their separate ways.

'Anyway, it had better not snow until after the Christmas Eve lunch,' I say, thinking of what a headache it would be for the pensioners to get there if it did. 'It can do what it likes after that.'

'It's a shame we can't order it on a certain date, as I'd like it to be on Christmas Day, after lunch whilst I'm watching *Die Hard*, which is bound to be on a channel somewhere,' says Sue.

'Even though it definitely isn't a Christmas movie,' I say, quickly getting into my car and closing the door before she can argue and Mum jumps into the passenger seat.

Sue waves a fist at me before she takes Barry's arm and, muffled up in their winter coats, they walk over to their house, which is literally across the road from the community centre.

Pulling out of the community centre, a black car approaches and makes its way into the car park. I can see that it is hot shop guy, and I wonder what he is doing here?

Before heading home, I make a detour into town to buy a few things for Dad, and Mum plans to call in at a charity shop to drop a Christmas card off for one of her friends who works there. In town I run into Audrey coming out of Boots.

'Lauren, hi.' She smiles warmly. 'Where are you off to?'

'Hi, Audrey. I'm just grabbing a couple of things for my dad for when I visit him tomorrow.' I tell her all about his heart problems. 'He's okay, but is scheduled for an operation early in the new year.'

'Oh no, I'm so sorry to hear that.' She frowns. 'My dad died of a heart attack,' she says, before covering her mouth with her hand. 'Gosh, I'm so sorry, what a stupid thing to say.' She looks mortified.

'Please don't worry, I know you didn't mean anything by it.'

'I'm always putting my foot in it.' She shakes her head. 'My mum says she's surprised I wasn't born with my foot in my mouth. Sorry,' she says again.

'I'm sure that's not true. You mustn't let anyone make you feel that way,' I say gently, realising that even the most innocent remarks can get to us.

'It's kind of true though. I kind of just say what's on my mind. Maybe that's why I don't have many friends,' she admits.

'Ah, but here's the thing. Real friends wouldn't mind, they would know that you don't mean to be rude. You know the saying, "Those that mind don't matter, and those that matter don't mind."'

'That's so true. But I guess it's making the friendship in the first place I find difficult,' she admits.

'You met me and Gemma, didn't you? Not to mention your new friend from the gingerbread evening,' I remind her.

'I did, didn't I? Fingers crossed I haven't messed things up so far.'

'Of course you haven't, and when you do make new friends, just be honest. Tell them in advance that you have trouble filtering your thoughts,' I tell her. 'I have always found that honesty is the best policy in any situation. They might even help you.'

'You are so wise,' says Audrey. 'I'm so glad I met you.'

'Well it's easier dispensing advice to other people.' I shrug.

'What are you up to tonight then?' I ask as we fall into step.

'I'm actually going to an arts and craft sale a few miles away with Ellie, my new friend.'

'Oh, that sounds like a nice place to pick up a Christmas gift.'

'That's what I was thinking. Um, you are welcome to join us,' she offers.

'Oh, I wasn't angling for an invite.' I laugh. 'And honestly? I have a ton of things to do. Thanks, though, I hope you enjoy it.'

'I will.' She smiles. 'I'm just heading home to drop this cough medicine off for Mum.' She lifts a bag. 'She's come down with a bit of a virus.'

'Sorry to hear that. Actually, if you have ten minutes I could give you a lift home? I'm just popping into Bentham's to buy

Dad a new dressing gown. I couldn't help noticing at the hospital that his current one is a bit well worn.'

'Sure.' She smiles. 'And thanks, that would be great.'

I choose a thick, maroon dressing gown for Dad, along with a spy thriller from WH Smith. Dad has always enjoyed a good spy thriller and as he is supposed to be taking things easy at home, hopefully he will appreciate it. Mum texts me and I tell her I will meet her in the car park and I introduce Audrey to Mum when she arrives.

'Actually, I was wondering,' Audrey begins when we pull up outside her house. 'Do you need an extra pair of hands at all at the pensioners' Christmas lunch?'

'We can always do with an extra pair of hands,' I tell her and Mum agrees. 'Why, are you offering to help?'

'I was thinking about it. To tell you the truth, I was trying to persuade Mum to go along, but she won't hear of it.' She fiddles with the strap on her bag. 'And I suppose it's too late now anyway.' She looks at me.

'No, really, there is always room for one more. Honestly, we have a mountain of food this year. Maybe you could ask her again?' I suggest.

'I will, because I think she needs to make some friends. She doesn't go out anymore since Dad died,' she confides. 'I think she feels a bit trapped inside the house.'

'But she encourages you to make friends?'

'She does.' Audrey nods. 'She told me she doesn't want me to end up like her,' says Audrey, and my heart goes out to her mum. 'She tells me I ought to be going out with people my own age, and not hanging around with her. But I just feel a bit mean leaving her alone every time I go out of the house.'

'Oh, Audrey, I'm sorry you feel like that, but you have to go to work, your mum knows that. And your mum is right in encouraging you to go and try different things, but maybe we could help her to do the same? You know, she is lucky to have a daughter like you.'

'Thanks,' says Audrey coyly.

'Try and get your mum to come,' Mum says gently. 'The first step is the most difficult but after that it isn't so bad. She will meet lots of nice people at the community centre.'

'I'll try.' She smiles.

'Anyway, try and let me know by tomorrow, just so we can set an extra place. But, of course, you are welcome to come and help out regardless. I can even arrange a lift for you both.'

'Really? Oh wow, that might be a good thing. Mum hates the thought of buses, and I imagine it will be difficult to get a taxi on Christmas Eve. Perhaps getting a lift might encourage her.'

'I will personally collect you both, I promise. So I take it you're not working Christmas Eve then?'

'No, I actually finish tomorrow until after Christmas, as I worked until late Christmas Eve last year. We have a rota.'

'Then you must definitely come along to the centre on Christmas Eve,' I tell her.

'Thanks, Lauren.' She smiles. 'I will almost certainly be there.'

'Great. Speak to you soon.'

I notice the net curtains part as Audrey's mum peers out and watches me drive off as Audrey walks up the path. I do hope they will both come along on Christmas Eve. I don't like the thought of them spending Audrey's Christmas holidays stuck inside the house, her feeling guilty about leaving her mum.

SIXTEEN

At home I realise I'm out of milk, so head to the corner shop to buy some. I'm walking along the pavement a little close to the road, when a car drives through a huge puddle of water and soaks me.

I stand there dripping and catching my breath, like in that scene from the *Bridget Jones* movie, cursing the idiot driving, and raising my hands in the air, when the car comes to a sudden stop. Oh heck, I hope there isn't going to be any trouble.

'I am so sorry.'

Hot shop guy is striding towards me, holding his hands up and at least having the decency to look genuinely sorry.

'Really? You're not just getting me back for soaking you in Prosecco.' I make a vain attempt to dab at my trousers with my scarf that I have unwound from around my neck.

'I'd like to think I'm not that childish,' he says in that annoyingly lovely Irish accent. 'Look, let me give you a lift, you can at least warm up for a minute in the car.' At least he has the decency to look a little contrite. 'I have heated car seats,' he adds.

'Is that a chat-up line?' I ask, annoyed and already beginning to shiver but as it's freezing and I don't fancy walking home soaked through, I reluctantly accept his offer.

'I hadn't thought of that,' he says with a laugh, before straightening his smile when I don't return it.

'And, actually, I was on my way to the shop,' I tell him. 'I am out of milk.'

'Then take a seat, I insist. I will nip into the shop and get your milk for you,' he says, fixing me with those eyes that are large and green, framed with dark lashes that any girl would envy.

'Oh, and I'm Kian, by the way,' he says when I am seated in his passenger seat. 'Just so you're not accepting a lift from a stranger.' He grins.

'Lauren,' I tell him.

'Pleased to meet you, Lauren, officially that is. After I get your milk, I will drop you home. How's that?' He smiles warmly.

I suddenly wonder whether I ought to let this guy know where I live. I don't really know him after all. Should I even be sitting in his car, even though I now know his name? Then again, I have seen him about town, I guess, and Jo has his details from when he booked the gingerbread evening. I tap out a quick text to Gemma to tell her who I am with all the same, in case I go missing. Maybe I should have hopped in my car, instead of walking here.

'Are you sure I am not keeping you from being somewhere?' I ask Kian as the warm air from the car heater washes over me.

'No, I've finished what I needed to do. I went into town to sort out a few birthday balloons. It's my daughter's birthday on Christmas Eve,' he tells me.

'The little girl you were with at the gingerbread evening?'

'Yes, her name's Bella,' he says, smiling proudly.

'She's super cute,' I say, recalling the little girl, and the excited look on her face when she won a prize.

'She is adorable, although I may be biased. She's really looking forward to her party,' he tells me.

'That's nice. Ooh, that's really nice,' I say as he gives me a puzzled look.

'The warm seat, I mean,' I say as I feel the warmth flood through my body. 'I could sit here for ages.'

'Be my guest.' He grins. 'You can give me a shopping list of things to buy if you like, although I'm sure you want to get out of those wet clothes,' he says, looking directly at me and I feel my cheeks flush.

'Of course I do, but I am warming up quickly,' I say, avoiding his gaze and wishing my car had such a feature.

Pulling up outside the shop, I reach for some pound coins in my pocket for the milk, rather than handing over my bank card.

'Don't worry about it,' says Kian, smiling. He has nice teeth I notice. 'It's the least I can do after soaking you.'

'So, it's your daughter's birthday Christmas Eve? I'm not sure if that's a good or a bad thing, being so close to Christmas,' I tell him, when he returns with the milk, and two large chocolate chip cookies.

'They were discounted at the counter,' he explains and I wonder why he has bought two. Surely he isn't expecting me to invite him in for coffee? But then, the other one is probably for his daughter.

'I guess, that's why I try to make it a bit special,' he explains. 'She is spending Christmas with me this year.'

I'm about to mention that I saw him near the community centre earlier, when a teenager walks into the road without even looking up from his phone.

'Are you trying to get yourself killed?' He winds the window down and calls to the startled teenager, after braking suddenly. The young man sheepishly raises a hand and mouths sorry, before darting onto the pavement.

'Jeez. What's the world coming to?' He shakes his head.

'Some people need their phones surgically removing from their hands.'

'I know what you mean. Do you know, someone made a purchase in the shop the other day, without even glancing up from their phone. It's plain rude sometimes.'

'So that's where I have seen you before,' says Kian. 'When I saw you at the gingerbread evening, I was racking my brains. You look kind of different out of that uniform.' He glances at me, dressed in jeans, jumper, and boots. 'It's quite a formal look in the shop, isn't it?'

'It is. Bentham's strives for the formal image alright. I kind of like getting dressed up for work though.'

'I like it. It's quite sexy in a way.' He gives me a sideways glance and almost has me blushing once more. 'Sorry, that probably makes me sound like a sexist pig.' He pulls a face. 'It's just you know, the tight black skirt and white blouse, it's reminiscent of the nineteen fifties. Especially with the red lipstick.'

So he has noticed my lipstick?

'Sorry if that sounds bad. I'm never sure what is the acceptable thing to say these days. I just mean, it's quite a glamorous look,' he explains a little awkwardly.

'I don't see how anyone could be offended by being told they look good,' I reassure him. 'Maybe words like sexy are a bit off though.' Which seems a bit like a double standard as he is known as hot shop guy to me and Gemma, but never mind.

'Duly noted.'

'Oh, and this warm seat is just too comfortable,' I say, changing the subject. 'I'd be worried I would fall asleep if I was driving any distance,' I say, enjoying the warmth around me.

'I never use it on a long journey for that reason.' He smiles. 'And I always start a long journey with a double espresso.'

It's a short journey to my house, and I ask him to drop me off at the corner, just in case, even though he seems perfectly normal. And a good father by the sound of things but you just can't be too careful, especially these days.

'Um, thanks for the lift then. See you around,' I say, before climbing out of the car.

'I think you made it home just in time,' says Kian, glancing up at the sky. 'Or you might have been in for a second soaking.'

I look up to see that dark clouds have gathered above.

'And maybe next time neither of us will soak each other.' He smiles that gorgeous smile once more before driving off, and thankfully not loitering to see which house I go into.

There's a brightness all around despite the grey clouds above, which can only mean one thing.

My clothes are almost dry as I turn the corner and head up the path to my house, just as a raindrop falls onto my face. Except it isn't a raindrop, but a snowflake. I glance upwards to see tiny white flakes fluttering towards the ground.

SEVENTEEN

It's the eve of Christmas Eve and it's crazy busy at Bentham's. The light dusting of snow yesterday didn't stick to the ground, leaving the roads a little slushy, but at least it means we won't have any issues transporting the pensioners to their party tomorrow. I'm mentally running through everything in my head, hoping there isn't anything I have forgotten, however unlikely that might be as I have been ticking things off my list.

I'm not sure why, but I find myself scanning the crowds in case Kian decides to pop in for some last-minute shopping this morning. I was also surprised that I found myself thinking about him last night when I got home. Halfway through the morning service a similar-looking bloke walks in, with the same easygoing, almost beaten-up look, wearing a brown leather jacket and accompanied by a good-looking redhead.

But it isn't him, and to my surprise I breathe a sigh of relief that Kian wasn't with a woman and wonder what on earth has got into me? I'd noticed him in here for the first time the other day, but maybe he has only just moved into the area.

'I'm really looking forward to Christmas Day this year,' says Gemma, spraying herself with a sample of a very expensive perfume that we have behind the counter. 'My family are coming up from Wales, there's going to be fourteen of us. I haven't seen my cousins for two years,' she tells me. 'We always have such a good laugh, I am really looking forward to it.'

'It sounds wonderful.' I smile, thinking of how this year it will be just me and Mum, which suits me just fine though after the craziness of Christmas Eve at the community centre. I wish Dad could join us too, but I know that is selfish of me. He has his own relationship with Rose. I just hope he heeds the doctor's words and doesn't overindulge on the day.

'Why don't you and your mum join us on Christmas Day?' offers Gemma as if reading my mind. 'The more the merrier, I say. Mum's dining room is huge, and everyone will be pitching in with the cooking. Apparently, one of my aunts is bringing half of Tesco with her.' She laughs.

'That's so kind, Gemma, but honestly? I'm quite happy quietly spending the day with Mum. And I'll be popping over to see Dad and Rose in the morning with their presents.'

Rose is quite difficult to shop for, not being one for perfumes or cosmetics due to a skin sensitivity, so I have bought her a new heated styling brush as she mentioned needing a new one last time I visited.

'Of course, but if you change your mind you will be more than welcome,' she says kindly as a man approaches the counter with a box of sparkly tree baubles. He could probably get them for half the price at the huge discount store on a nearby retail park, but obviously likes to support local business. It seems most of the patrons feel that way, telling us they would hate to see the store close due to the onslaught of discount shops as many other high street stores have done. I like to think that as we sell quality items, along with such wonderful sales, the customers are still getting great value for money.

'Thanks, Gemma.' I feel blessed to have such a good friend. I don't know what I would do without her.

The day rolls on with festive cheer as excited shoppers cram into the store for that last-minute gift. Christmas tunes are playing in the background and I feel a tingle of excitement myself, knowing that everything is prepared for tomorrow. I can't have forgotten anything, I have been over things so many times and it isn't as if it's the first time this is happening, so it should run like clockwork now.

A father with a little girl, who I presume to be his daughter, is picking out a gift and I find myself wondering how Kian's day will go with his daughter Bella on Christmas Day? Will it just be the two of them, or will they be joining in with the rest of his family? I wonder if he lives in an apartment or a house? Gosh, what is the matter with me?

I distract my thoughts by being busy serving customers, my thoughts occasionally turning to tomorrow. The other volunteers will arrive in the morning and Sue is cooking two huge turkeys in her oven overnight, on a low setting, clearly not worried about fires or anything like I would be – although I suppose everyone has fire alarms these days. The vegetables will be cooked when we arrive at the centre on the morning of Christmas Eve and I have some hand carved ready-cooked ham to serve along with the turkey.

After preparations are complete, we will make the short journeys ferrying the pensioners to the party, for the ten or so who are unable to make their own way there. The guests usually arrive at one thirty to enjoy a pre-dinner drink, before Christmas lunch is served around two. Santa will arrive around four thirty dispensing gifts to all and it gives me a warm rosy glow just thinking about it and the practised routine that always goes to plan. I know Gemma teases me about my lists and attention to detail, but something like this can't be organised on a wing and a prayer.

Taking a break later in the staffroom, I receive a phone call.

'Five o'clock today, okay great, thanks,' I say, confirming an appointment.

I'm just back at the counter serving a lady with a pair of leather gloves when a familiar face walks through the door.

'Mum, hi, what can I get you?' I ask.

'Nothing, love, you know I wouldn't pay the prices in here.'

An immaculately groomed woman behind her is holding a dress that I happen to know has a two-hundred-pound price tag.

'Especially when they have been made in some sweat shop in some undeveloped country, paying the workers a pittance,' adds Mum, with a shake of her head.

'Okay, Mum, but keep your voice down.' I steer her to the corner of the counter whilst Gemma serves the woman with the expensive dress.

'So what are you doing here?' I ask.

'I've been thinking about what you said about inviting your father over on Christmas Day,' she tells me.

'Really?'

'Yes, I don't want to cause any trouble, but do you think I ought to ask them? I can be very persuasive,' she says, which is definitely true. 'We're all adults here, aren't we?'

'Perhaps, but I definitely can't see Rose agreeing to it.'

'Well, there is no harm is asking.' Mum looks serious for a minute. 'What with your father's heart problems, you never know if it might be his last Christmas.'

'Oh, Mum, don't say that, I can't bear the thought.'

Mum's right though. We are all adults, and in a perfect world we ought to be able to sit around a table together, but, sadly, real life isn't always like that.

'Leave it to me,' Mum says firmly. 'Right then, I'll be off now. I'll call you later.' She lifts a pot of foundation from a nearby counter, and tuts at the price tag before leaving.

. . .

Town is bustling with shoppers when I finish work, and I pass a dozen or so wooden chalets adorned with Christmas lights. It's only a small square, with traders selling the usual food and drink, wooden toys and a few clothes stalls, one selling hand-made Peruvian hats and scarves. Once I have been assured that the products are eco-friendly and vegan, I pick out a colourful beanie hat and scarf for Mum to go with her earrings. There are stalls selling bottles of Gluhwein, offering shoppers a sample, alongside pungent cheeses, some with a Christmas twist with the addition of cinnamon and spices.

The smell of sizzling German sausage from a stall fills the air as shoppers stroll around the market, muffled in thick coats and hats. I say hi to lots of people who recognise me from the shop, as I walk. As I approach the end of the square, near a stone monument, I watch a group of carol singers dressed in traditional Victorian costumes, singing away, and collecting money for a local hospice.

I peel a ten-pound note from my purse and place it into a violin case, as the group break into 'God Rest Ye Merry Gentlemen', and a Victorian-dressed gent tips his top hat.

I try to shake the thoughts of a hospice from my mind as I head to my car, anxiously wondering what the outcome of the meeting with the doctor will be.

EIGHTEEN

After my meeting with the doctor, I grab a coffee from the café, realising I have hardly had a drink all day, apart from a few sips from a bottle of water. My mouth feels dry and I am a little nauseous, but I guess that was just down to nerves earlier. The news was positive I think, so I feel I can breathe again, but the earlier adrenalin is causing a headache to build.

I'm just walking out of the Blue Teapot with my takeaway decaff drink, and not looking where I am going when I bump into someone. The lid from my coffee comes loose, and a little bit of my drink splashes onto the pavement.

'Not again? This is beginning to become a little bit of a habit,' says Kian, standing in front of me. 'I'm thinking of walking around in a waterproof jacket at all times now,' he teases. 'Although this time, I managed to avoid being drenched.'

'I am so sorry,' I gasp, gazing into Kian's gorgeous eyes. He's dressed smartly and smells good too. I wonder if he is off on a date?

'At least you wouldn't have been scalded. It's more cream than coffee,' I tell him.

I'd absent-mindedly nodded when the girl behind the counter asked me if I wanted cream and sprinkles on my latte.

'Well, that's alright then. Can I buy you another?' he offers, but I just want to head home and take something for this headache, even though he is the most attractive guy I have seen around here in a long time. I hesitate for a moment, but he looks like he might be off somewhere important.

'Thanks, but really I must get home. And aren't you going somewhere yourself?' I can't help asking, given his smart attire.

'I do have a meeting with a client, but not for another half an hour,' he says, glancing at his watch.

'A client?'

'Yes. I'm a psychologist, but I also work as a hypnotherapist. I have an office near the library,' he tells me.

'How interesting,' I remark.

'It is. Well, most of the time. Some days it's just helping people to feel calm before they get on a plane, that sort of thing.'

Maybe I ought to have been to see him before I went to the doctor this evening.

'Right, I'll leave you to it. Maybe we can grab that coffee another time though?' he suggests.

'I'd like that,' I say, thinking I really would.

'Great,' he says, before standing in front of me for a few seconds and I wonder whether he is about to say something else.

'See you later then, and merry Christmas,' I say, turning on my heels.

As I walk away, he calls my name and I turn around.

'Merry Christmas to you too,' he says as he lifts a hand and waves.

If I was braver, maybe I would have caught up with him and asked him what his plans were over Christmas, but I've never asked a guy out in my life. Not that I think there is anything wrong with that, but I don't want to look foolish, especially as I don't really know his situation. One thing is for sure though, I hope it isn't too long before we run into each other again.

'Do you have a minute? I know you are busy though, so I won't keep you long.'

I call Gemma, who told me she will be spending the evening wrapping Christmas presents for tomorrow.

'Sure I do, but I'm going to have to run down to the late shop before it closes. Would you believe I have run out of wrapping paper? I hope they have some left.'

'What are you like? I'd have a nervous breakdown if I hadn't wrapped my presents weeks ago. Oh, and I have some Christmas gift bags here, if you can't get your hands on any wrapping paper.'

'I knew you would.' She chuckles. 'Anyway, what's on your mind?'

'Well, I took your advice and booked a private doctor's appointment. I decided I didn't want to wait until after Christmas, it would have spoilt everything and been on my mind the whole time.'

'You did? And what happened?'

'Well, I think I can breathe again,' I tell her. 'The doctor had a look at the lump, and said it didn't feel like a cancer. They have a particular shape apparently; he thinks it might be basal cell carcinoma.'

'Cancer?' she says in a quiet voice, the word always instilling fear in people.

'A non-cancerous one. They are contained in the cell, hence the name, but can spread across the face if not removed.'

'Oh, Lauren.'

'Don't worry, I'm trying not to. Obviously further tests need to confirm the diagnosis, but it will need to be removed. I felt quite reassured by the doctor, who told me he had years of experience. And he did say it was probably down to my love of sunbeds, which is a salutary lesson if ever there was one.'

'You never think when you're young though, do you?'

'Definitely not. Anyway, now that I have been checked over I can start to feel a little excited about the Christmas party,' I tell her.

'Well, I'm sure everything will be fine. As you say, maybe you can relax a little now. And I'm sure the party will be a wonderful day, with all your careful planning.'

'Thanks, although it isn't just me, it's a team of us. I'm so glad Sue cooks the meats, I think I would be panicking about the turkey being too dry.' I laugh. 'And before I go, I just wanted to say, I'm glad you urged me to get the lump checked out sooner rather than later.'

'That's what friends are for. And thank you so much for my gorgeous bracelet. I was going to call you tomorrow,' says Gemma.

'Wait, you have opened your present?' I ask, shocked. My gift from her is under the tree where it will stay until Christmas morning.

'You know what I'm like.' She giggles. 'There was no way I could see it there under the tree without ripping the paper open. I'll call you tomorrow night to see how it's all gone at the community centre.'

'I'll let you off. And I'm glad you love your present, even though it isn't officially yet Christmas. Thanks, Gem.'

'I hope you like yours too. Now, I must go or I'll end up wrapping presents in the pages of the local gazette.' She laughs.

'Okay. Speak soon.'

Eileen from next door has knocked to show me the dress she will wear tomorrow for the Christmas lunch.

'Oh, Eileen, it's beautiful, it really brings out the colour of your eyes,' I comment on the floaty grey dress that has a little bit of sparkle around the neckline.

'Thank you.' She does a little twirl. 'I was worried I might be a little overdressed, but it is Christmas after all.'

'Absolutely! I think it's just perfect.'

'Thank you. And it smells wonderful in here. What are you making?' she asks.

'A couple of date and walnut loaves. They contain no sugar, but taste absolutely delicious. I thought I would make it for Mum as she likes things organic and natural, although there's enough for everyone, of course. Maybe even healthy enough for Dad to have a slice.'

'Is there anything I can do to help?' asks Eileen.

'No, I think I've got everything covered, but thank you.'

'Oh right, okay,' she says, looking a little disappointed.

I recall Eileen's comments the other day saying she missed her working life and how she would make some biscuits for the café she once owned with her husband.

'Although actually, Eileen. Do you think you could whip up some of those lemon biscuits you told me about the other day?'

She told me of the melt in the mouth lemon shortbreads she used to make that sounded delicious.

'Oh, I'd love to, of course. I think I have most of the ingredients already.' With that she waves goodbye and heads back to her house.

I check my list for the millionth time, ticking things off. I have all the vegetables and Mum commented on the size of the sack of potatoes I bought, but I know how the old people like their roast potatoes. Mum is a dab hand at peeling vegetables so I will be grateful for the help tomorrow in the kitchen, along with Sue, Barry and a couple of other volunteers who live near the centre.

I feel lighter having seen the doctor as I check the gift bags for the pensioners, all of the gifts donated by local businesses.

They include things like toiletries, notebooks and pens and, of course, some additional freebies from the make-up counter at Bentham's. They also have a Christmas cookie in a box baked by yours truly and a miniature bottle of Baileys.

The phone rings and it is Audrey, telling me she has persuaded her mum to come for lunch tomorrow, if that's still okay.

'It's more than okay. We have twenty-five people and prob-ably enough food for twice that number,' I tell her.

'And I would love to come along and help, if I wouldn't get in the way,' she offers.

'Of course you wouldn't! The more hands on deck the better, really,' I assure her.

'Okay, see you tomorrow. I will look forward to it.'

I give the house a final scrub, so that on Christmas Day I can sit and relax with Mum and have a chilled day.

I give Dad a ring to ask if he has spoken to Mum yet. It's Christmas Eve tomorrow, and I realise that Mum hasn't actually got back to me about Dad and Rose joining us on Christmas Day.

'Hello, love, how's things? All ready for the pensioners' lunch?' asks Dad, who despite being invited has never taken me up on the offer of joining us, saying it's for people on their own and he prefers Christmas at home. Even though Rose's home isn't really his home. He has lived with her for three years though, and he has definitely put his stamp on the place with his favourite armchair, bookcase full of his books and a green-house that keeps him busy pottering when he isn't working on someone else's garden.

'Just about ready, yes, thanks. Are you sure you and Rose won't come? I always make far too much,' I offer once more. 'Although, you know you are welcome at my place Christmas Day too.' I throw that in, wondering whether Mum has manged to say anything.

There's a silence for a second before Dad speaks.

'Aye, love, your mother did mention that. It was very thoughtful of you,' he says. 'But I'm not sure Rose would be too comfortable with that, which is a shame really as you know I would like to spend Christmas Day with you.' He sighs, and I wonder why people can't just act like adults and dine together if they are invited to, regardless of their history. Maybe we all ought to practise peace and goodwill unto all men at this time of year. But maybe that is easier said than done.

'It is, but never mind. You know you are welcome anytime.' I make sure he knows that.

'I do know that, thank you, love.'

I don't add that I hope he doesn't eat too much of the wrong type of food. I worry about him, of course, being his daughter but I can't police his life twenty-four hours a day. It would be far too exhausting.

NINETEEN

It's Christmas Eve and finally the day of the pensioners' lunch has arrived and I can't wait to see all the happy faces later in the day.

I'm just parking at the community centre when Kian's black car pulls into the car park.

I step out of the car as Kian walks around to his car boot.

'Hi, fancy meeting you here,' I tell him as he looks up at me in surprise.

'Hello there. How are you? You aren't carrying any type of liquid, are you?' he asks, a smile playing around his mouth.

'Lucky for you, no. So what are you doing here on Christmas Eve?' I take in his dark, slightly curly hair almost touching the collar of his jacket, and broad shoulders.

'I might ask you the same thing,' he says.

'Well, I'm here to drop a few things off for the party,' I tell him.

'Today?' he asks, looking a bit puzzled.

'Umm, yes. It's the annual Christmas meal for the local pensioners.'

He flicks a button and his boot springs open to reveal a load of bags and boxes.

'Hmm. I'm not sure how that is going to work. What time is this party then?' he asks.

'One o'clock and will last pretty much all afternoon, and what do you mean by you don't know how this is going to work?' I ask with a feeling of anxiety.

'Because there is going to be a birthday party here in a couple of hours. Two o'clock, to be precise.'

He lifts a box from the boot and places it on the floor. There is the head of a donkey poking out.

'The piñata,' he informs me.

'Piñata?'

'Yes, for the birthday party,' he repeats. 'Keep up.'

'What? I don't think so,' I say as panic engulfs me.

'Oh really.' He raises an eyebrow. 'And why not?'

'Sorry, I just mean we will be cooking a roast dinner in the kitchen, so I'm not sure how it could work,' I say, flying into blind panic. 'Surely there must be some mistake here?'

'Nope. The party is at two o'clock,' he says calmly as he begins to unload the rest of the things that include bin bags full of inflated balloons in assorted colours.

'But... but... it can't be. There must be some mistake. Are you sure you have booked it for the right date?' I can feel myself becoming light-headed. I really should have had a more substantial breakfast than a cereal bar. 'It's the pensioners' party today, it is always at the same time every year,' I explain.

'I don't think I could mistake Christmas Eve.' He smiles, completely unruffled by my panicked outburst. 'I booked it two months ago, I have the keys and everything.'

He pulls the key to the centre from his pocket to show me.

'But I don't understand. We have the annual party for the elderly in the community every Christmas Eve. Surely the council must have realised that when you booked?' I ask, my head spinning.

'Maybe it was a newbie in the office.' He shrugs. 'Maybe it was an oversight. Whatever it was, my daughter is having her birthday party here at two o'clock,' he says, calmly but firmly, and I really feel as if I might faint.

I feel my heart pounding and the blood rushing through my ears. The date is booked out every year. It's booked almost as soon as the party is over. Everything is in place. I have a ton of vegetables in the boot and Sue is bringing the cooked turkeys later. This cannot be happening.

'Unless you want to be the one to tell my seven-year-old daughter and her friends that it isn't happening, of course,' he says, still completely unfazed and looking at me with those annoyingly piercing eyes.

He unloads another open box that contains a long string of bunting.

I can feel my heart sink. I remember him telling me his daughter's birthday was on Christmas Eve. And he has gone to the trouble of organising a birthday party for her this year which is sweet, but someone has messed up the bookings big time.

'Well, of course I understand that you can't let her down, but I can't let the old people down either. Is there anywhere else your daughter could have the party?' I ask desperately as I retrieve my phone from my bag.

'Yes, of course, the alternatives are unlimited on Christmas Eve,' he says sarcastically.

'I'm sure we can sort this out. I will just give the council offices a ring,' I say, sounding far more confident than I feel. And, of course, I truly do not want to ruin his daughter's birthday party.

'Good luck with that.' Kian shrugs. 'They have finished for the Christmas holidays. Yesterday, I believe.'

Sure enough, the call rings out, with a message that the

office will be open again in a week's time, followed by a selection of numbers to call to report floods, problems with refuse collection and unwanted pests. I have one right here standing opposite me, but I'm sure that's not what they mean. Strangely enough, there is no number to enquire about a problem concerning a double booking.

'I can't believe this is happening.' I pace the car park, wondering what on earth I am going to do? Everything is set for the pensioners' lunch, but then it is also the venue for Bella's seventh birthday party.

'Chill your bones,' Kian says as he pulls a lollipop from a packet. 'Want one?' he offers.

'No, thanks. And what do you mean, "chill your bones". This is a disaster!' I throw my arms up into the air. 'It's Christmas Eve, and we have two parties booked for the same time, at the same venue.'

'It seems we do.' He nods, his calmness really beginning to grate on my nerves. 'It's the first time I've done anything like this, but as Bella is spending Christmas with me, whilst her mother is on holiday with her boyfriend, I thought why not? I want her to feel special as her birthday generally just merges into Christmas, you know?'

'I can imagine. And, of course, it's lovely of you to do that. I bet Bella is really excited.' At least that much we can agree on.

'She is. And so are the parents of the children as it gets them out of their hair for a few hours on Christmas Eve, while they get things sorted for the big day.'

'I can imagine. I just can't think how this has happened though? What on earth are we going to do?' I ask as my fists automatically clench and my neck feels as stiff as a board.

'What do you suggest?' he asks. 'Flip a coin, heads or tails?' He sucks on the lollipop and shrugs his shoulders once more. Why isn't he flapping like a bird – as I am – instead of standing there like that lollipop-sucking TV cop from the seventies. Kojak, I think he was called.

'I really don't know, but I don't think flipping a coin is fair. Is there no way you could have the party at your place?' I suggest. 'A dozen kids is a lot less than twenty-five adults.'

'In a second-floor apartment? I don't think so. The neighbours below would have me evicted. Maybe you could have the old folks at your house? So much easier than an apartment, I'd say.' He surveys me for a moment as he takes another suck of that damn lollipop.

'I can't. My kitchen is too small, and so is my oven.'

Am I actually having this conversation with him?

He picks up one of the boxes and heads for the door of the community centre humming to himself. Humming! I walk beside him asking him what he thinks he is doing.

'What does it look like? I'm getting these boxes inside to decorate the hall. The caterers will be bringing the party food at eleven,' he informs me. 'And the cake. Oh, you will like the cake.' He smiles as he fiddles with the keys. 'It's a sea scene from Disney's *The Little Mermaid*,' he tells me, clearly oblivious to my heart palpitations and the possibility that I might lose control of my bowels.

'Caterers?' I stammer.

'Yeah, but don't sweat. It's sandwiches and cakes mainly,' he explains. 'I won't be taking over the kitchen. Don't you worry now,' he says, smiling. This guy is so laid-back he's horizontal. 'It's a bugger about the bouncy castle. It would take up half of the hall though, so I guess it will have to go outside. But it's not going to rain. I've checked the forecast,' he tells me.

'Bouncy castle?'

'Of course. What's a kids' party without a bouncy castle. Now, here I am making a sacrifice, so you might look a little more pleased. The kids will need to wear their coats, but I'm sure we can work together.'

'Yes, yes, I'm sorry. I truly don't want your little girl's birthday to be ruined,' I say, feeling as though I am about to burst into tears.

'Well, you would have to be heartless if you wanted that. And as you have organised a Christmas Eve party for the old folk, I don't think that's the case.' He smiles at me warmly.

I think of the mountain of vegetables in the car, and the bags of gifts waiting for all the pensioners back home. I can't tell them that it's all off, most of them have been looking forward to it for months. Many of them have no families to share their Christmases with at all.

As Kian turns the key in the door and enters the hall with me on his heels, he turns to me. 'Look, I don't want to be letting the pensioners down either, but you need to work with me,' he says, 'because we are agreed that I can't be ruining my little girl's birthday.' He looks at me with those green eyes. 'So here's what I am proposing,' he says, plonking the box down. 'The only solution is that we have a joint party.'

TWENTY

'We— What?' I can hardly believe my ears.

'We have a joint party. You could at least say yes, grand idea, why didn't I think of it? Not a bother!'

'Because I am trying to get my head around it. You're serious, a joint party?' My mouth is almost hitting the floor.

'Sure, why not. The hall is definitely big enough.' He gestures to the vast space around us. 'You can't argue with that. Besides, I'd say we have no choice in the matter.'

'Yes, but...'

'Twenty-five people you say.' He's marching off purposefully to a pile of chairs stacked in a corner. 'And there will be fourteen children, so there are more than enough chairs. And tables, I'd say.' He nods to a stack of tables. 'There will be plenty of space. I will draw a line down the middle of the hall if you like,' he offers.

'I don't think there's any need for that,' I say, although I secretly think it's a good idea to divide the space up a bit.

But could it work? I am coming round to the fact that there may be no alternative. Someone at the council has made a terrible error, but it shouldn't mean that anyone should suffer because of that. It is slowly dawning on me that there might not be any other solution.

'So, we're alright with sharing the space then?' asks Kian, setting down some boxes.

'I guess it will have to be,' I reluctantly agree, my head spinning.

'Good. Now, if you don't mind me taking a few of those ceiling decorations down so I can hang this piñata.'

'Take them down?'

'Yes. Not all of them, but we want it to look like a children's party too, right? And there are more Christmas decorations up there than Santa's grotto,' he says, glancing at the ceiling.

'No, of course not. I will grab a ladder for you,' I say, heading to a storeroom and praying that nobody minds the sudden change of plan. A kids' party and pensioners' party combined? Lord help us!

'That's grand, thanks. And don't look so worried. Things don't always go according to plan in life, but a party's a party.'

'I suppose so, it's just a bit of a shock, that's all,' I say, trying to steady my nerves. He's right of course, life doesn't always go according to plan, but this is a nightmare. An unplanned event that is bound to be a disaster. It can't possibly work. I feel sick.

'I can imagine. But if there's one thing I do know about, it's how to throw one heck of a good party.' He winks. 'So relax.'

And all I can do is I pray that he's right.

I decide not to tell the pensioners about the double booking just yet, as I don't want it to put them off coming. Maybe I can play it off as the perfect surprise, rather than an insane idea – kids running around all over the place while pensioners try to chat quietly as they munch on Christmas lunch. And a bouncy castle! My stomach is in knots as I step outside and call Gemma.

'You're kidding me.'

'I'm not. The centre has been double booked and the pensioners are going to be sharing the space with a bunch of seven-year-olds! Oh, Gemma, it's going to be awful, I just know it. A few of the pensioners have heart problems. One or two get a bit confused.' I sigh. 'Especially old Wilf, who is as deaf as a post.'

'Well, that's alright, at least he won't be able to hear them squeal after all the sugar they are likely to consume.' Gemma giggles.

'Oh don't, this is not funny. And some of them use sticks or walking frames. What if there's an accident? What if a child barges into one of them?'

I run through every scenario in my head. Spilled juice on the floor causing an old person to go flying. Pensioners trying to get on the bouncy castle after a drink or two. I can think of a couple of cantankerous old blokes that wouldn't think twice about giving an unruly child a clip around the ear and ending up in court.

'Will you stop right there,' she tells me. 'You're talking about a group of kids, mainly girls, I assume, not a herd of stampeding elephants.'

'I suppose so. Oh, Gemma, it's just I wasn't expecting this. Everything had been going perfectly to plan up until today. How could anybody have mixed up the booking?' I say in frustration.

'Who knows? But people are human and sometimes they mess up,' she reasons. 'It could have been a young apprentice or something. Remember when you worked on reception at that hotel, and you gave the wrong suitcase to a guest?' she reminds me.

'Oh my goodness, yes! Luckily, he returned it an hour later, although he wasn't happy.'

'I bet he wasn't. What good would a Boy George fancy dress outfit be to a fifty-five-year-old architect? Although it takes all sorts,' she says, and despite everything I can't help but laugh.

'Look, I know how hard you work to make this day perfect, but life doesn't always go according to plan, does it?' Gemma reminds me.

'That's what Kian said.'

I think about how he seemed to take it all in his stride.

'Kian?'

'Oh yes, I forgot to say, would you believe it's hot shop guy.'

'It never is!' she gasps.

'Yep. He's having a birthday party for his daughter's seventh birthday. She's spending Christmas with him this year and he organised a party for her. It just so happens to be at the same venue as the pensioners' party.'

'Well, it's a great opportunity to get to know him. And his daughter. Honestly, Lauren, I think everything will be just fine. And brownie points to him for being a good dad, hey.'

'Under any other circumstances, I would agree. But he's sabotaged my hall,' I say, feeling my blood pressure rise. 'And I do think it's nice that he has gone to the trouble of organising the party for his daughter, of course I do. She really is adorable and it must be hard when birthdays at this time of year just merge into Christmas. I just wish he had booked a different venue.'

'Maybe you are overreacting a bit. I'm sure everything will work out just fine,' says Gemma, yet another person who seems completely unfazed by the idea. 'A party is a party after all.'

'Kian said that too. Maybe I am overly stressing.'

'Possibly. And you never know, the kids might be a real tonic for the old people. You might even get a few of them to join in with a game of Twister.' She laughs.

'Oh stop. I don't think our ambulance service could cope with that, thanks very much.'

I know she is joking, but her comment fills me with dread.

'Maybe not. But honestly, it might be fun. As Kian said, you will have separate sides of the hall and he won't be using the kitchen if the party food is being delivered. Just try and go with it. I would come and give you a hand if I wasn't on shift today.'

Gemma works Christmas Eve and Boxing Day as she likes a couple of days off over New Year. With me doing the party here, we have kind of kept to that arrangement every year since.

'Oh, I'll try, really, I will. But it will feel so strange sharing the hall with children. And I'm not sure they will like the music. Sue's bringing her record player and her old vinyls too. I don't know if Glenn Miller will go down too well.'

'You might be surprised. Just stop worrying,' she tries to reassure me.

'Thanks, Gem. I'll try.'

'I'll call you later when I have finished work,' she says. 'When I'm sure you will tell me how brilliant it all was.'

'I can only hope. Oh, and did you manage to get some wrapping paper?'

'I did. Would you believe the last two rolls from the late shop. Adults and children alike will have their gifts wrapped in Grinch wrapping paper.' She laughs and I wish I had some of her attitude to life.

TWENTY-ONE

I'd been in a state of panic when Mum arrived at the centre and she'd taken a bottle of brandy from the cupboard – for medicinal purposes – and poured us each a measure to calm me down from stressing over the party situation.

'Yours for the shock, mine for the cold,' she'd said, rubbing her hands together. She'd walked over from her place in town and was wearing fingerless gloves.

'I'm not sure they offer much protection from the cold, Mum,' I'd said, commenting on her gloves.

'Ah yes, but they're so handy if I need to use my phone, or pay bus fare. It's a faff having to take gloves on and off.'

There's a million things to do, and the other volunteers will be arriving shortly, yet after calling Gemma, I find myself now stressing again to Mum.

'Don't worry, it might be a lot of fun,' she tells me. 'You know how much the old people like children.' She is yet another person who seems unfazed by the whole situation. Surprised, yes, but nothing like as panicked as I was about everything, so maybe I ought to try and relax a little. Try as I might though, I just cannot visualise the two groups sharing the hall space.

'Do you think so?'

'I do actually.' She smiles. 'Unless there is someone you know who absolutely hates kids.'

'No, at least not that I know of, although old Elsie has been known to grumble about children kicking the ball in her garden. And she has complained on several occasions about her great-grandchildren putting their fingers all over her ornaments when they visit,' I tell Mum.

'Oh, I know Elsie. She also complains when they don't visit, and doesn't seem to realise why that might be.' Mum laughs. 'I told her to get a few toys from the charity shop, and some colouring books and pencils. You can't really expect kids to sit there upright and silent, it's not the Victorian era.'

'I know, that's what worries me.' I sigh.

'Don't worry, I know most of the people attending and they are generally a jovial bunch. Eileen's coming, isn't she?' she asks, Mum having met Eileen many times.

'She is, yes, and looking forward to it.'

'There you go then. And most of the ladies are fun, especially when they have had a sherry down them,' Mum reminds me. 'Do you remember last year, Martha, I think it was, gave us all a rendition of "Stand by Your Man" on the karaoke machine.'

'Oh, I do. She surprised everyone with her voice, it was amazing!'

Once more I am reminded that old people have often once had a vibrant, fulfilling life that we never seem to consider.

'Anyway, there will be enough of us here to see things run smoothly,' Mum reassures me.

'Thanks, Mum.'

Whilst Mum is sorting a few things out in the kitchen, I call Sue and break the news about the double-booked party.

'I can't help freaking out a bit. Do you think I ought to let the old people know? Or just keep quiet?' I ask her.

'Oh, bloody hell.' Sue is laughing, seemingly unconcerned.

'I'd probably say nothing,' she advises. 'You don't want people not turning up and spending Christmas time alone. Hang on a minute, love,' she says, disappearing for a second. 'Sorry, I was just covering the turkeys in foil. Right, where were we?'

'I was wondering about telling the pensioners and you said I shouldn't, which makes sense, I suppose. I don't want to put them off coming.'

'I don't think they will be,' says Sue. 'In fact, I think they will probably love the idea. Most old people love children, and I imagine as the average age is eighty plus, that most of their grandchildren will be all grown up now. Sorry, love, hang on.'

I can hear Sue telling Barry that the salted peanuts are in the cupboard over the dishwasher, but to keep his hands off the mint Matchmakers.

I think about Sue's comments, realising she is right about the pensioners' grandchildren being older now or maybe teenagers at the least. Perhaps seeing the children really will be a tonic for them.

'I guess you're right. I think I was worried about the older people being safe, what with children charging about. Anyway, I will see you soon, thanks, Sue.'

'See you shortly, hun, and try not to worry.'

As the general consensus of opinion seems to be that a joint party might be rather a nice idea, maybe I ought to try thinking that way too. But despite the reassurances, I am still a bundle of nerves.

TWENTY-TWO

Hope it all goes well today. It's heaving in the store already!
Gemma. Xx

Gemma's text message is adorned with Santas, Christmas trees and snowmen.

It's one of those bright, crisp winter mornings with a clear blue sky and I pray it stays that way as the bouncy castle is arriving shortly, Kian informs me.

Mum has quickly rustled us up some organic scrambled eggs, even though my appetite has completely deserted me.

'You must eat,' insists Mum. 'And these are organic free range from a friend of mine who has a smallholding,' she tells me as she spoons scrambled eggs onto a plate.

'They do look good. Thanks, Mum.'

'We will have a busy day, so it will set us up nicely,' she sensibly advises.

My stomach is churning over, but I manage to eat some of the breakfast that is actually delicious. Mum has always been a good cook, and I think the idea she mentioned some weeks ago of some cookery lessons at the food bank is a great idea.

I still worry that I ought to have warned the older people that they are going to be sharing the space with children, despite Sue telling me otherwise. On the other hand, that might have caused them to stay away and miss out, which is the last thing I want.

My mind is swirling with thoughts of sharing the hall with Kian which, if it were under different circumstances, I would be quite excited about. I hate to admit it, but there is just something about his presence that captivates me. Maybe it's that seductive voice. Or those gorgeous eyes. Perhaps his easy-going, laid-back attitude. Whatever it is, I have to admit, I enjoy being in his company.

It's just after ten o'clock when I set out the vegetables, as well as making sure the plates and glasses are all squeaky clean. The other volunteers will be arriving shortly to begin the preparations for lunch. After that, we usually sing along to Christmas songs and generally get into the festive spirit. Everything is going to be so different this year. I take a deep breath as I head out of the kitchen, and gasp.

The right side of the hall has now been festooned with pink and mauve balloons and a giant cardboard cut-out of the Little Mermaid is standing close to a stained-glass window that is streaming morning sun into the hall. There is no denying it all looks beautiful.

On the other side of the room all the tables have been laid out ready for the pensioners' lunch.

'You did this?' I nod towards the tables.

'I did,' says Kian. 'As I was here, I thought I would lend a hand whilst you were in the kitchen.'

'That was a great help, thank you,' I tell him gratefully.

'Not a problem.'

I introduce Kian to my mum properly.

'I'm sure your daughter will love this,' I say, gesturing to the pretty decorations. 'It's all so beautiful.'

'Thanks. She's with her gran this morning so I could get things ready,' he explains. 'She's been up since the crack of dawn, bouncing with excitement.' He smiles affectionately when he talks of his daughter.

I offer to make him a coffee, and Mum takes her own herbal teabags from her handbag and hands me one.

'Probably sensible not to have too much caffeine, but I can't live without my coffee if I'm up early in the morning,' says Kian.

I give Sue a quick call and let her know that the tables are all set up, so if Barry has something else he needs to do that's fine. She tells me he will come with her anyway, otherwise he will sneak off to the pub.

When Kian heads to the kitchen, Mum starts to talk in a low voice as we get to work covering the tables in festive paper tablecloths.

'So that's the guy you told me about? You never said he was so handsome,' she says, nudging me.

'I didn't think it was relevant.' I shrug.

'And that lovely accent too. I went out with an Irish boy when I was seventeen,' says Mum, taping the paper tablecloth to the underside of the table.

'Did you?'

'Yes, it was in my first year of college. I later ditched the course but we went out for a few months,' she recalls. 'His name was Eamon. Oh, he was handsome.' She smiles wistfully.

I never think of Mum as having any other boyfriends other than my dad. I guess there's a lot we really don't know about our parents unless we ask.

I can hear Kian whistling in the kitchen and wonder what it must be like to be the type of person who just shrugs and catches the curveballs life throws at you. I must admit there are times when I wish I could do the same, but I guess we are all different.

Thinking about it, being organised has probably been the

key to me keeping any anxiety at bay. A place for everything, and everything in its place. Lists and organisation are the key to keeping things running smoothly. Until today, that is. Lists make things real to me, otherwise everything feels a bit abstract which makes me feel ungrounded. Add to that the fact that I don't have the best memory, so making lists has been my saviour. I can't imagine doing anything in life without a plan.

I once went on a weekend away with a friend who had forgotten half of her clothes and had to borrow mine. She also underestimated her spending money and had to message her dad to put some into her account. Then there was the fact that she failed to book a table at a smart restaurant as she had promised for my birthday. We couldn't get in anywhere decent at such short notice, apart from a dodgy-looking place down a side street. The weekend left me so stressed I vowed to make sure I would plan everything to the nth degree so that nothing can possibly go wrong. Until now, that is. It seems life happens anyway, regardless of my meticulous planning.

Kian returns with the drinks, just as Sue and Barry arrive.

'Morning, hun.' Sue kisses me on both cheeks in the hall-way. She has her dark hair up and is wearing a denim dress, looking at least a decade younger than her real age.

'Oh wow, look at that!' Sue glances at the not so little Little Mermaid cardboard statue. 'I bet your daughter will be thrilled.' She turns to Kian. 'I'm Sue, by the way. This is Barry.' She chats away. 'I take it you are Kian? Lauren has told us all about you.'

'You mean all about the predicament with the hall.' I can feel my cheeks colouring.

'Yes, that's what I meant.' She gives me a glance that says 'sorry'.

Maybe I have been talking about him a lot?

'That's a gorgeous Irish accent,' Sue says to Kian. 'Where-abouts are you from?' she asks.

'Wexford in south-eastern Ireland. Just outside actually, in a small village,' he reveals.

'Lovely. I've always fancied going to Ireland. We toyed with the idea of hiring a car in Ireland and exploring, didn't we, Barry? You can get really cheap flights to Knock apparently, and pick up a car from there.'

'True enough,' agrees Kian. 'It's around a four-hour drive from the airport to Wexford, but there are some lovely towns to visit on the way.'

'We did talk about it, yes,' says Barry. 'Well, we considered a camper van actually, which I don't think would have had enough space for all of your clothes and make-up. Anyway, in the end you said you prefer cruises,' he reminds his wife.

'I did, didn't I?' Sue concedes. 'Ireland just looks so wild and wonderful, so maybe one day. So, Kian, how long have you lived in the Lakes?' she asks. 'I take it you do live around here?'

'Ten years, and, yes, I do. I moved here for the love of a woman,' he explains. 'Although I have only recently moved here to Fellview. Before that I was living near Keswick.'

So he is with someone? I assumed when he said he was divorced that he was single. I feel my heart sink.

'The marriage didn't last, but I fell in love with the Lakes anyway,' he says. 'And, of course, my daughter is here. Anyway, I'm sure you would enjoy Wexford. It's a great mix of coast and town so definitely worth visiting if you do ever decide to take that trip,' he tells Sue.

'Lovely. I'll pick your brain if we ever do. Right, Barry, you're on meat carving duty,' Sue tells her husband. 'Lovely to meet you, Kian.'

'And the rest of us had better get ready for some serious veg peeling,' I say as we head off to our various tasks. 'The more potatoes the better.'

'Oh, the pensioners love their roast potatoes, don't they?'

Sue laughs. 'Right then, maybe we had better crack on instead of standing here chatting, or Christmas lunch will never be served.'

TWENTY-THREE

It occurs to me that Sue has been here all of five minutes and has managed to find out a lot more about Kian that I have this last week. Then again, maybe it wouldn't have seemed appropriate to be asking where he was from and chatting happily in a car the other day to the man who had just soaked me to the skin.

We are heading into the kitchen to begin preparations, when the door opens and in walks Audrey, carrying a large bag. She takes in the children's section with admiration as she enters the hall.

'Oh, wow. I wish I had had the chance to go to a party like this when I was little,' she says. 'In fact, even now I love Disney.' She smiles.

'Well, I'm sure Kian would more than welcome a hand with the children once the pensioners are settled with their food,' I suggest.

'I definitely wouldn't say no to that,' he agrees, smiling.

'Then I would love to,' she says, gazing at the giant-sized Little Mermaid.

The pensioners' side of the room is also looking great as my mum is a dab hand at turning red napkins into pretty fans, and

Christmas coasters featuring robins are set next to the cutlery. The rosy-cheeked Santa poster on the windows will be smiling down on them all when they arrive, creating the perfect festive scene.

'I guess you already have a central table decoration, but I wondered if you might like this,' says Audrey, pulling the most glorious centrepiece from her bag that has us all gasping in admiration.

'Audrey, it's beautiful,' I say, glancing at the huge show-stopper of a centrepiece.

It's a winter garden scene, adorned with silver pine cones and mistletoe berries. A robin is sat atop a snowy log, nestled amongst sprigs of holly and ivy and the whole sculpture is dusted in a sprinkling of silver glitter. When she places it in the centre of the table and adds a chunky red candle, it looks absolutely perfect.

'We have an old plastic one that looks nothing like that,' I tell her, thinking it another example of Audrey's creative talent. 'Thank you so much, it will take pride of place every year. If we can keep it, that is?'

'Of course you can keep it. And you are very welcome. I'm pleased you like it.' She beams proudly. 'Right, I have heard there are a mountain of potatoes to peel.' She produces a potato peeler from the pocket of her coat. 'I just can't use anything else,' she explains.

There is laughter coming from the kitchen, when I walk through and introduce Audrey to everyone.

'Oh, you're the girl who won the gingerbread competition, aren't you? Lovely to meet you,' says Sue warmly.

'Nice to meet you all too,' says Audrey politely, before rolling her sleeves up and getting stuck in to the potatoes.

. . .

An hour later, a huge pile of turkey has been sliced and arranged onto plates along with the cooked, sliced ham.

Barry glances at his watch and mutters something about the local pub opening in an hour and Sue slaps him on the wrist and tells him he can get stuck into chopping some vegetables first, before he even thinks about it. Apparently, it's traditional for the men to gather at the local pub on Christmas Eve and Sue doesn't really mind, but thinks it only fair that Barry stays and helps with the preparation first.

I keep glancing at Kian as I prepare some sprouts, noticing how easily he turns his attention to everyone in the room. Audrey is standing beside him looking completely at ease as he chats away to her.

'So, when did you get involved with the pensioners' parties?' he asks me as I pop some sprouts into a giant pan.

'Ten years ago now. I just hated the thought of anyone spending Christmas alone. I know it isn't exactly Christmas Day, but we are not allowed to open the centre then, so I thought, why not Christmas Eve?'

'It's a really nice thing to do.' He smiles. 'I mean, I know they have such things throughout the year, but most people want to be getting on with preparing their own Christmas than being here, I would imagine.'

'You're probably right. Although you would be surprised at how many people have volunteered in the past, just to give something back to society. Others, like Sue and Barry, began volunteering after retirement and have helped with the party every year since. And then there are the people who don't want to be alone with their thoughts at Christmas.'

'Which one are you?' he asks, before picking up a piece of raw carrot from a pan and popping it into his mouth. 'Although you are obviously not retired.'

'What? I'm not sure. I just enjoy doing it, that's all.'

I brush off his question, even though I do spend a lot of time thinking of Christmases past if I'm at home over Christmas. And it was a week before Christmas when I broke up with my boyfriend, and I took the rather expensive watch I'd bought him back to the shop for a refund.

We'd had a huge fight when he bought yet another bike having updated the one from the shed, then announced he would be going on a mountain biking holiday for a week after Christmas. We had to face facts then. We wanted different things, me wanting to save up to get married, him still a million miles away from that.

'Sorry, no offence meant.' Kian holds his hands up. 'I just imagined a young woman like yourself spending Christmas Eve getting ready for a big night out in town, or a party somewhere.' He smiles. 'Not giving their time to the old folk.'

'Well it just goes to show, we shouldn't have preconceived ideas about people.'

'Maybe not. That's me told.' He grimaces.

'Sorry, if that sounded a bit harsh,' I say, thinking I am probably still a little stressed about the party situation. 'I suppose I'm just as guilty of making assumptions about people at times.'

'You mean like thinking old folk won't want to be in the same room as children?' He raises an eyebrow.

'Perhaps.' I smile reluctantly. 'And as for being young, I'm not that young. I'll be thirty-three in January.'

'Positively ancient then,' he teases.

It's hard to say how old Kian is, but I'd put him in his late thirties, maybe even forty. He looks after himself though, that's for sure, managing to look good without looking too groomed, with that dark slightly curly hair and relaxed, yet stylish, sense of fashion.

We both go to pull a kitchen drawer out at the same time, and when our hands briefly touch, I feel my arm hairs stand on end.

'Sorry,' he says, allowing me to go first, before he reaches for a vegetable knife. 'I might as well give you a hand before the party food arrives,' he says kindly.

Kian tackles some parsnips and before too long, all the veg is in the huge pans.

'I think we're done,' says Sue, shaking a tea towel. 'Roast potatoes on in say, an hour, the other veg later. And you're definitely on the gravy.' She points at Mum. 'Mine could never be as good as yours.'

'No problem.' Mum smiles, pleased to be complimented on her gravy.

'So are you feeling a bit more relaxed now?' Kian asks, as we walk into the main hall and survey the room.

'I think I am,' I admit. 'The room looks wonderful, doesn't it? And everything seems to be under control.'

'I told you not to worry, didn't I?' says Kian, looking around at a place that unbelievably is set for a joint party.

'You told me to chill my bones as I recall.'

'I did, didn't I?' He grins. 'Well in my experience, being stressy never achieves anything.'

'Nor does lack of organisation,' I retort.

'Stress is a killer. No one ever died from forgetting something.' Kian shakes his head.

'What about forgetting to take life-saving medication?' I say triumphantly, and he rolls his eyes.

'Well okay, but you know what I mean. Maybe you should learn to lighten up and just go with the flow sometimes,' he says, but not unkindly.

Glancing at the two halves of the room makes me think of how the partygoers are at such opposite stages of their life. It also makes me consider how precious life is and how quickly it passes by. My mind flits back to a birthday party one summer, where I was blessed with a sunny day and a group of school friends came to my house and we had a wonderful time. It's hard to believe that was over twenty years ago now. I don't remember every single detail, of course, but Mum took lots of photographs. Whenever I leaf through the albums all the memories of that happy day return in an instant.

Thinking about it, perhaps everyone is right about the two groups sharing the space as I loved being around my grandparents, especially at this time of year. My grandmother had the patience to teach me things such as biscuit baking and making paper chains. And I remember the year my grandad made me a wooden doll's house, allowing me to help him by knocking nails into the wood and applying pastel-coloured paint. I have the doll's house to this very day. I am truly grateful to have so many happy memories to look back on.

'We both planned these parties, but I don't think we had any choice but to share,' says Kian. 'But you have to work with what you've got, has always been my motto. No good putting yourself into an early grave through stress.'

'Well I can't argue with that, although sometimes it is easier said than done,' I reply just as a large van pulls into the car park.

'That will be the bouncy castle,' he says. 'Thank goodness for the blue sky, hey?'

There is no sign of rain on this beautiful, but frosty morning and I pray it stays that way.

'It's still cold though. I hope the children will all have coats with them,' I say, feeling a little guilty that they can't have the bouncy castle inside but there simply isn't the room.

'I did think about that, so I had the foresight to text the parents that the bouncy castle will be outside,' he tells me. 'I realised that children like to wear next to nothing when I picked Bella up from school last week on a non-uniform day. One kid was wearing nothing but a thin sleeveless dress and fairy wings.' He gives a little shiver. 'A couple of boys wore football kits, and not a coat or hat in sight. Sure it's up to the parents, but I don't want them catching their death of cold on my watch.'

'I can't blame you for that,' I agree.

TWENTY-FOUR

All the food prepped, I walk outside with Kian as we continue chatting. The truck reverses carefully and in no time at all the giant castle has been erected in the large rear yard of the community centre garden that has been fake turfed.

'That's pretty impressive,' I say, eyeing the giant purple structure adorned with stars and musical notes.

'It is, isn't it? It's called the party dome. Music plays out from some speakers, flashing lights, the lot. Watch this.'

He presses a button and music blasts out. He invites me to look inside and with the press of another button, the interior of the dome is lit up with stars and looking like a night sky. It's so beautiful I'm reluctant to move for a minute, just taking it all in.

'Fancy a go before the kids arrive?' he asks, and I'm not sure if he is being serious or not.

'Tempting as that is, I think I'll pass,' I say.

'Maybe later then. It might do you good to let your hair down.'

I'm not sure what to make of that. Is he suggesting I need to loosen up a bit?

'I hope Bella likes it,' he says then, before I have a chance to overthink his remark. 'They were all out of princess castles, as I left the booking a little late,' he admits. 'Luckily my daughter is mad about space. She's loving a project she's doing in school, so I think I am off the hook,' he tells me. 'Plus, the princess castle didn't have an inbuilt disco.'

'Then this is definitely the winner. The kids will absolutely love it, I'm sure. And, of course, inside the hall looks very girlie with the Little Mermaid and the pink balloons.'

'That's what I was hoping.' He nods.

'A kids' party is nothing without a bouncy castle, although Gemma tried to give me a heart attack when she said the pensioners might like to have a go.' I shake my head.

'They might do.' He gives a wicked grin. 'Just joking. I imagine you don't want any broken hips.'

'Definitely not. Not on my watch.'

'Gemma,' says Kian. 'Was she at the gingerbread evening with you?' he asks.

'That's right. We work together at Bentham's.'

'Of course.' He smiles. 'It's hard not to notice that beautiful red hair,' he says and I agree with him.

His comment makes me wonder whether it was Gemma he was looking over at during the gingerbread evening, and not me as she thought? And would it really matter if it was?

I don't have time to dwell on that with so many things to do, and soon enough the potatoes are roasting in the oven and it's time for me, Sue and a couple of other volunteers who have just arrived, to go and collect the pensioners who are unable to make their own way here.

My stomach is churning, praying everything will be alright this afternoon when a catering van arrives, no doubt filled with the goodies for Bella's party. All I can do is pray that today turns out to be a good day for everyone.

. . .

The giant snowman has been erected in the entrance hall of the centre, and has the pensioners laughing as they come in, with its rather slow rendition of 'Frosty the Snowman'.

'Well, would you look at that.' Eileen claps her hands together and gazes at the swathe of pink and mauve at the window inside as the light is shining through the pretty stained-glass window. 'It's just magical.'

'Ooh, it is,' say a few of the others as they file into the room.

'What's happening here then?' asks Wilf. 'It looks like a kiddies' party to me.'

'We're actually sharing the room,' I explain once more.

The children's table is laden with cakes, sandwiches, sausage rolls and all the usual party treats. The cake takes pride of place in the centre of the table, setting off the scene beautifully.

'Is it a buffet this year then?' someone says with a frown. 'I thought we were having a traditional Christmas lunch.'

'No, our table is this way.' I guide the group to the other side of the room.

'Hmm,' sniffs Elsie. 'I should hope it isn't a buffet.'

We'd told the older people about the double booking in the car and thankfully, most of them were fine about it. Wilf, it seems, hadn't heard what was said, but seems okay about sharing the room. One or two were even excited at the thought of seeing the children, so maybe the day won't be as bad as I have been envisaging. Perhaps Kian is right. Sometimes, you just have to work with what you have got and make the best of it.

'Oh gosh, I'm a bag of nerves,' I say to Sue as Barry is placing large slices of meat onto plates.

'Why? Everything is just tickety-boo,' she says, opening the oven door and the rich aroma of roasting potatoes fills my nostrils.

'These veggies are almost done now,' says Audrey, poking at veg in pans with a knife.

'Looks like it's time for your gravy,' I tell Mum, who is happy to oblige.

Everyone is quickly served and during the main course, the children start to arrive clutching presents for Bella. My heart melts at the sight of the girls in their pretty party dresses, and smartly dressed boys, with their hair fashionably styled.

'Well, that was wonderful,' Eileen says, placing her knife and fork down. 'You all work so hard.'

'It's worth it. It's such a joy seeing everyone meet up,' I tell her.

'Feet up?' says Wilf. 'Surely you can't put your feet up just yet, we haven't had our pudding yet.'

'Lauren was saying it's nice to MEET UP,' says Eileen, almost shouting down his ear and rolling her eyes.

'Oh aye, it is, yes.' He chuckles. 'I can't argue with that. It's my favourite day of the year.'

His comment brings a lump to my throat and reminds me why I am involved in this every year. Wilf has carers call around since his wife died, and a daughter who calls on him regularly but is away for Christmas this year, so today is a special day for him.

The meal is going down a treat and Sue has played some vinyls much to the delight of the guests.

'I'll get you up for a dance in a minute.' Gerald winks at Eileen. Gerald is dressed smartly in a suit and blue tie that matches his twinkling eyes.

'Oh, I'm up for that,' says Eileen, looking delighted.

We're having a little break before dessert, everyone chatting away. At the other end of the room, Bella is opening her gifts wide-eyed with excitement.

'Little people,' says Flora, an eighty-five-year-old, looking up from her plate. 'What are they doing here?'

'I told you children would be joining us,' says Sue gently.

'Did you? Oh right, yes,' she says and Sue and I exchange a glance. Flora's daughter has been concerned that she is forgetting things and repeating herself a lot, so is keeping her eye on things.

An excited Bella is still receiving her gifts from the children, mainly girls, who are taking in the decorations with wows, oohs and aahs.

'Would you like to say hello to our other people who are having a party here today?' I ask the children before they sit down at their table and they nod.

'It looks like a Christmas dinner, not a party,' says a boy with black hair as we escort them across the hall towards the old people.

'Well, when you get older parties are more about sitting and eating I suppose,' I tell the boy.

'And drinking. At least the dinner parties I go to,' Kian whispers to me.

'I don't want to get old then,' the boy says and Kian laughs.

'I don't suppose anyone does really. But it doesn't mean you stop enjoying yourself,' I tell him, but he looks unconvinced.

The children say hello to the old people and they all wish Bella a happy birthday when I tell them she is the birthday girl.

'How old are you?' asks Wilf.

'Seven,' says Bella proudly.

'Are you? You don't look eleven.'

'SEVEN,' Elsie shouts at Wilf.

'Oh seven.' He laughs. 'Very nice.'

'I remember being seven,' says Elsie. 'We went to the seaside and I had my first ride on a donkey,' she reminisces, her harsh expression turning into a smile. 'Blackpool, it was.'

The pensioners look delighted to see the children, apart from Flora, who is busy asking when the dessert will be served.

'Oh, she looks just like my granddaughter when she was

little,' says a grey-haired woman, her eyes misting over. 'I do miss that age, they grow so quickly, and then they rarely visit when they become adults,' she laments.

'I miss the children at my old school,' says another lady, a retired headmistress from the village. 'My one regret in life is not having children of my own,' she says, almost bringing a tear to my eye. 'This is a real tonic seeing all of these children.' She beams. 'Thank you.'

'It's a pleasure and I am sure we will all have a chance to mingle later, so let's enjoy our respective meals,' I say, leading the kids towards their party table. So far so good.

'So it seems the old folk don't think the children are the spawn of the devil?' says Kian, with a grin.

'It would appear so. And I'm sorry if I was a bit over the top, I just didn't want any accidents or for anyone to get upset, that's all.'

'Not a problem, I can understand that.' He smiles warmly and I feel a definite glow inside.

The kids are seated and about to tuck into some food, when Kian makes an announcement.

'Right, kids, get yourself some food and then you can all go on the bouncy castle outside,' he says and there is a squeal of excitement from the children.

'Actually, Kian,' I say. 'Do you think the children ought to have a bit of a play outside before the food? It will be like a washing machine in their tummies jumping up and down on the castle after they have eaten.'

'I never thought of that. But Bella's been telling me she's starved.' He scratches his chin, thinking.

'Okay, change of plan,' Kian tells the children. 'Maybe just have one sandwich and then we'll go outside to the bouncy castle and—'

He barely has time to get the words out of his mouth when there is a chorus of 'yay', before the children jump up from their chairs and stampede towards the outside area, almost pushing me and Kian up against each other as they run past.

'That was good advice,' he says, standing so close to me I can take in his scent and my heart rate soars. Both of us just stand there for a moment, before I break away and follow the children.

'I kind of forget what children are like sometimes,' he says as we reach the outside area.

The children's excitement reaches fever pitch as they take in the scene in front of them, as disco music begins to fill the space outside. I can't resist slipping my shoes off and climbing inside. I listen to the squeals of joy from the children at the sight of the colour-changing sky inside the castle, dotted with swirling stars.

As I step back outside, Kian realises that none of the children are wearing coats and makes a vain attempt at getting them back inside.

'I guess it's an undercover castle,' I reassure him. 'And all that bouncing around will have them overheating if they are wearing coats, and we don't want that, do we?'

'Yes, you're right.' Kian smiles. 'What would I do without you?' His green eyes meet mine and I feel a warm glow inside again.

'I dread to think,' I tease. 'Maybe you would have to deal with a load of kids stuffing their faces, then vomiting in the bouncy castle,' I say and he pulls a face.

'That would be awful.' He pauses for a moment. 'I would never get my deposit back if that happened.' He grins.

'Do you want me to stay out here for a bit?' I ask him, not wanting to move and enjoying standing next to him far too much, before giving myself a shake. I am here for the pensioners' party. I also remind myself that maybe Kian was staring over at Gemma on the gingerbread evening. I am simply the woman who has double booked the hall for a party, so I guess he has to be polite. It's just a shame he is so good-looking.

'I think I'll be grand, they seem to be having a right old time. Although maybe, if I need to, can I give you a shout?' he adds.

'Of course,' I tell him, and when he places his hand on my arm and thanks me, annoyingly there go those zingy feelings again and I wonder if he feels it too?

I think about the men I have come across over the last few months, in the pub, at Bentham's, or just generally out and about and it occurs to me that no one has really caught my eye recently. It's not that I am particularly picky, but men haven't even been on my radar as I was so bruised by my last relationship, I decided I would be better off on my own. And where do you meet men these days? I know lots of couples meet online, but it's not something I have really thought about. Perhaps that's after listening to a woman at work who has experienced one online dating disaster after another. Usually because some people like to use profile pictures that are not exactly representative of how they look. When she met up with Guy from Kendal, he told her he had forgotten to update his profile picture, which she said must have been at least ten years out of date if not more, as he had hair in his profile picture.

I'm preparing the desserts in the kitchen and, half an hour later, I hear the sound of children so it seems Kian has managed just fine on his own. A bunch of rosy-cheeked children have returned to the table and are ravenously tucking into food as if they have never been fed.

'Are those children having a party?' asks Flora as I am about to ask everyone what they would like for pudding.

I really must talk to her daughter, much as I don't want to. But Flora's memory is a cause for concern, so I think it only right to mention what has happened today.

'They are. See the little girl in the blue dress.' I point out Bella. 'It's her birthday.'

'Oh, it's nice having a birthday.' Flora smiles before telling me she would love some Christmas pudding. Bella catches my eye then and waves over and Flora waves too.

'I think it's my birthday in June. The sun usually shines then,' Flora tells me. 'Although June seems rather a long way off.'

'Well, that lunch was simply wonderful,' says Eileen, pushing her dessert away from her having enjoyed a nice slice of red velvet cake. She then taps a spoon against her glass.

'If I could just have your attention for a bit,' she asks the assembled pensioners. 'I am sure you would all like to join me in thanking Lauren and all of the volunteers for making today possible,' she says. 'Every year we are lucky to come together with friends old and new, and celebrate Christmas time. So thank you all.' Everyone duly raises their glass in a toast, before bursting into thunderous applause.

'Oh, I agree, it was the best meal I've had in a long time,' says Gerald. 'You can't beat a good roast. I used to love a decent curry too but I can't do that without a side order of Gaviscon these days,' he says and everyone laughs and empathises.

After coffee and mince pies the group are sat around chatting at the table. Sue is playing a variety of golden oldies on vinyl and Gerald, as promised, is whizzing Eileen around the dance floor. She looks beautiful in her grey dress, the sequins on the neckline sparkling as they catch the light. Her husband has been gone for two years and I guess she must feel lonely, so it's nice to see her looking so happy. She throws her head back and laughs at something Gerald has said and I feel proud that she has this opportunity to dress up and have a dance with a handsome man. I can't help wondering when I might have the chance to do the same.

Having pulled Christmas crackers earlier, the rest of the

pensioners are wearing party hats and some are now also dancing to the music. Others are happy to sit and chat, especially those who are not so great on their feet.

'Oh, isn't this wonderful,' I say to Kian.

'It's great to see,' he agrees. 'I hope I have someone like you to look after me in my old age,' he says, as Sue and Barry are impressing everyone with a vigorous jive.

'Actually, sorry, that came out wrong. I was just thinking how anyone would be lucky to have you watching out for them, is what I meant.' He looks slightly embarrassed.

'Don't worry, I know what you mean. I guess we all want to feel safe and needed as we get older.'

'Can the old people play musical chairs with us later?' asks Bella, who is tucking into a sausage roll and I feel slightly faint at the thought of an elderly person racing to find an empty chair. On a wooden floor. Maybe not racing exactly but I think musical chairs is a dangerous game given the age demographic.

'I'm not sure,' says Kian. 'What do you think?' He turns to me.

'Don't put this on me. Oh nooo,' I say, thinking I don't want to be the one responsible for the broken bones of the older partygoers. 'Maybe pass the parcel is a safer bet. You do have some prizes, I take it?'

Kian slaps his forehead with his hand. 'The parcels! I've left them at home on the kitchen table where I was wrapping them last night.' He glances at his watch. 'I can be there and back in ten minutes if you can hold the fort?'

'You want me to look after the kids on my own?' I say, although at that very moment Audrey is striding towards me.

TWENTY-FIVE

'I'll watch them with you,' Audrey says, having caught the end of the conversation about the parcels. 'I've just poured everyone a drink, and quite a few have said yes to some more of your red velvet cake,' she informs me. 'Who knew old people could eat so much?'

'I'm so happy everyone is enjoying themselves,' I tell her.

'Thank you so much, I shan't be long,' says Kian to us both, already heading for the door.

'My mum is really enjoying herself too,' says Audrey. 'Thank you so much for finding a place for her today and picking her up. I think she has found a new friend.'

I glance over at Audrey's mum, who is deep in conversation with Eileen, who has taken a break from her dancing. They are about a similar age and I really hope there is the possibility that they might become good friends.

Even though there are enough volunteers, I hope Kian doesn't hit too many red traffic lights. I walk over to the children's party table then and make a suggestion.

'Before you go outside again on the bouncy castle, would

you like to dance with some of the old people?' I ask the children.

'Old people don't like our music,' says the boy with the mop of black hair as he licks frosting from a cupcake off his fingers.

'They do.' Bella frowns. 'My nanna likes Rihanna and she went to a concert with my mum to watch Harry Styles.'

'My mum fancies him,' says another child, grinning.

'Do you think they know the dance to "Gangnam Style"?' asks a little girl in a red dress. 'My grandad dances to that when he's drunk and makes us all laugh.'

'I'm not sure about that,' I say, although I suddenly have an idea.

'Bloody hell, I need a drink, I'm knackered,' says Sue, before unscrewing the top of a bottle of lemonade and pouring herself a long drink after her vigorous dancing.

'You're a very good dancer,' Mum tells Sue as she begins clearing the table, and placing debris from crackers into a bin bag whilst I collect up some plates. Audrey is already in the kitchen stacking up the dishwasher.

'Runner up in regional dance competition in nineteen seventy-six,' says Sue proudly. 'I fell off the back of a motorbike the following year, so that put paid to that. My leg wasn't right for ages.'

'I used to like a dance when I was younger,' Mum says with a wry smile. 'Although more disco dancing. Me and a friend had a job in a nightclub dancing in a cage. It's where I met Lauren's dad.'

'You really are full of surprises,' says Sue.

'I used to be,' says Mum. 'I was the one who was always up for adventure as a teenager. I think I surprised people the most when I settled down and got married at the age of twenty-three.'

I wonder for a second if I was actually planned, or if I was responsible for putting paid to Mum's adventures. She sounds like her life was full of fun before I came along. Then again, I wasn't born until many years into their marriage, my parents taking for granted the fact that they wouldn't have a problem having children. And the doctors couldn't find anything wrong either. Eventually, they fostered a young child for a few months, and lo and behold six months later Mum was pregnant with me.

'Okay, everyone, I was just wondering if any of you would like to have a game of musical statues?'

'Musical statues.' Elsie frowns. 'Are you joking?'

'With the children,' I add, in case they think it a strange thing to suggest. 'And you never know, you might enjoy it.'

'Musical statues!' say the children, jumping up and down with excitement.

'That's boring,' says the black-haired boy.

'I'm sure it is what you make it.' I paint on my brightest smile.

I grab a huge tub of Celebrations. 'Sweets for everyone who takes part, and, um, maybe some small prizes,' I say, and grumpy boy looks a bit happier.

I had gathered up all the discarded gifts from the Christmas crackers that I can give out, although I'm not sure what the kids will do with a nail clipper or a tape measure. At least there are a few plastic toys in there though.

'Can't we go back on the bouncy castle?' says the boy with the black hair as he stuffs another cupcake into his mouth. 'That was much more fun.'

'Yes, of course, but after a game of musical statues,' I say firmly, wondering whether I ought to have trained as a teacher.

'Musical statues?' says one of the older guys. 'I don't know about that, I might seize up if I stand in one position for too long,' he says and the others laugh.

'Oh, come on, it will be fun,' says Eileen, getting to her feet.

'If you say so,' huffs Elsie. 'Although I thought this was supposed to be a pensioners' party.'

'Kids keep you young,' says Mum but Elsie looks unconvinced. 'Honestly, whenever children come to the food bank with their parents, they always make me laugh. Little treasures they are. They grow up so quickly.'

'Go on then, let's give it a go,' says a tall bloke, whilst a lady who needs the assistance of a Zimmer frame asks if it will be alright if she acts like a statue from her chair.

'Of course it is. We want you all to have a good time here despite any handicaps.'

'I don't think you're allowed to say that word,' says black-haired boy.

'Oh right, sorry.' I smile. 'For anyone who has limited mobility.'

The music plays and we soon get into the mood. Audrey helps me to judge and after a while, everyone is showing their competitive spirit, arguing that they weren't moving when they are called out – and that's just the pensioners!

Audrey and I hand out sweets for winners, and Audrey mistakenly hands a whistle to the black-haired child that I thought I had hidden. He then proceeds to blow it loudly.

'Man the lifeboats, man overboard,' says Wilf, looking startled, and Sue settles him, before miraculously managing to prise the whistle from the boy's hand.

'And it was all going so well,' Mum says laughing as the boy bursts into tears. I hand him a red plastic elephant and a yo-yo that he pulls a face at, but accepts all the same. A few minutes later, Audrey has shown how to successfully glide the string of the yo-yo up and down, and he is smiling happily. She really is a godsend. I feel so pleased that I ran into her on the evening of the forest moon walk, which reinforces my belief that it is sometimes a good idea to push yourself out of your comfort zone. You just never know what might happen if you do.

Some of the older folk are getting right into things, competing with two children that now remain in the game. Glancing at my watch I realise twenty-five minutes have passed and there is still no sign of Kian. I'm not exactly sure I will be able to keep the children entertained if he takes much longer. What do I know about kids? I think to myself with a feeling of rising panic. It's not as if I even have any nieces or nephews, the only interaction with children being at Bentham's. Deep breaths, just go with the flow.

We are down to eight people on the floor, so I pause the music for a little longer, eliminating two at a time. They are all poised in various positions, the ones who have been called out are walking slowly back to their chairs, rubbing their backs. Just then, Kian walks through the door.

'Bloody hell, have I stumbled upon rehearsals for "Thriller",' he says, his eyes wide and Audrey and I burst out laughing.

TWENTY-SIX

'Everything okay?' I ask Kian as he places a bag full of parcels down on the floor. An old guy moves then and Audrey pronounces him out of the game much to his disappointment.

'Sure, yes, I just ran into someone I know,' he tells me. Am I imagining it, or does he look a little stressed?

'Right. Well, the good news is the kids have all been fine but I think they are ready to go outside again and run around,' I tell him, thankful that there have been no incidents in his absence.

'Sure thing.'

'Maybe when they come back inside, they can have a game of pass the parcel. Something nice and calming,' I suggest.

'Sounds like a plan.' He grins. 'Then we can light the candles on Bella's cake.'

A couple of the people on the floor move then and are asked to sit down, protesting that Kian made them turn around when he walked through the door. Finally, we have joint winners in Gerald and the birthday girl, Bella. Gerald receives a tape measure, and Bella a bath bomb, which was left over from the pensioners' gift bags.

'It seems like everyone is having a good time, so maybe you

were right all along,' I tell Kian when I finish refreshing drinks. Elsie is actually beginning to loosen up a bit after her second sherry and is kind of chair dancing, moving her body from side to side and smiling.

'No sense in worrying over things you can't control.' He gives what I think is a bit of a forced smile, and I wonder whether everything with him really is okay?

'I guess not.'

'Dad, what about the piñata,' says Bella, looking up towards the pink straw donkey above her head.

'Oh sure, shall we do that first then?'

'Yes, please,' squeals Bella. And I imagine the amount of running around the kids will need after another load of sugar from the contents.

Kian passes the stick to Bella, and she takes the first whack at the piñata, before each of the children have a turn. Robbie, the black-haired boy, whacks the donkey with such force that a stream of sweets come cascading down over Elsie's head as she walks past.

'Oh my goodness!' she exclaims, and to my surprise she laughs. 'It's raining sweets.'

Their pockets full of toffees, the children have a game of pass the parcel, before going outside once more to the bouncy castle, with strict instructions from me not to eat any toffees whilst bouncing up and down.

'Is everything okay?' I finally ask Kian, who looks deep in thought.

'What? Yes, sure. It's just something has cropped up that I wasn't expecting, that's all,' he says without elaborating.

He heads outside followed by Audrey, and I will join them when I have made sure all of the pensioners have everything they need. I wonder what could have made Kian's mood shift in such a short space of time?

.   .   .

After the tired-looking children return to the hall and Kian lights the candles on the beautiful cake, the old people join in the singing of 'Happy Birthday', and Bella looks like the happiest little girl in the world.

It's a joy to watch some of the children head over to the pensioners' table and sit with them, others are dancing to some modern songs, with Gerald still on the floor busting some moves with Eileen. Black-haired Robbie takes a seat next to Elsie.

'How old are you?' he asks her as he plays with a plastic elephant, walking it across the table.

'Don't you know it's rude to ask a lady her age?' she replies, but there is a smile playing around her mouth. That sherry has definitely loosened her up a bit.

'Is it?' asks the boy. 'But grown-ups always ask kids how old they are, don't they?'

He throws the plastic elephant up in the air, failing to catch it, and it lands squarely in a discarded glass of lemonade. Elsie smiles at it lands with a plop. 'It's a good job elephants can swim,' she says. 'And, yes, I suppose adults do ask children how old they are, but it's different,' she explains. 'So how old are you then?'

'I'm seven, nearly eight. I might have a party in a play centre when it's my birthday,' he tells her.

'That sounds nice. And since you asked, I will tell you that I am eighty-four years old.'

'That's really old. Will you be dead soon?' he asks and I close my eyes in mild frustration.

'Well I sincerely hope not!' She frowns. 'I would like to see my son next year,' she tells him.

I'm sitting enjoying a drink and watching their conversation unfold. Hopefully it can't get any worse.

'Why can't you see him now?' he asks as he winds the string around his yo-yo.

'Because he lives in Australia and it's a very long way away,' she explains.

'They have kangaroos there, don't they? And koalas. We have been learning about Australia at school. Bad people got sent there for committing crimes. Is your son a bad person?'

Oh Lord.

'Goodness me, no!' Elsie exclaims. 'Criminals got sent there hundreds of years ago. These days it's a very nice place to live apparently.'

'So why don't you go there? Are you too old to go on a plane?' he asks innocently.

'My goodness you do like to ask a lot of questions, don't you? But, as a matter of fact, yes, I probably am too old for such a long flight,' she tells him.

'Couldn't you go and live there?'

'It's not really as simple as that. But he's coming over here next year for a visit. He was too busy with his work this year.'

She quietly takes a sip of sherry as she stares ahead wistfully and I fear Robbie might have upset her.

'I hope he does. But if he doesn't you can still talk on the phone, can't you? My uncle lives in Canada and my mum speaks to him a lot.'

'Yes, I do, of course.' She smiles. 'And we video call so I can see his face.'

'That's good then. My mum does that too.'

He retrieves the elephant from the glass and dries it with a napkin before handing it to her.

'You can have this if you like,' he says and he might as well have handed her a gold nugget, such is the joy on her face. 'Elephants never forget. Even if you don't see your son you will never forget each other,' he says, before sliding off his chair and running back to the party table.

I watch Elsie close her eyes and clutch the elephant in her hand like a prized gift.

A while later, I chat to the retired headteacher of the local primary school and ask her if she knows the current head-teacher. When she tells me she does, I have an idea.

I glance at my watch and realise it's almost time for Santa's visit, so manage to get everyone inside.

My dad usually does the honours dressing as Santa, but I had to find a replacement this year, in the form of my neighbour Martin, who kindly dashed out and bought a load of selection boxes to dispense to the children when I learned we would be sharing the hall.

'Boys, girls and grown-ups alike. We have a special visitor arriving any minute now,' I announce, after Sue has switched the music off. 'If you listen carefully, you might be able to hear the sound of bells somewhere.' I cup my hand to my ear.

Right on cue, there is a tinkling of bells, courtesy of Spotify being piped through the speakers.

'Is that the reindeer bells!' says an excited Bella.

'I think it might be,' I say and she jumps up and down with excitement.

A few seconds later, a burly bloke bursts through the door with a ho ho ho! And quickly begins handing out selection boxes to the children.

'Are you the real Santa?' asks an excited girl in a sparkly party dress.

'Yes, yes, I am,' says Martin, doing his best to disguise his voice. Not that any of the children here would know him, I'm sure. Kian is standing next to me, grinning.

'Because I know there are fake ones in the grotto in the town square,' says the little girl. 'Well, my brother says so anyway. Because the real one lives in Lapland.'

'Ho ho ho. Yes, I have come from Lapland,' he says, edging away as politely as possible as the children move in, circling him like vultures.

'Then where are your reindeer?' a boy demands. When he

tells him they are resting for a busy evening later, and that he took an EasyJet flight, I struggle to keep a straight face.

'You organised this then?' says Kian, nodding to Santa, who is surrounded by children and looks completely out of his comfort zone. 'You really did think of everything, didn't you?'

He looks at me with open admiration, and I can't help feeling thrilled.

'I tried. And although it wasn't quite what I was expecting, I have to say that so far today has been a success, despite my initial reservations,' I admit.

'I'd have to agree.' He takes the empty glass from me, asking if I would like a refill and when our hands brush together, it takes all my composure to answer him.

'Bella and her friends are having the best time. And I've enjoyed your company,' says Kian. 'Actually, I was wondering if...'

'Yes?' I can feel my heart beating that little bit faster.

Before he has a chance to answer, I hear an almighty crash coming from the kitchen followed by a cry.

Kian and I race to the scene to find Mum lying on the floor.

'I slipped on some fat that must have dripped from a roasting tray,' she says, rubbing at her hip and grimacing in pain. 'Sorry to spoil the party, but I think I might have broken something.'

TWENTY-SEVEN

'Sorry, love, fancy landing you with this on Christmas Eve,' says Mum as she is strapped onto a stretcher and wheeled into an ambulance to be checked out at hospital. She is putting on a brave face, but every now and then I see her wince in pain.

'Oh, Mum, don't be silly, you're not landing me with anything. The party is going well, but I'm more worried about you,' I tell her, anxiously hoping she will be alright. My parents are not even what you might call particularly old, but it reminds me of how our health changes as we age.

Audrey and Sue are standing beside me outside in the car park, Barry having sneaked off to the pub for a quick one a short while ago.

'You go with your mum in the ambulance,' says Kian, appearing from inside then. 'The party will be winding up soon, so when the children have all been collected by their parents, I will help Sue get the pensioners home who aren't being collected. I will come to the hospital later and take you home.'

'Really, Kian, you don't need to do that,' I protest. 'I can get a taxi home later, hopefully with Mum, if she hasn't broken anything.'

'On Christmas Eve?' He looks doubtful. 'No, you've been a great help here today, even with your own party taking place. It's the least I can do. Can I put my number in your phone?'

'Sure.'

I hand over my phone and he adds his contact details.

'What about Bella though?' I ask.

'I'll make sure she is sorted, don't worry.' He smiles.

'Well, only if you're sure? Although I will only call you if I can't get a taxi.'

'Make sure you do,' he insists. 'Honestly, it's not a bother.' He leans in and, to my surprise, kisses me gently on the cheek, sending an electric shock running through my body. 'See you later then.'

I can hear the music coming from inside, thankfully everyone is still enjoying themselves, Mum having put on a brave face, and telling her friends it was just a little sprain.

Inside the ambulance, Mum gives in to her discomfort and is given some pain relief, and I pray it isn't anything too serious. I also find myself stroking my cheek where Kian had kissed it, and wondering how it would have felt if his lips had landed on mine.

'Oh, thank goodness for that.'

I am on the phone to Gemma, who has called to see how the day went. Mum has been X-rayed, and thankfully her hip is not broken as she first feared, but the doctor has advised her to rest and told her she will likely have some bruising tomorrow.

'So at least I don't need to be worrying about both of my parents needing operations right now,' I tell Gemma, thinking of Dad.

'Thank goodness for that. Can you imagine them both being laid up over Christmas?'

'I know. I've persuaded Mum to stay over with me tonight.

She's a little sore but I'm just so thankful that nothing is broken. She's fast asleep now, courtesy of her pain meds.'

'I'm glad she's okay. And Kian came and picked you up?' she says. 'That was very decent of him. I told you he fancied you, didn't I?'

'I'm not sure about that,' I tell her, although he did kiss me on the cheek. 'He just seems like a good bloke.'

'Who would give up his Christmas Eve, yeah right.' I can imagine her smiling.

'I must admit I thought it would be a right inconvenience on Christmas Eve, but he said Bella was exhausted after the party, so her grandparents watched her for a couple of hours, I think. He was back in time to say goodnight before she went to bed to wait excitedly for Santa.'

I think of our journey home in his car, Mum thanking him and asking him if he was sure she wasn't putting him out and he'd said it was no bother and that we would be waiting ages for a taxi on Christmas Eve. He arrived before I even texted him, buying us both coffees whilst we waited for Mum to come out of X-ray.

He'd even bought a coffee for an old lady sitting next to us and they chatted about their favourite Christmas films, whilst waiting for her husband, who was being assessed after falling over in the garden, and putting his back out. She'd told him her favourite film was *Home Alone* and that she bet he expected her to say something like *It's a Wonderful Life*.

'Not necessarily. I was once told not to make assumptions about people,' he says, turning to me and smiling.

The lady explained that *Home Alone* just brought back so many wonderful memories of spending time with her children and grandchildren when they were growing up.

'I'm hoping my great-grandchildren will enjoy it too, if any come along.' She smiles.

I noticed how Kian also opened doors for patients using

walking sticks, bought a load of chocolate bars from a vending machine and left them at the nurses' station, wishing them all the best, and just generally seemed to put a smile on people's faces. He also made nice comments about someone wearing a snappy outfit, and commented on my coat and how red really is my colour, which against my dark hair, I have been told before. I think back to his commenting on Gemma's beautiful hair and realise that he is just the man he is, generous with his compliments. The kind of person who has the ability to make you feel good about yourself with a few choice words.

I wonder whether he could be a bit of a charmer, as I know nothing about him really, yet his comments on the things he observes do seem perfectly natural.

We chat for a while longer, Gemma telling me that the bag she has her eye on is still unsold, and that it will be going in the January sales.

'I'll be in early Boxing Day morning, nabbing it as soon as the discount has been applied,' she tells me and I think she deserves it, having coveted it for so long.

'So what are you up to tonight then?' I ask.

'I'm going to get in a long hot bath, then flop in front of the TV. It was one long, busy day,' she says, after I ask her if she feels like coming over.

'Okay. Same here. Merry Christmas, Gemma. I hope you all have a wonderful day tomorrow.'

'Thanks, you too. I actually envy your quiet one tomorrow,' she says.

'You'd be bored after an hour.'

'That's probably true.' She giggles.

'I'll call you tomorrow when I have opened my present,' I tell her.

'Okay. Night then, sweet dreams. Give my love to your mum.'

. . .

It's almost after nine thirty, and Mum has taken herself to bed with some painkillers, when there's a knock at the front door. I wonder who it could be at this time on Christmas Eve, so glance through my Ring doorbell, glad that I have had it installed.

'Dad, what on earth are you doing here?' I ask open-mouthed as I see him standing on the doorstep and carrying a holdall.

'Room for a small one?' he asks.

TWENTY-EIGHT

'Are you okay, Dad? What on earth has happened?' I ask as he drops his bag down and takes a seat in the lounge. 'Have you had an argument with Rose?'

'You could say that.' He exhales deeply. 'Although maybe a bit more than an argument. We have decided to go our separate ways.'

'On Christmas Eve?' I say, shocked.

'Let's just say, it's probably been a long time coming.' He sighs.

I make tea and we sit together on the large sofa.

'Sorry to pitch up like this, but I was wondering if I could stay for a few nights, until I sort myself out?' he asks.

'Dad, of course! This is your home too, there is no need to ask. And there's plenty of room as you know.'

Four bedrooms in total, always ready made up should anyone decide to stay, usually my parents. It's kind of an arrangement we came to when my inheritance was gifted to me early, as my parents went and pursued their own lives, Mum preferring to live in the centre of town now and Dad moving in with Rose. It's lovely having them breeze in and out of my life though.

'So, how's your mother?' Dad asks as he sips his tea.

I'd texted Dad and told him about Mum's fall as I thought he might like to know.

'She's fine, no broken bones and sleeping soundly upstairs.'

'What, she's staying here?' He sounds surprised. 'Now I feel like a bit of a burden.'

'Don't be silly,' I reassure him. 'Anyway, Mum is fine, but I'm more interested in what has happened with you and Rose right now.'

'Hard to pinpoint one thing.' He shrugs. 'We've been arguing a lot lately, she always seems to be having a go at me over something or other. She complains if I spend too long in the greenhouse when she's home, other times I think she would like me to sleep in there.' He rolls his eyes. 'But I'm okay, love, don't you worry. All I want is a bit of peace at my time of life.'

'Did something happen for you to walk out though, especially it being Christmas Eve?'

'She brought a fish supper home earlier, saying she wasn't cooking on Christmas Eve,' Dad tells me. 'I told her that was a bit inconsiderate, given my heart condition and we had a huge row.' Dad sighs. 'She said it wasn't her responsibility to police whatever I eat, and she wasn't going to give up her treats for anyone, or words to that effect.'

'She said what?' I can feel the anger rise inside me. Not very supportive, I'm sure. Although maybe she wasn't quite as harsh as that, taking into account Dad saying 'words to that effect'.

'Honestly, love, as I said, the break has probably been a long time coming, the final straw if you like,' he says, seemingly resigned to the situation. 'And I wouldn't mind, but I'd made a big pan of soup.'

'You did?'

'Yes, your mother taught me how. And she made me some

lovely vegetable soup last week, from some winter veg I've been growing at the allotment.'

'Mum never mentioned anything about that,' I say in surprise. 'Did she take it to your house?'

'No, she dropped it at the allotment. I've been down there getting rid of some old stuff from the shed and the greenhouse.'

'In this weather?'

'As I said, in my shed and greenhouse mainly, although maybe I have just been wanting to get out of the house,' he admits.

'Oh, Dad. You should have said something. Promise me you won't go down there again until the spring, especially with your heart condition,' I say gently. 'And are you sure you're okay?'

'I'm fine.' He manages a smile. 'As I said, the split has been a long time coming. I don't really think we have that much in common, to tell you the truth. She can't stand *Countdown* for a start,' he says, and I think of how Mum and Dad used to watch it together, competing with each other, especially on the word round.

'Well as long as you're alright, that's the main thing. And I will look after you after your operation, so it makes sense for you to stay here for a while.'

Dad's operation is scheduled for early January.

'You're a good daughter.' Dad reaches across and squeezes my hand.

'That's because I have had good parents,' I say, thinking it unexpected but lovely that we will all be spending Christmas Day under the same roof.

TWENTY-NINE

'Kian, hi,' I say, surprised and thrilled to be receiving a call from him on Christmas morning.

Mum, having got over the shock of seeing Dad this morning, is having breakfast with him in the kitchen.

'Good morning and merry Christmas,' he says, the sound of his voice delighting me.

'Merry Christmas to you too and Bella, of course. Are you okay? You sound a little out of breath,' I comment.

'What? Oh yes, I'm just walking quickly to the corner shop. Would you believe I forgot the golden rule of checking that toys don't need batteries, so Bella has a barking, walking dog that currently can't do either of those things.' He laughs.

'Oh no. Thank goodness for the shop hey, it should be called Open All Hours. I don't think that place ever closes, even on Christmas Day.'

'And as you say, thank goodness for that,' he says.

'Is Bella with you?' I ask, thinking I might wish her a merry Christmas.

'No, she's at home with a family member while I nipped out,' he tells me.

'Well wish her a happy Christmas from me,' I say, hoping they have a lovely day together.

'I will do. So how is your mum?' he asks and I fill him in, also telling him about Dad pitching up here last night.

'It's a long story,' I tell him.

'Well I'd like to hear it sometime. That's why I was calling actually,' he says. 'I know we are both busy at Christmas, but would you like to go out with me one evening when we are both free?' he asks and my heart soars.

'Yes, I think I would like that.'

'You think?' I can hear him laugh.

'Sorry, yes, that would be really nice. Is that better?' I ask, feeling thrilled. I can't wait to see him again and wondered when that might be.

'Much better. Okay, well, I'll call you again soon. Have a wonderful Christmas Day.'

'Thank you, you too.'

'Something, or should I say someone, has put a smile on your face,' Mum comments as she swallows down some painkillers with a glass of water.

'It was Kian,' I tell her.

'I thought as much. Is he okay?' she asks, smiling.

'He is. He called to wish me a merry Christmas. Oh and he asked after you,' I tell her as I pour myself a coffee from the cafetière.

'Is Kian the bloke who shared the hall for his daughter's party?' asks Dad, Mum obviously already having filled him in about the events of yesterday.

'That's right. He only lives a couple of miles away, having moved into town from a place near Keswick.'

Victoria Apartments are quite upmarket overlooking the

river and with glimpses of the forest beyond. I imagine his apartment to be stylish, yet relaxed, a bit like Kian himself.

'Well you should get yourself out on a date with him. It's been a while since you had a boyfriend,' says Dad with his usual forthrightness.

'I'm well aware of that, Dad, but where do you meet blokes these days? Besides, I am perfectly happy on my own,' I tell him, which of course is true. But Dad's right, it has been a while since I've been out with anyone and I rather like the feeling of anticipation, wondering where Kian might take me.

'Although, in fact, he has just asked me out.' I can't help smiling as I tell my parents the news.

'Oh lovely,' says Mum. 'Asking you out on Christmas Day, how romantic.' She claps her hands together.

'Do you remember when I asked you out?' asks Dad, pouring himself another coffee.

'Of course I do. Easter Saturday, when I was dancing at that club.' She smiles. 'We spent Easter Sunday going to Morecambe on the back of your motorbike.' She smiles fondly at the memory.

'You were quite the adventurous couple then, by the sound of things.'

'We were. As anyone should be if they get the chance,' advises Dad. 'Life goes by so quickly.'

As we sit chatting, I know I am going to enjoy every minute of today, with unexpectedly both of my parents sharing it with me. I do think about Rose for a minute though, and hope she isn't spending it all alone. I also have her Christmas gift here.

'She's gone to her sister's for the day,' Dad tells me when I ask about her. 'To tell you the truth, we had both been invited, but she only mentioned that to me a few days ago, for some reason.' He shrugs, painting a picture of how strained their relationship must have become. Maybe living with the tension wasn't good for his heart either.

We have porridge and berries for breakfast, as later we will be enjoying a delicious roast with meat left over from yesterday. Mum may have a little Turkey, as she is, (when it suits her) a Flexitarian, although her diet is generally meat free. There will be extra vegetables and lean turkey for Dad too.

We have a little bit of a tradition of opening our gifts after breakfast, so first of all I open up Gemma's gift in the silver paper. I think of her family receiving gifts wrapped in Grinch paper then and can't help but laugh.

Inside is a pretty silver bracelet, dotted with pearls. There is also a gift card for afternoon tea for two people at a posh hotel in Grasmere.

Mum and Dad have bought me some beautiful silk pyjamas, and a bottle of my favourite perfume, and Dad is thrilled with some rare tomato seeds for his greenhouse and a new wristwatch.

'Oh, it's perfect,' says Mum, trying on the beanie hat and scarf. 'And handmade too.' She also loves her earrings.

After the present opening, I call Gemma.

'Merry Christmas! And thank you so much for the bracelet, I love it, it's just so me,' I say as I admire it on my wrist. 'But afternoon tea as well. Haven't you gone a little bit over the top?' I ask as we never normally spend too much on each other at Christmas, saving the bigger gift for our birthdays.

'Merry Christmas to you too! And I haven't actually, it was a deal on one of those online sites. I thought you might like to take your mum. Maybe you both deserve a bit of a treat, especially after your mum having a fall.'

'Oh, Gemma, that is so thoughtful, thank you.'

'No problem. It might cheer her up, we can do something like that too, another time, if you fancy it?'

'I'd love that.'

'So how is your mum doing?'

'Not too bad, thanks. A huge bruise on her side but I'm just so thankful that she has no broken bones. I don't think she would be able to cope with being laid up for long.'

I quickly tell her about Dad being here too and that I will fill her in more when I see her.

We say our goodbyes, Gemma off to spend the day with her large family, me here with Mum and Dad and I couldn't be happier to be with them both. And to look forward to my date with the delectable Kian.

'You've done us proud, love,' says Dad, pushing his plate away after Christmas lunch.

Mum said it still feels very strange having King Charles deliver the Christmas Day speech, rather than the queen but that she thought he did a good job all the same.

'Those parsnips from the allotment tasted good, didn't they? And the carrots. Was there something sweet in them?' asks Dad.

'I roasted them with thyme and honey,' I tell him.

'Really? Well, they were delicious.'

I roasted some potatoes in olive oil along with the veg, so Christmas lunch for Dad was quite healthy.

'I don't suppose you have any of that red velvet cake left, do you?' asks Mum, having declined some Christmas pudding.

'I do actually.' I head to the fridge.

'Maybe I could have a small slice.' Dad joins his hands together in prayer pleadingly.

'Well, alright, just a small slice as your lunch was pretty healthy.' I smile. 'I even have some vegan cream substitute to pour over it that tastes exactly like cream, but healthier,' I say, except when I open the fridge I realise I forgot to buy some.

'Right, I'm just nipping to Open All Hours for that cream. And don't worry, Dad, it tastes really good,' I say, before he can complain. 'Back in two ticks. Keep your hands out of the Quality Street tin.' I wink.

'I hope you're going to enjoy a Christmas dinner later,' I say to Alf at the shop, placing my cream and a packet of playing cards down onto the counter. I remember how we all used to play a game of cards and thought it might be something we could enjoy later.

'Very soon actually.' He glances at his watch. 'I am closing up in five minutes, so you have made it here in the nick of time.'

'Thanks, Alf,' I say, lifting my things from the counter. 'And merry Christmas.'

'And to you too.'

I'm about to get into my car, when I notice Kian at a zebra crossing further up the road, and I freeze. Because this time he isn't holding Bella's hand alone. A willowy blonde is holding her other hand and chatting to her. I watch the cars slow down at the zebra crossing as they make their way across the busy road, all three of them with a smile on their face.

THIRTY

'Are you alright, love?' asks Mum as she watches a Christmas movie with Dad. Her leg is propped up on a footstool as she told me that her leg had been hurting her.

'That's because you keep getting up and doing things,' I'd told her firmly. 'You are supposed to be resting completely. Doctor's orders, remember?'

Dad and I had done the washing-up and put all the dishes away, telling Mum firmly to sit down.

'So, are you alright?' asks Mum again. 'You look as though you have seen a ghost.'

'What? Yes, I'm fine.' I force a smile. I don't want to ruin Christmas Day, but I can't get the image of Kian with another woman holding Bella's hand out of my head.

'You're sure?' Dad presses.

'I'm sure, really. I think I'm just a little tired, that's all.' I muster up my best smile.

'Well, that's hardly surprising, you do so much. Sit down and watch the film with us,' Mum insists. 'You used to love watching films with us when you were little.'

'I will, Mum. I just want to knock and make sure Eileen's

okay. I was going to invite her in for a drink later, if you don't mind.'

'Of course not.' Mum smiles. 'I always have time for Eileen.'

It turns out that Eileen has other plans for this evening, in the form of Gerald, who has invited her to his place for dinner.

'He's picking me up at seven,' says Eileen. 'Would you believe we are having a fondue evening? We got chatting at the party yesterday, and I mentioned how I used to love a good fondue party. Anyway, he called me this morning, having tracked a fondue kit down last night.' She grins. 'I think it's a chocolate dipping thing really, for marshmallows, but near enough.' She laughs.

'That's wonderful, Eileen. I hope you have a lovely evening. Gerald is a lovely bloke.'

I fill her in on both my parents staying with me for Christmas.

'That's the spirit of Christmas, having family around, isn't it?' she says. 'Sounds like some of us oldies are having one of our best Christmases ever.'

Back inside, I keep thinking about my forthcoming date with Kian, whilst also wondering who the mystery woman was? Perhaps it was Bella's aunt? When he'd said earlier that a family member was looking after Bella when he'd nipped to the shop, he never specified it was his parents. I decide I am overthinking things and try and put it out of my mind. He's hardly likely to ask me out if there is someone else on the scene, surely?

I'm mulling this over when Gemma calls.

'I'm just having five minutes outside with a secret cig,' she tells me.

'I thought you had quit?' I say, surprised, having never seen her smoke when we have been together lately.

'I have. Well, almost. I only have one very occasionally. Not enough to say yes when doctors ask me if I smoke.' She giggles. 'I'm playing hide and seek with two of my nephews. I'm around the corner near a row of garages. I'll go back in a bit. So how is your day going?'

'It's going great. We've done the usual, eaten far too much. Mum and Dad are watching *Deck the Halls* for the umpteenth time. I'll be joining them in a minute.'

I long to tell Gemma about seeing Kian earlier, she always manages to say the right thing. But I decide against it.

'And yours?'

'It's been a lot of fun actually. The kids are wearing me out though. For some reason, I seem to be the unpaid entertainment whenever we are all together,' she whispers, determined not to be found just yet. 'We've played Twister, pin the tail on the elf and now hide and seek, whilst everyone else is getting pissed,' she moans. 'Especially my gran, who insists she doesn't drink, but is knocking back the sherry, "as it's Christmas".' She giggles.

'Well you could hardly expect your gran to play Twister,' I say, thinking of the party at the community centre and her teasing me saying the old people might like it. 'And it's your fault you are nominated as children's entertainer. You are far too much fun.'

'True, that is. And I'll miss them when they have gone, so I guess I should make the most of it.'

Gemma has made no secret of the fact that she would like to have children one day and I think she would make a wonderful mum.

'Right, I'd better go. I can hear the boys shouting my name loudly, they might call out a search party if they can't find me soon.'

'And discover your dirty little secret.' I laugh, thinking of her furtively smoking behind the garages.

'Exactly. Speak to you soon. Bye.'

That evening, I make sure everywhere is spotless, even though Dad keeps telling me to sit down and relax, which I do eventually with a large glass of red wine.

Despite reassurances from Dad that Rose had gone to her sister's, I messaged her anyway to wish her a merry Christmas and ask if she is okay, but she never replied. I wonder then whether things really are over between them, although, in all honesty, Dad doesn't seem to be too upset, so perhaps their split really was a long time coming.

Just after eleven, Mum retires to bed, with Dad not far behind her. I realise then that I haven't seen Tony since early this morning. He's generally miaowing at the back door around nine, having been out all day. He's always been more of a day cat, who goes to bed around the same time I do, although sometimes his routine changes.

I walk outside and call his name but there's no sign of him. I put the contents of the inside bin into the large outdoor one, when he appears wrapping himself around my legs.

'Oh, I see, you smelt the leftovers, did you? There's some turkey left in the fridge if you want some.'

He miaows and I wonder if people would think I had gone mad, hearing me having a full-on conversation with a cat.

Back inside, after a slice of turkey, Tony curls up into his bed and I wonder what my life would be like without him. I also wonder vaguely whether or not Kian likes cats.

THIRTY-ONE

I wake early and glance at my phone. I can hardly believe it's nine thirty!

I'm just stretching out my arms before a shower, when there's a tap on the bedroom door. Dad enters then, carrying a cup of tea.

'Why didn't you wake me?' I stretch my arms out over my head.

'I thought you deserved a lie in. You do enough running around.' He smiles warmly, sitting at the edge of the bed. 'Me and your mother had a lovely day yesterday, we were just chatting about that in the kitchen.'

'What did you have for breakfast?' I narrow my eyes at him.

'Bran Flakes.'

'Really?' I ask doubtfully.

'Yes. Ask your mother. I'm not sure I could get a taste for them but they weren't too bad with a few raisins,' he tells me.

I head to the shower and after breakfast I decide to wrap up well, and take the fifteen-minute walk into town to meet Gemma for a coffee at the Blue Teapot, one of the few cafés open on Boxing Day.

The wind bites as I walk along, the roads deserted apart from a few hikers heading for the hills decked out in walking gear, and a couple of families with children enjoying their bikes or scooters, probably Christmas presents.

I pass a couple carrying coffees, linking arms, and smiling up at each other. I think of Kian then, and wonder when I might hear from him to arrange our date. I also fleetingly think of the woman I saw him with and how they were all laughing together, reminding me of a family.

Turning into the market square, I bump into Audrey and her mum coming out of Bentham's.

'Hi, how are you both?' I ask, thinking it nice that Audrey's mum is out of the house.

'Really good, thanks. Mum and I just nipped into town, so Mum could have a look at the sales in your shop,' says Audrey. 'Well, not your shop, obviously, but you know what I mean.' She smiles.

'And I got this,' says Audrey's mum. 'Almost half price, it was.'

She pulls part of a checked woollen coat from her bag to show me.

'Ooh very nice. I'm sure you will get your wear out of that in this cold weather.'

'Yes, I think I will. I have a couple of padded coats but nothing smart. I'm going to watch the Fellview brass band with Eileen on Tuesday at the civic hall.'

'That sounds lovely. Enjoy yourselves.'

I'm happy for Eileen too, who certainly seems to be out there living her best life right now.

Gemma is waiting at a window seat in the café, and waves as I approach.

'I'll get you a coffee,' she says, jumping up to the counter.

'Thanks.'

I unwrap my scarf from my neck and hang my coat on the back of my chair.

'So did you have a nice Christmas?' she asks, returning with my drink. 'And what's the story with your mum and dad being under the same roof?'

I tell her all about what happened with Rose and how Dad said things hadn't been right for a while between them.

'Your poor dad. He has his big op coming up soon, doesn't he? Will he be staying with you for a while then?' She pops a marshmallow from the top of her hot chocolate into her mouth.

'He will. You know how it is, there is a room for Mum and Dad whenever they want to stay. I still see it as their house really, despite them pursuing their own lives.'

'That's such a lovely arrangement, isn't it? Well, maybe it wouldn't be for everyone, but I know how close you all are.'

'Anyway, I have something to tell you.'

We both say this at virtually the same time, and burst out laughing.

'Go on, you first,' says Gemma.

'Okay.' I take a deep breath. 'Well, you know Kian, aka hot shop guy?'

'Yes.'

'He has asked me out.'

'Has he?' Gemma stirs the cream on the top of her drink.

'That wasn't quite the reaction I expected,' I tell her, wondering why she isn't excited for me, as she normally would be.

'What, gosh no, I'm really pleased for you.' She smiles then, but it feels like she is holding something back. 'And lucky you, he really is a cutie. I told you he fancied you, didn't I?' she says, sounding like her usual bubbly self but I'm not quite convinced.

'So, what's your news?' I turn the conversation to her, wondering why her reception to the news of my date with Kian was so lukewarm. I will try and prise it from her once she has told me her news.

'I'm thinking of leaving,' she says as she takes a sip of her drink.

'Leaving. What, you mean Bentham's?' I ask in surprise. Gemma has loved working there for as long as I can remember. She has always been in retail, and when she first joined the staff, she told me it was pretty much the best establishment she could hope to be employed by.

'No, not just Bentham's. Here, as in Fellview.' She looks up at me.

'Leaving?' My hot coffee suddenly feels cold in my mouth, 'But what's brought this on? And where would you go?' I can think of a dozen questions I want to ask.

'I suppose it was over Christmas, spending time with my extended family,' she explains. 'One of my older cousins brought his friend along who would have been on his own over Christmas. Anyway, long story short, we hit it off.'

'And you are thinking of moving to Wales?' I ask, hoping it's North Wales, which isn't too bad a journey, but it turns out it's mid-Wales, a three-hour drive away.

'It could be worse,' Gemma says. 'South Wales is more like five hours.'

'It is a long way,' I say quietly. 'Although if it's what you really want, I support you. I don't suppose you can be like Gavin and Stacey, can you? Commuting all that distance.' I manage a smile.

'Oh, it's not about Brad, that's his name, I barely know him. I am thinking about it though,' she says. 'I guess us all being together made me realise how much I miss my family, especially my young nephews, even though they do wear me out.' She laughs. 'My aunt said they have regular get-togethers, and I don't know, I think I would like to be part of a big family. I hadn't realised how much I missed that. Mum is seriously considering moving back to Wales, too.'

Gemma moved up here as a teenager when her dad took a job in the area. She'd protested and demanded to stay with her aunt in Wales at the time, before settling here and eventually being happy. Until now it seems. Her dad has passed away since, so I guess it makes sense for her mum, who lives a few miles away, to also want to be closer to her sister and extended family.

'I can understand that,' I tell her, even though my heart breaks at the thought of my best friend not being around anymore.

'Anyway. As I said, I'm just thinking about it. I might be over it tomorrow. I'm always the same after a big family get-together.' She laughs. 'It will probably soon be business as usual. Talking of which, I should probably get going.' She glances at her watch.

Gemma is on shift today, for the Boxing Day sales, starting work at twelve, finishing at eight, whilst I don't return until tomorrow. It's worked out well really, as I can look after Mum for an extra day, although I didn't quite expect Dad to be around too.

'We'll chat more later. Still on for drinks when I finish work?' she says, picking her bag up from the floor and looping it over her shoulder.

'Yeah, sure. See you tonight.' I smile.

The door opens and the family I saw earlier enter, the young boy placing his scooter in a corner near a coat stand. They find a nearby table, all of them red cheeked and smiling and I can't help but smile myself. It's a lovely place to raise a family, with the river walks and fells to climb, not to mention enjoying long walks and picnics in the summer months.

I order myself another drink, then mull over what Gemma has

just told me. I can imagine her thriving amongst a huge family, and think of how different we are. Maybe I ought to take up more invitations, from some of the work gang, and explore more opportunities. Just before Christmas, they went on a canoeing day in Windermere and even though I was tempted to join them, I thought of all the things I needed to do that weekend, and declined in the end. Audrey is also a new friend I could spend more time with if I chose to. I love Gemma like a sister, but she must do what it takes to make her happy, I realise that. Life has to change if we are to grow.

Sipping my coffee and staring at the square outside, I also wonder why Gemma was less than thrilled when I told her that Kian had asked me out. But maybe I will ask her more about that later.

I am just finishing my second drink, glancing out of the window, when I notice Rose walking past with a lady around her own age. I tap on the window and she gives a little wave, so I head outside and say hello. She briefly introduces her sister, who smiles before walking inside a shop.

'How are you, Rose?' I ask.

'I'm fine,' she says a little stiffly. 'You?'

'Yes, fine. Sorry to hear about you and Dad.' Despite their differences they did spend several years together. Before he met Rose, he frequented the local pub a lot, meeting friends, and probably drank too much beer.

'Thanks. If I'm honest, though, I don't think we were making each other happy just lately,' she says, echoing Dad's sentiments. 'I don't really think we had that much in common, to be honest,' she admits. 'How is your dad?'

I think of Dad's love of being outdoors, whether it be mowing someone's lawn or spending hours in the garden or greenhouse. Even as a youngster, he often took me on long country walks, telling me about the various forest plants and listening out for birdsong. Mum came along on those walks too, seemingly enjoying them just as much as Dad, and I wonder when things started to go wrong between them.

'He's okay. I think he will feel relieved when his operation is over though. He's staying with me at the moment.'

'That's nice for him. I'm staying with my sister over Christmas, which has been lovely actually as she is on her own too.' She tells me.

At least neither of them have been alone over Christmas.

'Anyway, I must go.' She points to the shop her sister has just walked into.

'Of course, yes. Look after yourself, Rose. Oh, by the way, I do have a gift for you,' I tell her. 'Maybe next time you pop in Bentham's I could give it to you.'

'That's very kind of you.' She smiles. 'I hope your dad's operation goes well.'

'Thanks. Bye, Rose.'

I take a quick browse of the village shops, though some of the shops and cafés are closed, except for the Blue Teapot. Alf's general store is open, and, of course, Bentham's for the Boxing Day sales.

I pass a children's clothing store, with a banner across the window announcing a sale. There are balloons in shades of pink and mauve in the window alongside the display of clothes and I think of Bella's party at the community centre. I also think of the trouble Kian went to in order to make his daughter's birthday special at this time of year, and how he was sure we could host a joint party without any problems.

It turns out he was right all along. Everyone had a wonderful day, well, apart from Mum, who ended up in hospital. I picture him in the kitchen getting stuck into the preparations whilst he calmly awaited the arrival of the party food. I also find myself picturing his handsome looks, his charming accent and just about everything else about him. Annoyingly, I can't seem to get him out of my head.

I push harder with my steps on the way home, walking quickly and breathing deeply. I do enjoy walking and remind myself that I ought to try and get more steps in every day. I used to enjoy walking a lot and joining the dance class every Tuesday at the community centre, but when it changed from Zumba to aerobics, I kind of stopped going. Maybe I ought to give it another go. These days my time seems to be taken up with work and meeting Mum or Gemma for lunch or, of course, assisting with the local pensioners, which I enjoy and always find time for, but I need to stop making excuses and find new pursuits to shake myself out of my usual routine, especially in the light of what Gemma has just told me.

Sometimes life gives us a little reminder to think about our own self-care from time to time, without the need to rely too heavily on others. It's something I will take on board seriously in the new year.

THIRTY-TWO

'You off out tonight then?'

It's almost seven thirty when I walk into the lounge.

'Yes, I'm meeting Gemma when she finishes work. We are going out for a drink.'

'I'll give you a lift into town,' offers Dad. 'Don't be getting a taxi.'

'Thanks, Dad, I'll get one home though.' I smile.

'Don't be doing that, it will be busy on Boxing night. I'll come and collect you. Unless you're thinking of going clubbing, that is, I won't be able to stay awake until the early hours of the morning, but I'm a night owl as you know.'

Dad has always enjoyed staying up late watching movies and enjoying a little bit of a lie in.

'Thanks, Dad. It won't be too late though, think my clubbing days are over.' I laugh.

'Oh, have you heard yourself?' Mum laughs. 'Too old for nightclubs at your age? Although, I'd stay away from the Blue Angel, I've noticed some right dodgy-looking characters going in there when we've been on our protests,' she says, referring to her protests outside the Co-op which is close by.

'I know, that's why I don't bother,' I say.

There are two nightclubs in Fellview, one frequented by teenagers barely out of school, the other by the so-called 'dodgy characters' Mum mentioned.

'You look nice by the way. Red is definitely your colour,' she says, remarking on my red woollen dress.

'Thank you.'

I think of Kian saying the same thing about red being my colour. The thought of him crossing the road with the other woman pops into my head then, and I wonder who she was? I'm also aware that he still hasn't called me to arrange a date. I'm not going to let that ruin my evening out with Gemma though.

I nip upstairs to grab a handbag, when my phone rings.

'Kian, hi.'

'Lauren, how are you doing?'

'I'm good thanks. How are you?' I'm thrilled by the sound of his voice.

'I'm well, really good. So what are you up to tonight?' he asks.

Surely he isn't going to ask me out at this short notice?

'I'm off out into town. I'm meeting Gemma for a drink at the Grapes,' I tell him.

'Nice. I imagine it will be pretty full in there, being Boxing night,' he says.

'I guess so. I think there is a live band, who are pretty good by all accounts.'

'That sounds good.'

There is a pause for a second, and I wonder what he is going to say next. Maybe he would like to join us?

'Come along if you like,' I say. 'Or maybe we should make arrangements for that date you mentioned,' I say, taking the bull by the horns.

'I most certainly would. I was about to ask you when you

are free,' he says. 'I was wondering, do you like the cinema?' he asks.

'The cinema? Yes, I do.'

'In that case, do you fancy dinner one evening this week? Whenever suits you. We could eat at a restaurant near Keswick, then watch a movie.'

'Tomorrow suits, if you are free. And that sounds lovely, I haven't been to Keswick in ages.'

The last time I went there was with Mum to watch a doomed love story and we both cried.

'It's a date then. The film has had great reviews,' he tells me. 'It's about a refugee chocolatier who makes a new life in Britain. I'm told it's very uplifting.'

'That sounds like something I would enjoy. I look forward to it.'

'Me too,' says Kian. 'Anyway, enjoy your evening with Gemma. I'll text you to tell you what time I will pick you up tomorrow.'

'Okay. Night, Kian.'

I skip downstairs with a huge grin on my face.

'Are you ready then?' asks Dad, picking up his car keys from the counter.

'Ready.' I beam, looking forward to spending time with Gemma, and to telling her all about my forthcoming date.

The Grapes is already busy, but I manage to find a table in the corner, and order a bottle of white wine for us to share, while I await the arrival of Gemma.

'You smell nice,' I comment as she arrives five minutes later and plonks her bag down on an empty chair.

'I helped myself to a spray of that new Dior fragrance, a sample obviously.' She smiles. 'And look!'

She proudly shows me the handbag she has had her eye on for ages.

'You got it.! Cheers to that,' I say, pouring us both a drink.

'I did. It actually got discounted an hour after I started work, so I nabbed it,' she tells me triumphantly.

She unzips it and shows me the interior of the gorgeous butter-soft brown leather bag. 'It's got loads of handy compartments,' she says excitedly. 'It was marked down thirty per cent and, even better, I used a gift card I got for Christmas to pay another chunk of it. It ended up only costing me twenty-five pounds.'

We chat about our respective days, and Gemma tells me it's been hectic at Bentham's and that I was lucky to have had the day off.

'I so need this,' she says, taking a long gulp of her wine. We chat away, and half an hour later there is a tap of a microphone as the pub manager announces the arrival of the band who are going to play some live music. The pub slowly begins to fill, and as the sound of music fills the bar, it becomes more difficult to continue our conversation.

A bloke smiles at Gemma across the bar, and she returns his smile before telling me he is fit.

'And what about Brad?' I raise an eyebrow. 'Have you forgotten about him already?'

'Brad who?' She laughs. 'I'm only joking, really, but it's nice to be noticed occasionally. Something you never need to worry about, all eyes are on you whenever you enter a room.'

'I'm sure that's not true,' I say, even though if I am entirely honest I did notice a few men glancing in my direction as I walked in the pub, but maybe that was because I was alone.

We finally manage to have a chat whilst the band take a break from performing. The band had played a rousing set, covers from rock bands mainly, but one or two slower songs that really showcased the lead singer's great voice.

'You don't think guys notice you? Well just look at the lead singer checking you out.' She nods towards the small stage at the end of the room.

I glance over at the long-haired singer, who raises his pint and winks at me.

'Well, it's very flattering but I'm not interested.'

'Why not? He looks as sexy as hell to me,' says Gemma.

'Possibly, but he's not really my type. Besides, I am going on a date with Kian. We're going to the cinema.' I feel a tinge of excitement as I tell her this. Once more, there is a bit of a lukewarm response from Gemma at my news.

'Oh right,' she says, taking a sip of her drink.

'You don't think it's good idea?' I say, now wondering if there really is something she is keeping from me.

'I never said that.'

'You didn't have to. The look on your face said it all. Gemma, is there something you are not telling me?' I almost demand.

Just then, the band fires up once more, and an ear-splitting rendition of a Freddie Mercury song reverberates around the bar.

Gemma mouths something, but I can't really make out what she is saying.

I'm puzzled by Gemma's response. I've never known her to be anything but happy for me when I've had a new boyfriend. And she is always making me aware when a man glances in my direction.

I'm mulling this over, ready to resume our chat, when the guy who had been looking at Gemma across the bar walks over and asks her if she would like to dance. A few people have already jumped up and are dancing away on the small dance floor. She agrees, and is soon up there waving her arms in the air and really going for it with the tall, fair-haired guy and I wonder when I will have the chance to talk to her properly about Kian.

I don't have to wait long though, as Gemma returns to the table after a couple of dances, and the band finish their set to rapturous applause.

'Mike has gone to buy us both a drink,' she says, looking over at the guy, who is waiting at the busy bar to be served.

'Good, because I need to ask you something and I want you to be honest with me. Why don't you seem happy about me going out with Kian?'

'Oh, Lauren, it's not that I'm not happy for you, it's just... well...'

'Well what?'

She pauses for a moment before answering.

'I served him the other day with a gift. For a woman,' she tells me.

'And what's wrong with that? It's Christmas time, it could have been for anyone,' I reason.

'Which, of course, is exactly what I thought, but then I saw him with Bella and another woman. She was tall with blonde hair,' she tells me in a quiet voice. 'The three of them were coming out of that American diner across town.'

'It might be a relative,' I say casually, although I swallow down a feeling of disappointment. Kian never mentioned another woman, although there is no denying that I also saw him with a tall blonde woman. Perhaps she is Bella's aunt or something, but he never mentioned her on the phone. Then again, why would he?

'I know that, but I guess I am just looking out for you, like you do with me. But you're right, I'm sure she is probably just a friend or a family member. I'm sorry.' Gemma reaches over and covers my hand with hers. 'Maybe I'm a bit mistrusting of blokes after that last one who turned out to be still married.' She sighs.

'Well I can understand that. Yet here you are accepting

drinks from strangers.' I smile as I gesture to the guy who is making his way towards our table with some drinks.

'I'm just letting my hair down, it's Boxing night,' she says. 'Besides, I vaguely recognise him from around town, he lives locally.'

'Well just be careful,' I advise her.

Mike, having managed to push his way through the crowd, places a pint and two glasses of wine down onto the table, even though there is still wine in the bottle.

We chat for a while and it turns out Mike is a really nice bloke who works locally in a garage. His friend was supposed to join him this evening, but has ended up being on call at a local fire station.

Having finished my drink, I explain I am in work tomorrow morning, so politely decline the wine Mike bought.

'You two stay on and enjoy yourself,' I tell Gemma, even though she has work tomorrow too.

'I will, if you fancy keeping me company?' She turns to Mike, who is more than happy to do so. 'If you don't mind me not sharing a taxi home with you, Lauren?'

'Of course I don't. Knock yourself out.' I smile.

It's just before eleven, so I decide to call Dad, who I know will still be awake as he's always been a night owl who likes to watch films until well after midnight.

'Let us at least wait with you outside then,' says Gemma, following me into the car park with Mike in tow.

When Dad arrives, Gemma wishes him a merry Christmas, before darting back inside with Mike when she hears the sound of a dance tune being played.

Having spoken to Gemma, I realise she was just showing concern as Kian bought a woman's gift and then she saw him with someone around town, as I did too, so I can't really blame her for putting two and two together I suppose.

Putting it out of my mind, I decide there must be a simple explanation for the mystery woman we both spotted him with. He would hardly be walking around town with her otherwise, knowing he could bump into me at any time, surely? All the same, I can't help wondering if I am doing the right thing in going out with him. I certainly don't want to go get my heart broken again.

'Have you had a good night, love?' asks Dad as we drive along. The streets are quiet for a Boxing night, although maybe most people are still indoors partying somewhere.

I feel a bit like a teenager being driven home by her dad. I'm half expecting him to ask if I met any nice boys at the disco.

'It was nice thanks, and the live band were really good.'

Really good, in fact. It's a pity I didn't find the lead singer attractive, but maybe that's because I have someone else on my mind.

As we drive past the fish and chip shop Dad glances at me hopefully.

'A fish supper is off the menu for you at the moment, I'm afraid,' I tell a disappointed Dad. 'Especially at this time of night,' I say, even though my own stomach is giving a little rumble.

When I'm home and getting ready for bed, I recall Gemma's lack of enthusiasm for my forthcoming date and fleetingly wonder if I am doing the right thing? What if he is seeing someone else, not being the type to date someone exclusively? But then, would he really introduce his daughter to someone he wasn't interested in? Maybe I am just overthinking everything as it's my first step into the dating world in a long time. I dearly hope it won't be the last.

THIRTY-THREE

'So how was your evening?' I ask Gemma after I have served a customer with a discounted jacket in the sale. There are some real bargains on offer, but I rein myself in as I have a wardrobe full of clothes, some I have only worn once.

'Really good.' She has a kind of dreamy faraway look in her eyes. 'Mike is lovely, and he makes me laugh.'

'I'm glad you enjoyed your night. Will you be seeing him again?' I ask and she shrugs.

'Gosh I hope so, oh, I don't know.' She sighs. 'I really liked my cousin's friend, didn't I? I mean I was considering moving to Wales.'

'But now?'

'Then Mike comes along and kind of makes me realise there might be some nice men around here,' she says, tidying a jewellery stand, someone having carelessly flung a necklace over the top of it.

'But surely you would need more reasons to move back to Wales than a bloke you fancied?'

Out of the corner of my eye, I see two women arguing over something, so head over to investigate. They both have their hands on a dress, claiming they saw it first and refusing to budge.

'I definitely picked it up first,' says the slightly aggressive brunette with tattooed eyebrows.

'You never did,' says the older woman calmly. 'I definitely picked it up before you. I only placed it back for literally a second to retrieve my purse from my bag.'

'But you put it back on the rail,' the brunette reasons.

'I placed it over the rail, it was obvious I wanted it. You just snatched it up,' says the woman, losing a little of her calm.

'I don't see how it would even fit you,' says tattooed-browed brunette, flicking her eyes over the woman's body. She has a point though. The lady is definitely not a size ten.

'It's for my daughter, if you must know!' says the woman indignantly.

'Well, it was on the rail, so still for sale in my book,' says the brunette defiantly.

Both the women still have hold of the dress and I hope they don't start a tug of war. I think it's going to take all my powers of diplomacy to sort this one out, as I know we have no more of that particular dress in stock.

'I can see how tricky this is.' I smile charmingly before rifling through the rail.

'But honestly?' I turn to the brunette. 'I really think that this is more your colour.'

I show her a similar dress, red in colour rather than the green they are arguing over.

'You have similar colouring to me, and I suit red,' I explain, using all my powers of persuasion.

She eyes the pretty dress that has a further five per cent discount than the green one they are fighting over.

'Hmm. I never noticed that,' she says, taking it from me and placing it against her body, moving this way and that in front of a nearby mirror. 'And, yes, people do tell me that I suit red.' She considers it for a moment. 'Fine, I'll try it on.'

She lets go of the other dress, before giving the older woman a filthy look and flouncing towards the changing rooms.

The woman hurriedly pays for the purchase before the brunette returns.

'And that is why you are the best member of staff here,' says Gemma, having watched the situation unfold. 'I would never have had the patience to deal with anything like that.' She shakes her head.

Thankfully, the brunette returns with the dress smiling, saying it fitted like a glove and the colour was perfect.

'Anyway, where were we?' I say, drama over and both women having left the store.

'Oh, you were saying, surely I wouldn't consider moving to Wales for a guy.'

'I never said that exactly.' I pause for a minute to serve a customer with some nail polish.

'No, but maybe that was half of the reason, pathetic right?' Gemma sighs. 'Am I really that desperate for a partner?'

'Not at all,' I say gently. 'And I do recall you saying that you missed all the camaraderie with the family.'

'I guess so, but realistically how often would those type of get-togethers be likely to take place? Probably little more than on special occasions. Everyone has jobs and busy lives. Perhaps I got carried away with the festive atmosphere,' she admits. 'I'm always the same when we all get together.'

'Well only you can make that decision, just make sure it's for the right reasons,' I advise.

'I will. Good job I have you as the voice of reason.'

Gemma is friends with a couple of the other staff here and is always up for a night out with them, even though I sometimes decline if I have other plans. Maybe her life would feel complete if she had a significant other, whereas I have never felt like I need a man to make my life complete. Until Kian came along, that is. I enjoy my work and my downtime with family and friends, although the possibility of Gemma moving away has definitely made me think about taking up a regular hobby.

I still get goosebumps when I relive the moment Kian's lips briefly met my cheek, and my stomach flips over when I think of our date tonight. I am currently stressing over what to wear and can't wait to get home and rifle through my wardrobe. The cinema is kind of a casual date although we are dining too, but I can't really justify buying anything new, although I have noticed a gorgeous grey silk blouse that has been hugely discounted. The last one just happens to be in my size too.

I don't talk too much of my date tonight and Gemma doesn't really ask about it as I think she still has her reservations about Kian. I'm not exactly sure why she has assumed he can't be trusted, just because of a purchase. But then, Gemma does tend to jump to conclusions at times. One thing is for sure though. I will be sure to tell Kian that Gemma mentioned serving him the other day, then maybe the truth will come out. At least I hope so.

THIRTY-FOUR

As the day rolls on, I feel nervous and excited about this evening. Gemma and I had sat in the staffroom earlier and I hadn't managed to eat a thing, Gemma asked me if I was feeling okay and I'd told her I was fine, just not hungry. She never really said much about my date with Kian, but then she has spent half of the afternoon trying to suppress yawns, so she clearly had a really late night last night.

The afternoon ticks over, with me trying to quell the nerves in my stomach, and soon enough it's time for me to finish my shift and I grab my coat and bag ready to head off for home.

'I hope your date goes well,' says Gemma. 'And I'm sorry I haven't said much about it, but you're my best friend and I can't bear the thought of you being hurt, you are so good to everyone else, you deserve nothing but the best.'

She throws her arms around me and squeezes me.

'Oh, Gem, I know. And thanks. I promise to get to the bottom of the mystery woman, don't worry, and I am touched by your concern, really.'

Back home, I find Dad knocking nails into a wall, repairing a shelf in the kitchen that was ever so slightly wonky.

'Dad, what are you doing? You are supposed to be taking things easy,' I tell him as I shrug off my coat.

'I know, but that shelf was annoying me. Whoever put that up mustn't have owned a spirit level,' he says, with a shake of the head.

Dad has the same eye for detail as me, and I had also noticed the ever so slightly off-kilter shelf that my previous boyfriend had erected, his one contribution to any DIY in the house. I didn't want to comment on it at the time, in the hope it might have encouraged him to do a bit more but that never happened. I must have become accustomed to the shelf being like that over time, although maybe my cookery books lining it had obscured the imperfection slightly.

Dad straightening the shelf has somehow removed any final reminder of my ex, which seems fitting as I am out on a date for the first time in ages.

'Thanks, but take it easy now. You have your operation in a few days,' I remind him.

'I'm fine, love, just a bit bored,' he confesses. 'And there was no heavy lifting involved,' he assures me. 'And your mother won't let me lift a finger, even though she's only just about on her feet herself.' He nods towards the kitchen. 'And no one wants their gardens doing with this ground frost.'

'I'll tell you what you can do then,' says Mum, emerging from the kitchen, a tea towel thrown over her shoulder. 'You could pop down to the allotments and get a couple of parsnips, if you have any left. I've found a lovely recipe for parsnip and apple soup.'

'I'm on my way,' says Dad, looking pleased. 'There are plenty left as I always grow far too many.'

'And don't be doing any work down there,' she shouts after him as he collects his coat from a hanger in the hall.

'Your father never did like sitting around,' says Mum, pouring me a cup of tea a few minutes later.

'That's true. Talking of which, are *you* not doing too much?' I ask, although Mum seems to be healing remarkably well.

'I'm absolutely fine. I had no broken bones remember, just bruising which is fading fast. Look.'

She pulls her jeans down slightly and reveals the large bruise that is already beginning to turn a pale yellow.

'I'm pleased you healed so quickly, Mum. I hope I have your genes when I get older.'

'Just look after yourself, that's the trick. Although good genes do help, of course.' She winks.

'Right, I must go and get ready,' I tell Mum as another fluttering of nerves take hold. 'Will you give me your honest opinion on my outfit?' I ask.

'You know I will.'

I shower and change, finally having settled on a pair of wide-legged black trousers, paired with my new purchase, the silver-grey blouse. I decide to gel and smooth my hair back into a ponytail and a slash of red lipstick completes the look. When I make my way downstairs, Dad has just returned, smelling of fresh air and earth.

'Just look at you.' Dad gives a low whistle. 'This Kian is a lucky bloke.'

'Thanks, Dad.' I am happy to have his approval, although Mum will give me an honest appraisal.

'Oh yes,' she agrees. 'You look really beautiful, classy but not overdone.'

'Thanks, Mum, that's exactly the look I was aiming for.'

'Although...' She cocks her head to one side and studies me for a moment. 'Maybe you could do with a necklace. What about that silver one?'

I nip upstairs and put on the silver necklace. Mum was right. I was worried the outfit looked a little businesslike, but the necklace has transformed it into evening wear. I feel fully dressed for a date now.

I take a glance at my watch, ten minutes before Kian is due to collect me. He had texted earlier, checking if I was still okay for this evening, and I'd told him yes and that I was looking forward to it. I fleetingly wonder who will be looking after Bella tonight, and whether it might be the female relative I saw him with. Assuming that's what she was. I lightly spray some perfume onto my wrists before I head downstairs.

I consider having a quick glass of wine before Kian arrives, but if I rush it my face will flush, so decide against it.

'You look perfect now,' says Mum kindly. 'I hope you have a lovely evening, you really deserve it.'

Before I know it, Kian has pulled up outside the house to collect me. He says hi to Mum, and I quickly introduce him to Dad before we leave.

'Wow,' he says, when I am seated in the car. 'You look amazing.'

I take in his appearance, his dark jeans and a crisp light-blue shirt beneath a charcoal woollen coat. It seems he has left his battered leather jacket at home. He smells good too.

'So do you.' I smile, fastening my seat belt and looking forward to spending the evening with him.

It's around a half hour drive to the venue and we chat easily as we drive along, asking each other about how our day has been. I tell him about the dress fiasco. He tells me he had seen a client who was terrified of washing-up liquid.

'It was a strange one indeed,' he confesses. 'But I think I managed to get her to relax and face the washing-up, for today at least.' He smiles. 'She tells me her kids think it's just an excuse to get them to do the dishes.' He laughs that easy laugh. 'Please don't repeat that in public,' he adds. 'Confidentiality and all that. Although I never actually mentioned their name, but you just never know who is listening.'

'Oh definitely, and I don't suppose many people have that particular phobia,' I remark. 'And don't worry, I have learned discretion from working in a shop,' I tell him, before immediately thinking about the gift he purchased. I don't want to mention it though, at least not right now.

'Would you like some music on?' Kian asks.

'Sure, that would be nice.'

He finds Classic FM and the sound of something familiar fills the car.

'Was this on a TV advert or something?' I ask.

'That's right, it was on an airline ad, I think. George Gershwin's "Rhapsody in Blue".'

'Maybe that's where I have heard it. Are you into classical music then?' I ask.

'Not particularly. I just thought it might set a nice mood.' He smiles.

'You could try Smooth Radio,' I suggest.

'So you like smooth guys, huh?' He turns to me.

'Not smooth guys, no, just the radio station. They play nice ballads.'

'I know they do, I am playing with you. Smooth Radio it is then,' he says, finding the station, where Boyz II Men are belting out one of their biggest hits that says something about coming to the end of a road.

'Blimey, I hope not. We're only just getting started, both metaphorically and literally.' He laughs.

So he thinks this is just the beginning of something? I find myself feeling excited by that thought.

We drive down a forest road, a silvery moon shining through the branches of the trees. It makes me think of the evening of the moon bathing where I first met Audrey, and I tell Kian this.

'She seems like a nice girl?'

'She is. And she is super talented at making things,' I say, recalling the centrepiece for the dinner and winning first prize at the gingerbread evening.

'Well, she is lucky to have met you, and so am I,' he says.

'It wasn't maybe under the best circumstances.' I pull a face.

'Do you mean dousing me in Prosecco, or stealing my hall space?' he teases.

'Probably the former, and I didn't steal your space, you stole mine,' I stubbornly tell him. 'Although it all worked out in the end.'

'Which I told you it would,' says Kian. 'Even though on paper you might think that would never have worked out. I was worried it would be a complete disaster.'

'You were?'

'Of course. I didn't tell you that though, no sense in us both flapping, was there?' He grins. 'Anyway, the old people seemed to love having the children around, didn't they?'

I think of Elsie and how the little boy handed her the plastic elephant.

'They really did. And the kids enjoyed it too.'

'Oh, they did,' agrees Kian. 'Bella giggles every time she tells me about the old people playing musical statues.'

'Your face when you walked in.' I can't help but laugh as I recall the moment Kian returned to the community centre to see old people in various stages of stillness, and his comment about 'Thriller'.

'And just seeing how much the pensioners enjoyed mingling with the children gave me an idea,' I tell Kian.

'Oh right, what are you thinking?' he asks as we drive, the radio playing another cheesy ballad.

'Well, I was thinking they could be invited into the local school hall, say once a month and the children could do some singing. Maybe even play some music. I know the local primary school was always quite encouraging about music sessions.'

'That sounds like a lovely idea.' Kian smiles. 'And maybe

the other volunteers could help out with lifts, given plenty of notice. I would be happy to do so too,' he offers.

'You would? Oh, that's wonderful. I've asked the old head-teacher to run it by the new one, who she is friends with.'

'Do you always think about other people?' Kian asks as we drive along.

'I just see it as giving something back,' I tell him. 'I mean, I have everything I want. A lovely home, a job I enjoy and so on. I consider myself quite fortunate compared to many.'

'Those around you are the fortunate ones, I'd say,' he says, casting a glance at me.

I blush and look out of the window as Kian turns into the restaurant's car park.

Kian walks around to the passenger door and opens it for me. He takes my hand as I step out, and I feel as though I am in an old Hollywood movie.

'Thank you.'

I wrap my fashionable black shawl around me as we make our way inside.

Kian has chosen a French restaurant with dark wooden tables and red lamps at the centre. The walls are adorned with an assortment of mirrors and black-and-white photographs, and the people seated at tables are sipping drinks from vintage glasses. The whole place is glamorous, yet unstuffy. Kian has booked a table near a window that a friendly waiter leads us to.

'This place looks amazing,' I comment as I sit down. 'You chose well.'

'Thank you. To tell you the truth I haven't been here before, it's pretty new, I believe, but the online reviews were great. I hope you like French food.'

'Oh, I do, omitting the frogs' legs, that is.'

I'd been to a French restaurant with Gemma, and although a high-street chain, the food was actually very good. Kian orders us each a glass of red wine and some water, whilst I peruse the menu.

'You suit being in a place like this,' says Kian, closing his menu. 'You look beautiful this evening.'

'Thank you.' I can feel the colour creep up my cheeks, thankful for the muted lighting.

'So how is Bella?' I ask, after I have ordered.

'Really well. She's having a sleepover at my parents' tonight.' He holds my gaze as he lifts his wine glass, and my stomach gives a little jolt, wondering if he will invite me inside his place at the end of the evening? And what will I say if he does?

'Do you have any other family living nearby?' I ask as I take a sip of my wine.

'No one other than my parents, who are a ten-minute drive away.'

I wonder then about the willowy blonde who is obviously not a family member.

'They moved from Ireland to be closer to Bella,' he explains. 'They have two older grandchildren from my sister, who started young. Seventeen, to be exact. As you can imagine, the reaction from a Catholic Irish family wasn't the best,' he reveals. 'But my parents came around in the end. My two nephews are twenty-two and twenty respectively, and doing their own thing now,' he tells me. 'Mum was delighted when Bella was born. She always wanted a granddaughter and wanted to be a part of her life, so they moved to the Lakes.'

'I can understand that,' I say. 'And Bella is adorable.'

'She is. I think after my parents retired, they realised they could be more involved with Bella, which is working out well.'

I'm about to say I saw him in town on Christmas Day, yet something stops me. I don't want to ruin this perfect evening, so keep telling myself that surely he would not be sat here with me if there was anyone else on the scene.

Our order arrives then, and we dine on the most delicious food. It tastes a lot nicer than the chain I visited with Gemma, the chicken tarragon tasty and melt in the mouth. I can't resist a tarte Tatin to finish, and soon Kian is settling the bill and we are taking the short walk to the cinema.

'Are you cold?' asks Kian as I wrap my shawl tightly around me as we walk.

'Not really,' I tell him. 'Why? Would you have given me your coat if I said yes?'

'I'm not that much of a gentleman.' He laughs. 'It's cold out here.' He shivers.

'Charming.' I laugh.

The sky is clear this evening, a silvery moon casting its light on the pavement. Christmas lights adorn shops and houses as we pass through the town reminding me that it is still very much the holiday season. A couple pass us, their hands entwined and I wonder how it would feel to have Kian's hand in mine.

After a short walk, we enter the cinema and are greeted by a huge Christmas tree in the entrance. A queue of adults are waiting to pay so whilst Kian insists on buying the tickets, I grab us both a coffee from a kiosk.

Seated in the comfortable seats, I am soon immersed in the film, trying to dispel any uneasiness in the back of my mind about the mystery woman. Kian told me that he had no other family nearby, so maybe that's why I am curious as to who she is. Perhaps she is just a close friend, men are allowed to have friends, aren't they? She could be someone from the apartment who was just walking home from town and ran into them both, but then, why would she be holding Bella's hand?

If anything is going to distract me from my thoughts it is the beautiful film that has dual locations both in the British countryside and Syria. A chocolatier who ran a coffee shop in Damascus selling handmade truffles had been displaced by war many years ago, so opens a shop in a sleepy Cotswolds village. It had tones of the movie *Chocolat*, but with some heartbreaking flashbacks from his life in his homeland before the atrocities. Overall, it was a story of triumph over tragedy, and left me with a smile on my face at the determination of the human spirit.

'That was wonderful.' I sigh as we take the walk back across town to the car park. 'The film deserves those awards and to think it was based on a true story.'

'I know, the guy uprooted his family from their homeland and took a chance, and it all worked out. I'm glad you enjoyed it, I loved it too,' says Kian. 'I did check the reviews carefully, as I didn't want to take you to a flop of a movie.'

'I think the restaurant would have made up for it, it was wonderful. And surely a film featuring chocolate could never be that bad.' I laugh.

It is the nicest evening I have had in a long time, and I hope Kian will ask me out again. As we walk the town is still busy, music pulsing from a bar somewhere, people out enjoying the festive period.

'Would you like a drink?' He gestures to a quieter bar with a Christmas tree outside strung with white lights. 'A soft drink for me, but you might prefer something stronger?'

'Sure, why not, but I won't have an alcoholic drink if you aren't.'

'We could always have a nightcap at my place instead?' he suggests.

He stops and looks at me, before curling his hand around mine and even in the coldness of the night my body is flooded with warmth.

'I'd like that, thank you.'

We walk, almost wordlessly to the car and I feel as though I am floating on air, as any doubts I may have harboured have disappeared.

'I've had a lovely evening,' I say as Kian opens the car door for me to step inside. Not before he has pulled me into his arms for a gentle, yet thrilling kiss, in the quiet car park shrouded by trees.

'Wow that was unexpected,' I tell him, when we pull apart.

'Was it really?' he asks. 'I've been dying to kiss you all evening.'

'I'm glad you did,' I tell him as I slip into the passenger seat.

'This is me then,' says Kian, fifteen minutes later as he turns his key in the lock of the front door.

I step inside the apartment, which is almost how I imagined it in my mind's eye. White walls, decorated with stylish art and a huge sofa that dominates the room. Potted plants are dotted about, including an impressive-looking bonsai sitting on a black wooden unit. A huge stripy coloured rug covers a grey-coloured wooden floor.

'Nice place,' I comment as he invites me to sit down.

I feel suddenly nervous as I relive that kiss in the car park. How is Kian expecting the evening to pan out? How am I expecting it to?

'Drink?' he asks.

'A glass of red wine, if you have it?' I ask.

'Of course.'

He heads to the kitchen, a glimpse of which I can see from the sofa. It is fitted out with sleek navy cupboards and pale marble worktops.

He returns with a whisky for himself, and passes me a glass of wine.

'Thank you.'

Kian plays some music from speakers and I sit back and relax. He comes and sits next to me then and slips his arms around my shoulders. But it's no good. I must ask him about the woman I saw him with in town.

'I forgot to say, I saw you in town on Christmas Day as I was driving.' I sip my wine.

'You did? I never saw you. Why didn't you stop and say hi?' he asks, looking puzzled.

'Because you were with someone.' I can feel my heart beating wildly.

'Oh, right,' he says, his face adopting a more serious expression.

'Was it a friend?' I ask, twirling the stem of my wine glass.

'Not exactly, but I don't want you to get the wrong idea if I tell you,' he says, looking a little sheepish.

'Tell me what?'

'Who the woman was with me and Bella.'

THIRTY-FIVE

'Well now I am worried,' I tell him, placing my wine glass down on an occasional table. 'I take it there is something you are not telling me?' I say, my heart sinking.

'I might not have mentioned anything, as it wasn't relevant. But I won't lie to you either. The woman you saw me with was Bella's mother. My ex-wife.'

I recall the smiling faces of the three of them as they stepped onto the zebra crossing and feel all the joy of the evening evaporate. And didn't he say his ex was going on holiday with her boyfriend for Christmas, which was why he was having Bella to stay?

'But let me explain,' pleads Kian.

'Go ahead,' I say evenly.

'Sally, that's my ex-wife, ended up not going on holiday with her boyfriend after all. Their flights were cancelled until after Christmas, something about a baggage handler dispute at the airport they were heading to,' he explains. 'But they only discovered this when they got to the airport, which was actually in Birmingham. They have rescheduled to go tomorrow.'

'I see,' I say, absorbing the information quietly.

'So she called me and asked if I would mind her spending Christmas Day with Bella after all. She said it didn't feel right, not spending the day with Bella when she was still here in the country, and only an hour's drive away.'

I can understand that I suppose. Maybe she rang him on the day of the party, explaining his sudden change of mood.

'So she came here for Christmas Day?' I ask.

Once more, I recall him saying a family member was watching Bella when he nipped out for the batteries on Christmas morning. He never actually lied to me, he just failed to say who the family member was.

'And did her boyfriend come too?' I ask, although I think I already know the answer to that.

'No.' He takes a sip of his whisky. 'He spent the day with his parents.'

I try my hardest to be accepting of the situation and recall me and Mum saying it was a pity people couldn't put their differences aside for Christmas Day, but this feels different somehow. Bella is a little girl, and if there is any possibility that Christmas Day has stirred memories for Kian and his ex, I would not want to stand in the way of a reconciliation.

'I'm glad you both got to spend the day with your daughter.' I smile, even though I can't think straight. 'Bella deserves it.'

'I'm glad you understand. I could hardly say no when she asked to join us, could I? What with it being Christmas Day.'

'Of course you couldn't.' I smile reassuringly.

Glancing at my watch I see it is just before eleven. I think of calling Dad, but decide to call a taxi instead. I don't want any questions when I get home.

'You're leaving?' Kian looks visibly disappointed when I tell him I am going to call it a night. 'Have I done something wrong?' he asks.

'No, Kian, you haven't, although maybe you ought to have told me earlier that you were spending Christmas Day with your ex,' I tell him. 'And not because I am the jealous type, but rather the cautious type.'

I don't add, *who doesn't want to get my heart broken having already started to fall for you.*

'Perhaps I should have mentioned it,' he says, running his fingers through his hair. 'But, to be honest, I didn't really see the point in telling you. Sally came here purely to spend time with Bella and I didn't want to ruin things with you. We have been divorced for two years, she's hardly going to be staying over.'

'Sorry, I just assumed it when I saw you together and then Gemma said she saw the three of you in town.'

'We were shopping with Bella. Look let me explain, please.'

I have an alert on my phone announcing the arrival of my Uber so I stand ready to leave.

'Bella had some birthday money and asked if Mummy could come along when she spent it,' he says as he escorts me out. 'We went to that toy store on the retail park just outside town, then an American diner, all at Bella's request, I might add.'

I did wonder whether he might mention the diner that Gemma noticed him leaving.

'Bella stayed on here with me after Sally's flight was postponed. I'm usually so busy with work, I never have her for sleepovers,' he explains. 'And I miss her.'

'I can imagine.' I smile. 'And I really did have a lovely evening, so thank you for that, but I really think I ought to leave.' I say as brightly as I can, before I make my way outside.

'I'm sorry you're leaving.' Kian sighs. 'I had a wonderful evening too. I only want the best for Bella. Can we meet up again and talk this through?' he asks as I am about to climb into the cab.

'It's plain to see how much you love Bella.' I touch him gently on the arm. 'And don't worry, we will talk soon. Goodnight, Kian.'

. . .

As Kian closed his front door he thought, with hindsight, that he ought to have told Gemma who the gift was for when she had served him with the red scarf, but he wanted it to be a surprise for Lauren. He'd hoped to give it to her tonight, before things had ended so disastrously. And had he been foolish in not mentioning the fact that he had spent Christmas Day with his ex-wife? How would he have felt if it was the other way round and she had been spending Christmas Day with her ex? He was worried he had blown things, which was the last thing he wanted as he hadn't been so attracted to a woman for a long time. She caught his eye when he first walked into Bentham's with Bella, standing statuesque and pretty, with her dark hair and red lipstick, she stood out from the other staff.

He poured himself another drink and flicked on the television. The relaxing effects of the pleasant evening had almost deserted him. But perhaps that was his own fault, he thought to himself as he sipped his drink. Only time would tell if things would work out between him and Lauren.

THIRTY-SIX

'You're back early,' Dad comments when I walk through the door.

Mum has retired to bed, having always been an early to bed, early to rise type of person.

'It isn't that early. And I do have work tomorrow.' I smile at Dad as I hang up my coat.

'Of course you do,' says Dad as he mutes the sound on the television. 'So how was your date?' he asks.

'Great thanks, Dad. I had a lovely evening.'

I tell him a little about the French restaurant and the moving film at the cinema, thinking of what a perfect first date it was. Before I maybe started overthinking things.

'I'm glad you had a nice time, love, you deserve it. Will you be going out with Kian again?' asks Dad.

That is the six-million-dollar question.

'I hope so, although we haven't actually arranged anything yet. Anyway, I'll be off to bed then. Night, Dad, enjoy the rest of your film.'

'Night, love.'

As I leave the room, I hear the sound of gunshots as Dad resumes watching his action movie.

Getting ready for bed, I think about the lovely evening I spent with Kian and wonder if I was right to be so cautious. What he said made perfect sense about Sally wanting to spend time with their daughter on Christmas Day, but I can't seem to get the image of the three of them smiling in the road out of my head. They looked so happy together and I can't take the risk of being hurt, despite them being divorced. It isn't unknown for couples to rekindle things, given the time and the opportunity. Especially when there are young children involved. I wonder if Sally is on social media. Maybe I could message her and ask, woman to woman, if she harbours any hopes of her and Kian getting back together.

Sleep doesn't come easily, as I toss and turn and go over the events of the evening. I also think of that kiss too, gentle yet passionate, and allow myself to think that he enjoyed it as much as I did.

Maybe it's about time I do something I never normally do, and throw caution to the wind, and just go with the flow, even if that puts me at risk of being hurt down the line, but then what would life be like if we were too afraid to ever take risks?

I am finally nodding off, when I hear the ping of a text. It's from Kian.

I really enjoyed this evening, hope you did too. I'll call you tomorrow. Kian. X

Okay. And I enjoyed this evening too but I think we need to have a chat. I'm in work tomorrow, so maybe we can talk in the evening? Lauren.

Sure. Speak soon. Goodnight. X

I feel a little more settled then, and soon drift off to sleep, ready to see what tomorrow brings.

Bentham's is as busy as ever with the sales continuing as we count down the days to New Year's Eve. Sparkly party dresses are flying off the rails, along with men's shirts and discounted leather shoes. There are steady sales of luxury mince pies and fruit cake that have been discounted and displayed on a table, alongside shortbread and whisky marmalade.

We are so busy, I don't have to time to chat with Gemma about my date, although she did ask me how it went earlier. I assured her it was lovely, and that I would fill her in a bit more later when we have a break.

I just finish serving a lady with some cotton handkerchiefs for her husband – the type that come in a box and have an initial embroidered at the corner – when I see a familiar face standing in front of me.

'Mrs Evans, hi, how are you?' I greet the ex-headmistress of the local primary school, who attended the Christmas party at the community centre.

'Judy, please.' She smiles, although I always feel like addressing her formally.

'Of course, it's nice to see you again, Judy.' I smile.

'And you too. I know you are busy, but I thought you might like to know that I ran the idea of the children performing at an assembly to invite the elderly residents in by the current head-teacher.'

'Oh, you did?'

She stands aside for a second as I quickly serve a customer.

'Yes, and she thinks it's a wonderful idea. I told her that I saw first-hand how well the older people interacted with the children. I also realised how much I missed them.' She smiles.

'And apparently, some of the children are only too keen to show off their recorder skills.' She laughs.

'Really? They still teach recorder in schools?' I ask, thinking back to my primary school days, and how proud I was when I learned to play the theme tune to *Match of the Day*.

'Not many, I don't think, but the headteacher was determined it wouldn't be a forgotten skill, so she bought in some recorders and even teaches the children herself.'

'How great is that?' I smile as another customer approaches the counter.

'Anyway, I can see you are busy, so maybe you could call the school and speak to the head sometime. She is definitely on board with the idea of involving the children in a concert, or at least regular assemblies.'

'I will. Thank you so much, Judy, I know plenty of people who will really enjoy that.'

She was right in saying the pensioners mixed well with the children. Even Elsie thawed out in the end, saying what a marvellous party it had been when she left.

'Myself included. Bye then.' She lingers at a stand and feels some leather gloves before heading off out of the store.

During my lunch break I call the school, forgetting that they are still on their Christmas holidays, so pop a reminder on my phone for January when I will give the headteacher a call.

Gemma is sipping a green tea and trying to resist the Christmas boxes of chocolates and shortbread that people have brought in. It would appear most of the staff, including Gemma, are on a post-Christmas diet.

'Ugh this tastes awful, but apparently it helps with weight loss,' she says, pulling a face as she sips her drink. 'Anyway, you said you would fill me in on how your date went,' she says, her resolve already gone as she takes a fantail shortbread from a tin.

'It was really lovely. We went to a gorgeous French restaurant, then on to the cinema.'

'And did you invite him in for coffee?' She raises an eyebrow.

'No actually, he invited me to his place. Besides, Mum and Dad are staying with me at the moment remember.'

'Ooh tell me more,' she says, throwing half of her biscuit in the bin after feeling guilty.

'We had a drink and a chat. His place is lovely, just as I imagined it to be. Anyway, I was home and in bed by eleven thirty, what with being in work this morning.'

'And that's all you're going to tell me?' She looks visibly disappointed.

'There is not a lot else to say.' I sigh. 'Other than Kian is calling me this evening so that we can talk.'

'Just talk? Are you not going out again?' Gemma eyes me suspiciously.

'Maybe. Oh, Gemma, I really do like him, but I'm wondering if I ought to get involved with someone who is so friendly with his ex-wife.'

'Is he?' She frowns.

'Apparently so, although he tells me they are not friends exactly, and the only communication they ever have is about Bella.'

'Which is understandable, I guess.'

'And I totally get that. She was the mystery blonde we spotted him with in town,' I tell her as I sip my coffee. 'She spent Christmas Day with him and Bella.'

'So, that was his ex-wife?' she says. 'Maybe they are just friendly for the sake of Bella. It is Christmas time after all.'

I tell her all about the cancelled holiday flight, and how Sally is now sunning herself in the Caribbean with her boyfriend of over a year.

'I understand your caution,' she says eventually. 'But she sounds pretty loved up to me.'

'I know you're right. But then I also can't help thinking

about the present he bought for a woman. What was it, do you remember?'

'A beautiful silk scarf,' she tells me. 'And not cheap as I recall.'

'Right,' I say, draining the last of my coffee.

'I suppose it could have been for anyone, as you said.' Gemma shrugs. 'I kind of wish I hadn't mentioned it now.'

'No, you did the right thing. It's just that if it was for his wife, and they are still buying each other expensive gifts, it feels like there is unfinished business between the two of them.' I sigh.

'It does seem a bit odd to be buying an ex a costly gift,' she agrees. 'But then again, that scarf could have been for anyone. There is only one way to find out and that is to ask him,' says Gemma, gathering up our cups and placing them in a dishwasher.

Glancing at my watch, I see break time is almost over, so I nip to the ladies. I reapply my signature red lipstick before returning to work and mull over what Gemma has just said. Maybe I will just have to come right out and ask him who the gift was for? Without sounding like some sort of weirdo, that is.

Finishing work at four, I'm driving home when my phone rings. It's Kian. I answer on hands-free and tell him I will be home in ten minutes, so he agrees to call me back then.

I arrive home to the sight of Mum and Dad watching *Countdown* on the television and Mum boasting that she got the long word.

'Nine letters. It's the best I've done in the history of watching the show.' She beams.

'It was a fluke,' teases Dad. 'You told me you didn't even know if it was a word, you just put all the letters together and hoped for the best.' He laughs, and she shoves him on the arm.

'What was the word?' I ask as I shrug my coat off.

'Jumboizes. Which is a shipping term for enlarging a ship by adding another section to it,' she says knowledgably.

'You only know that because Susie Dent explained it.' Dad giggles.

Mum rolls her eyes, and offers me a cup of tea. She is healing remarkably well and is almost bustling about at her usual pace now. I've enjoyed having her here, and Dad too, but knowing Mum, she will be wanting to get back to her flat soon, a ground floor one with a pretty garden that she has worked hard on and enjoys spending as much time as possible out there, especially in the summer months.

I take my tea upstairs and wait for Kian to call. I'm just out of my uniform and about to take a shower when my phone rings.

'Kian, hi, how are you?' Despite my uncertainty about the future I am thrilled to hear his voice.

'I'm okay. I was calling you about that chat, but I thought we could do that in person? Are you free later?' he asks.

'I could be, I suppose.'

Some of the work gang are going for drinks this evening, including Gemma, but I can meet up with them later at the pub.

'Can I pick you up in say... an hour?' he asks. 'I'll drop Bella off at her grandparents' first, she's been wanting a sleepover there to show them her Christmas toys. We could come back here to my place, or go for a drink, whatever you prefer.'

'I'll come to your place, if that's okay,' I tell him, thinking it the best place to have a private conversation.

'Okay. I'm looking forward to seeing you, Lauren. See you shortly.'

I'm dressed and downstairs, nerves building at the thought of meeting Kian, when my parents say they have something to tell me. My heart sinks for a moment, my first thought being that Dad is more ill than I first thought.

'I'll be out of your hair tomorrow,' says Mum. 'I should be completely on my feet by then. I'm actually okay now, just a little stiff when I stand up,' she explains.

'But there's no rush, surely?'

I kind of thought they would both be here until at least New Year's Eve.

'I know that, love, but I'm missing my place. I don't like the apartment being unoccupied for too long,' she says. 'And I have a couple of indoor plants that will need watering by now.'

'Well, I can understand you wanting to get back home, as long as you feel okay to look after yourself.'

'I will be.' She smiles. 'But I will have someone watching out for me, so don't worry.' She takes a glance at Dad. 'Your father is coming to stay with me for a while.'

'What? Are you telling me you are getting back together?'

I am standing with my mouth open. I know they have been getting along well lately, but I assumed that was just because they were thrust into the same space together.

'We've talked about it, and we just thought, why not?' says Dad, smiling at Mum.

'Neither of us are getting any younger, and as I'm retired, I can look after your dad after his operation,' Mum tells me.

'But I wouldn't have minded you both staying here, you know that.'

I take in the news that my parents are going to spend their later years together, which fills me with joy, mixed with a touch of trepidation. They say you should never go back, but I guess love doesn't work that way, does it? I am filled with emotion at the thought of my parents spending the rest of their lives together. I do hope things work out, as I want nothing but the best for them both.

'Of course you would, Lauren, but you have your own life

and a full-time job. It would be too much for you. I'm sure we will be just fine, and we know where you are if we need you,' Mum reassures me.

The three of us are standing there then in a group hug and I feel a silent tear trickle down my cheek. I'd always worried about Mum being on her own as she gets older, if I'm honest. I had no idea things were bad between Dad and Rose, so assumed they would be together for the duration.

'I'm so happy for you both,' I tell them, when we finally stop hugging. 'I hope you can make each other happy again.'

'We'll do our best. And I actually think I might be developing a taste for all that veggie food,' says Dad. 'I'd forgotten what a good cook your mum is.'

I grab my coat, and head out with a huge grin on my face. Now it's time to go and find out if my own love life has any chance of progressing.

THIRTY-SEVEN

'Lauren, hi, come in.'

Kian is dressed in jogging pants and a tight grey T-shirt that shows off the physique of someone who works out regularly.

'Fancy a drink?' he offers.

'Maybe just a tea, thanks,' I tell him as I came over in the car, and I want to keep a clear head.

'Sure,' he says as he walks into the kitchen area of the large, open plan space.

I glance around the lounge, for any sign of a woman's touch, but can't find any evidence of that. There are no photographs of anyone other than Kian and Bella on a black-and-white canvas, hanging on a wall. No flowers, or scented candles, but then, I don't suppose there would be any evidence of an ex-wife if Kian was expecting me.

'I'm glad you came,' he says, returning to the lounge with a pot of tea in a clear glass teapot and two mugs.

'I wanted to see you,' I say. 'I meant it when I said I enjoyed our evening, but it left me feeling a little confused.'

'Which I completely understand,' he says gently, sitting next to me on the sofa. 'But I've told you, Sally is Bella's mum, nothing more. I'm sure she isn't giving me a second thought whilst she is sunning herself in Barbados, nor me her.'

'Are you certain?'

'Of course I'm certain,' says Kian, taking hold of my hand and looking me in the eyes. 'I've relived our date, I don't know how many times. It was perfect.'

I think back to the beautiful restaurant, the moving film, and the twinkling lights in the town as we walked. And then there was that unexpected kiss in the car park.

'I thought so too. But I have to be certain there are no lingering feelings towards Sally.'

'I promise you there aren't,' he says, sounding sincere. 'I'm not one to play games, that's for sure. Yes, Sally is Bella's mother, but we have our own lives now. We are civil to each other, but I don't love her anymore. We are divorced after all,' he reminds me softly.

'I know.'

'And if the plane had taken off on time, I would have barely seen her. It was just the circumstances of her wanting to see Bella on Christmas Day, that's all.'

'I had to be sure,' I tell him, believing that every word he is speaking is the truth. I have to believe that.

'Well now you know.' He edges closer to me on the sofa. 'Lauren, I had the most wonderful evening the other night, magical even. When I kissed you, it felt so right and I hoped you felt the same way too.'

'I did, Kian, really,' I tell him, my heart soaring. 'Although I was hoping you might have told me about the woman's gift you bought from Bentham's.'

'Gemma told you, of course!' He shakes his head. 'It's a shame really, as now it has kind of gone and ruined the surprise.' He stands up and disappears into his bedroom.

. . .

'For me?' I say, accepting the silver gift bag, the top covered with black tissue paper. 'You shouldn't have. I don't have anything for you, I'm afraid. I didn't think we would be doing gifts.'

'Not a problem. Maybe you can buy me a drink sometime.'

'I can definitely do that.'

I remove the tissue from the bag and pull out the most glorious red scarf, and slide my hands over the silky fabric. Looking closely I can see it is dotted with tiny silver hearts.

'Kian, it's absolutely beautiful. Thank you. So the gift was for me?' I say quietly.

'I always told you red was your colour. As soon as I saw it, I thought of you.' He smiles. 'What do you mean, so the gift was for you?' He looks puzzled.

'Oh, Kian, I'm afraid I may have jumped to the wrong conclusion.' I sigh, holding the scarf in my hands. 'Gemma told me that she served you with a gift for a woman, and well...'

'You put two and two together, and came up with five?'

'Something like that.'

'You have to believe me when I say that I am interested in you only. From the moment I walked into that shop, I haven't been able to stop thinking about you.'

'Really?'

'Really. I wanted to talk to you at the gingerbread evening, but I was with Bella, and you were with a table full of women, so...'

'And then I soaked you in Prosecco.'

'Yes, there was that.' He laughs. 'But you are here now.'

He takes the gift bag from my knee, and places it on the floor, before gently taking my hand in his.

'So I'm hoping you aren't going to dash off this evening?'

'Well, I don't have work in the morning,' I tell him. My heart beating so loudly I'm sure he must be able to hear it.

'Good to hear. Maybe I can open the wine I bought,' he says.

'Why not?'

I tap out a text to Mum, telling her I will be staying out tonight, which makes me feel like a teenager once more. She sends me a thumbs up sign, followed by a kiss and says she will see me in the morning.

Kian has taken the teapot away, and replaced it with two large glasses of Merlot.

'Everything okay?' he asks as I drop my phone into my bag.

'Fine.' I smile. 'Just telling Mum not to wait up, which is a bit weird at my age.'

'So you're staying over?' A slow smile spreads across his face.

'I mean I can't drive if I have a drink, and I might need to wait a long time for a taxi, so...'

Before I can finish the sentence, Kian takes me in his arms and kisses me deeply. And I think that maybe it's time to just go with the flow and see where this whole thing goes.

THIRTY-EIGHT

Mum and Dad have packed their things and are ready to leave when I arrive home. Kian and I had taken Bella for a hot chocolate in town, and we are taking Bella to the theatre tomorrow night to watch a pantomime.

'I'll miss you both,' I tell them as Dad loads their cases into his car.

'We will only be up the road, love.' Mum squeezes me tight.

'I know.'

'Besides, it will be nice for you to have your own space again. Especially now that you are seeing someone.' Mum winks.

'Well he certainly seems to make you happy, that's the main thing,' says Dad. 'I haven't seen you smile so much as in these last couple of days.'

'Thanks, Dad. Oh and would you like to take some food?' I offer. 'I have plenty in the freezer.'

'No, love, we will be fine.' Mum smiles. 'We will go shopping tomorrow, but tonight it's a takeaway, I think. A healthy one,' Mum tells Dad as his eyes widen in surprise.

I had a call earlier to say my minor surgery is scheduled for the middle of January. I run my finger over the slight bump on my left cheek and think of how I was tempted not to bother getting it checked, with it being quite small. It was Gemma who persuaded me, and I'm thankful she did, after the doctor telling me it could silently spread and cause nerve damage beneath the skin if it isn't removed.

I'm so grateful to have people around me who watch out for me. And hopefully there will be someone else who might stick around for a while too.

I sleep well, and I am woken by the sound of a knocking at the front door. I rub my eyes and glance at the clock. It's a little after eight, so I must have turned my alarm off and gone back to sleep.

I'm wrapping my dressing down around me, running downstairs to answer the front door, and when I open it, I can barely believe my eyes.

Silently overnight, a heavy snow has fallen and blanketed the ground. My car is covered in snow too. Kian is standing in front of me with Bella, and carrying a large spade.

'I thought you might need a path digging.' He smiles. 'And I brought Bella to build a snowman in your garden, if you don't mind that is.'

'Oh my goodness! I hadn't even realised it had snowed overnight,' I gasp, taking in the sight of the white front garden.

'It will give you a good excuse for being late for work,' says Kian, glancing at his watch and smiling.

'I cannot be late,' I say firmly. 'And, of course, Bella, have fun building a snowman.' I smile.

'The downside of an apartment is having no garden,' Kian says with a shrug. 'But we will be going sledging later.'

'Really? I almost wish I wasn't due in work now.'

Inside, I shower and dress at lightning speed, before stepping outside, where Kian has already almost cleared the footpath.

'I think it might be quicker if I take you to work in my car,' says Kian, pointing to mine that is covered in snow.

'Good idea.'

'And we will get a hot chocolate in town,' he tells Bella. 'Can we come back and finish the snowman though?'

'Of course you can.' I smile. 'I look forward to seeing it.'

THIRTY-NINE

'What are your plans for New Year's Eve then?' asks Gemma during a rare lull in sales. 'I imagine they include Kian.' She smiles.

'Do you know we haven't actually discussed it, but I hope so, yes. I was kind of just going to go with the flow.'

Gemma had told me that Mike had invited her to a family party, but she wasn't sure she was ready for that and would have preferred the pub.

'And I didn't know what your plans were, but I imagined you would be spending it with Kian.'

I think back to last year, when Mum went to a party hosted by one of her friends from the food bank and Dad and Rose spent it together quietly, and I wonder if things were strained between them then? Gemma and I went to the local pub and danced the night away. Some of the staff from Bentham's were there, and we all had a ball. A handsome guy who worked in the men's clothing department took a bit of a shine to me and asked me out. I let him down gently, as I wasn't ready for any sort of relationship at the time, although I do remember we shared a rather nice kiss at midnight.

'Actually,' I say, after I have finished serving a young woman with a dress, 'I might have a party. You know, just a small gathering. Mum and Dad, Audrey if she is free, and one or two neighbours. Obviously, you and Mike if it doesn't sound too tame as I know you prefer the pub on New Year's Eve.'

'Honestly? Normally yes, but I have heard they are not even having a band this year.' She pulls a face. 'And it takes ages to get served at the bar. Of course I will come to your party! Maybe you could invite Sue and Barry too, Sue is such a laugh.'

'That's a great idea.'

I also need to ask Kian what his plans are.

'I must say I'm shocked,' says Gemma, spraying herself with some perfume. 'You thinking of having a party, the day before New Year's Eve, without weeks of careful planning,' she teases.

'It's hardly a party, more of small gathering.' I laugh. 'But I take your point. Anyway, I'll see what people are up to first, it's a bit short notice so they have probably already made plans.'

That night, Kian collects me from work and when I stroll up my path I'm greeted by an impressive-looking snowman in the garden wearing a flat cap and scarf, and with a smiling mouth that has been made from dark pebbles.

'I love him.' I smile. 'I hope the snow doesn't thaw too quickly.'

'Bella had a lovely time building him, before we went sledging. She's at my mum's now, as I had a meeting with a client this afternoon.'

'It must be tricky juggling work with childcare whilst Sally is away,' I say, turning the key in the front door.

'I had plenty of notice, so I blocked out my diary quite a bit over Christmas,' he says. 'I'll be making up for it in the new year though.'

'Talking of the new year, do you have any plans for New Year's Eve?' I ask as I unwind a scarf from my neck.

'Well, I was hoping they would definitely include you,' he says, snaking his arms around my waist and pulling me to him.

'Pleased to hear it. I was thinking of having a little gathering here,' I tell him.

'Sounds wonderful,' he says, kissing my neck, and making me forget what I am about to say next.

'So I was thinking,' I say, gently pushing him away. 'I ought to make a few phone calls. Only a small party, including my parents. What do you think?'

'I think it sounds lovely.' He smiles. 'But I have Bella New Year's Eve. Mum and Dad are going to a party at Dad's golf club.'

I vaguely remember Sue telling me that her and Barry were having their granddaughter over on New Year's Eve this year, so I decide to give her a call first.

'Hold that thought,' I tell him, retrieving my phone from my bag, and running upstairs to change, instructing Kian to pop the kettle on.

Five minutes later, I join him in the lounge where there are mugs of tea on the coffee table.

'So, what are you up to?' he asks.

'It looks like the party is on.' I smile. 'Mum and Dad are thrilled, as is Audrey, who asked if her mum could come too, and of course Gemma and Mike will come,' I say excitedly. 'And the best news is Sue and Barry are going to bring their granddaughter, who it turns out is the same age as Bella. She said she will bring her Barbie Dreamhouse, so they can play together.'

'That's wonderful.' Kian is smiling at me, and slowly shaking his head.

'What?'

'You're amazing,' he says. 'You think of everything.'

'I'm just practical.' I shrug.

'You're more than that. You're kind and thoughtful. Not to mention beautiful.'

There are no more words then as he kisses me.

FORTY

The house looks beautiful, strung with fairy lights across the windows and a thick holly wreath adorns the fireplace, dotted with chunky cream and red candles.

Bentham's food hall provided the finest of nibbles which are laid out on the kitchen table, and I have a chilli simmering away in my giant slow cooker. I have also baked my popular red velvet cake, along with cupcakes, and stocked up on soft drinks for the children.

I am pouring some crisps into a bowl, when the doorbell rings and it's Bella and Kian.

'Oh wow. Just look at you. You look beautiful,' I say to Bella, who is wearing a pretty silky blue dress, with a tutu-style skirt. 'And you don't scrub up too badly either.' I turn to Kian, who looks gorgeous in a light-grey suit and dark shirt, without a tie.

'Thanks,' he says, handing me a bottle of champagne. 'And it goes without saying that you look amazing.' He kisses me on the cheek. 'The scarf really suits you, I knew it would.'

I'm wearing a sleeveless black dress, the beautiful red scarf setting it off perfectly.

A couple of minutes later, Sue and Barry arrive with their

granddaughter. When the little girl takes her coat off, she and Bella burst out laughing as they are wearing exactly the same dress.

'Do you want to play Barbie?' asks Chloe and Bella's eyes light up when Barry, having nipped to the car, returns with an enormous Barbie house that he places in the corner of the room close to the Christmas tree.

'They would be mortified about wearing the same dress to a party if they were ten years older,' Sue says laughing as she accepts a glass of white wine from me, whilst Kian is in the kitchen, finding Barry a beer. 'And thanks for asking us over.' She smiles. 'Much as we love having Chloe, I'm sure she would much rather be playing with someone her own age on New Year's Eve, than us pretending to be interested in all things Barbie and Disney.' She laughs again. 'Although we have been building a snowman in the garden. Well, when I say we, I mean Barry mainly. I think he might have nodded off in the chair about nine o'clock if we had stayed home.'

An hour later, all of the guests have arrived, and introductions are made, although most people know each other, apart from a new couple who have not long moved in across the road, and were delighted to be asked over. We chat so easily to them that I think they could become good friends.

I'm delighted Audrey's mum agreed to accompany her here tonight, and Audrey tells me she has been getting out and about a little more.

'I think the Christmas party really gave her a confidence boost,' she tells me when we are in the kitchen eating a bowl of chilli.

'I'm pleased to hear it. Sometimes people just need that little bit of encouragement.'

Gemma and Mike arrive just after nine having been to the pub for an hour and Gemma immediately gets the party in full swing with some upbeat music. We laugh as Gemma and Sue start dancing in the lounge and are joined by Barry, who does some dad dancing, which mainly involves pointing at things, and has us all laughing.

'I'm not sure the girls will make it to midnight,' says Sue a little after ten thirty. She glances at Chloe, who has started yawning. 'She's done well to stay awake this long. Perhaps we ought to get going shortly,' she tells Barry.

'I could drop you off if you like,' says Dad, who has only had a couple of alcohol-free beers. 'We will be making a move soon ourselves. Sorry if we didn't make it until midnight, love.' He turns to me. 'But you can do that with the young ones, if you don't mind us leaving shortly.'

'Of course I don't mind. I'm just thrilled you came. Mum is only just getting on her feet after all. I'll call you tomorrow.'

I wish them an early happy new year, as I escort them to the door.

With not long to go before midnight, Eileen knocks on the door, brandishing a bottle of rosé.

'Eileen! You made it before midnight.' I usher her inside.

'I did.' She waves the bottle. 'But only because I had a long nap this afternoon.' She winks. 'Gerald took me out for an early dinner, but he's home now and probably well away.' She laughs.

It's nice to see Eileen dating, although she tells me she will never give up her independence and live with anyone again.

Audrey's mum looks delighted when she spots Eileen and quickly engages her in chat over a glass of something.

Bella is tucked up in bed in the guest room, as Kian will be staying over tonight. She pleaded to stay up until New Year, but after Chloe left, Kian found her on the sofa in the kitchen sleeping soundly, and gently carried her upstairs.

'You have such a lovely home,' says Eileen kindly. 'And it's wonderful to see it filled with so many people.'

'Do you know, you are right,' I tell her. 'Maybe my New Year's resolution ought to be to have more parties.'

Her comment makes me realise that you have to reach out to people if you want them in your life. And I am lucky enough to know a lot of wonderful people.

With several minutes until midnight, I tell everyone to make sure they have a glass as we make our way outside to the garden.

Kian had popped out earlier and got the fire pit started, and the fence is threaded with lights.

'Ooh isn't this lovely,' exclaim our new neighbours, taking in the garden with its wooden pagoda and water feature and winter shrubs that are dotted about in glazed pots. They tell me they were thinking of doing something similar with theirs, and that they will invite us to a BBQ in the warmer weather.

'That would be lovely,' I say, thankful for the possibility of making new friends in the street who are around my age.

'I've had a wonderful evening,' says Audrey's mum. 'Thank you so much for inviting us, but we should probably try and get a taxi shortly.'

'I don't think there will be much chance of that, without having pre-booked one,' Eileen says with a frown. 'I tell you what, stay at mine if you like, we can have a good chat in the morning. And you, of course, Audrey.'

'We couldn't possibly impose,' says Audrey, looking doubtful.

'You wouldn't be,' says Eileen kindly. 'I have the room. You will be waiting hours for a taxi, trust me.'

I make certain everyone's drink is refreshed, as at almost midnight Kian leads a countdown.

On the dot of midnight, fountains of colour appear above, every whoosh turning the sky into a sea of pink, silver and green. Kian pops the cork on a bottle of champagne, and offers it around.

There is a chorus of 'Happy New Year', and soon enough everyone is hugging, and wishing each other well for the forthcoming year. Kian and I share a long kiss beneath the pergola and I feel happier than I have in a long time.

What a difference a year makes, I think to myself as I glance up into the sky, Kian standing beside me, his hand in mine. I know there are a few things to overcome in the new year, but with Kian by my side, I feel like I can face anything.

As we make our way inside, Gemma threads her arm through mine. 'I'm glad things seem to be working out with Kian, you deserve to be happy,' she whispers.

'So do you, my friend. And Mike seems lovely.'

'He is. A little too keen maybe, but we shall see. I'm heading to Wales next month, so maybe that will clarify things. I agree he is lovely though.'

'Maybe tell him sooner rather than later then, if he isn't the one,' I advise her.

'Of course.' She nods. 'I would never hurt him.'

'I know you wouldn't.'

A rocket shoots into the sky then, followed by a cascade of silver stars. I have come to realise that we don't know in which direction life will take us, but we owe it to ourselves to explore every possibility. After all, life is a glorious gift.

EPILOGUE

It's late January and I'm sitting at home reading a book, with a surgical plaster across my face. Thankfully, the surgery wasn't too invasive, and the incision was quite small. I may have a faint scar, but as Gemma pointed out, Bentham's has the best make-up foundation money can buy.

I have taken a couple of days off work, and Mum has just returned from the kitchen, after making me a cup of tea.

Kian has been wonderful too, but is busy at work with back-to-back appointments as he told me he would be.

'You don't need to fuss, Mum, I'm fine really. I haven't had major surgery like Dad,' I tell her, looking up from my book. 'I'm not ill.'

'I know that, but I don't mind popping in, now that your dad is up and about. You did enough fussing over both of us when we were laid up as I recall.' She smiles.

Thankfully, Dad came through his operation okay, and is feeling the benefit of his surgery, saying he is already feeling less breathless. I think he has rather enjoyed having me and Mum fussing over him.

'Anyway. I will be off now. It's cookery afternoon at the

food bank. We are making soup today,' she tells me as she pulls on her coat.

'Sounds good, especially in this weather.'

The snow has long gone but there is a bitter chill outside.

'I'll save you some if you like. Anyway, see you later at the concert.'

'See you later. Bye, Mum.'

At six thirty we will be attending a concert at the local primary school, where some of the children will be showing off their recorder skills.

Most of the pensioners from the party will be attending, and just as on the day of the party, Sue and I will collect those who cannot make their own way there.

Gemma went to Wales last weekend, and bumped into her cousin's friend in the local pub. With his new girlfriend. Luckily, she had already decided that Mike was the one, having missed him terribly over the weekend.

Taking my seat next to Eileen at the school concert, I glance around at the packed-out hall, and feel a warm glow inside.

The evening is a roaring success, and Elsie has a tear in her eye when black-haired Robbie plays a solo piece on the recorder. When she catches his eye after he has finished to thunderous applause, he gives her a wave.

'Aren't children a joy,' Eileen says over cake and coffee in the school hall later.

'Oh, they are,' says a smiling Elsie, who seems far more cheerful than I remember. 'And the good news is the head-teacher told me they are going to do a concert once a month. She said it pulls the community together.'

'I couldn't agree more.' I smile as she goes off to chat to someone else.

'Pub?' asks Gemma, linking her arm through mine as we file out of the school hall.

'With this on my face.' I point to the giant plaster. 'The school hall is one thing, but the pub is different.'

'Fair enough. I have gin at my place?'

'Lead the way,' I say as a text pings through on my phone from Kian. I tell him I am heading to Gemma's and he says he will collect me later on after his last meeting around nine thirty if I like.

I tell him that would be great, before linking arms with my best friend and truly counting my blessings.

A LETTER FROM SUE ROBERTS

Dear reader,

I want to say a huge thank you for choosing to read *The Village Christmas Party*. If you did enjoy it, and want to keep up to date with all my latest releases, just sign up at the following link. Your email address will never be shared and you can unsubscribe at any time.

www.bookouture.com/sue-roberts

I hope you loved *The Village Christmas Party*, and if you did I would be very grateful if you could write a review. I'd love to hear what you think, and it makes such a difference helping new readers to discover one of my books for the first time. Positive reviews really can influence readers when choosing a book!

I love hearing from my readers – you can get in touch through social media.

Thanks,

Sue Roberts

facebook.com/Suerobertsauthor
x.com/SueRobertsautho

ACKNOWLEDGEMENTS

I would like to thank every single one of you, for choosing to buy this book. I do hope you have enjoyed it!

Christmas has always been a favourite time of year for me.

Perhaps it is because I dislike the dark evenings of winter, and the twinkling lights from trees and festive decorations just seems to cheer everything up! And then of course, there is the day itself. I love to spend it with family, and count my blessings to have such lovely people in my life.

A huge thanks, as ever, to my wonderful editor Natalie Edwards, and all the Bookouture staff that have had involvement in this book. It goes without saying, that I appreciate every single one of you, from the editors, the publicity team and design staff behind the scenes.

Finally, a huge shout out to all of you book bloggers and reviewers. It really is a good feeling when you have enjoyed my books, and shout about them to other people. I thank you all so much.

PUBLISHING TEAM

Turning a manuscript into a book requires the efforts of many people. The publishing team at Bookouture would like to acknowledge everyone who contributed to this publication.

Commercial
Lauren Morrissette
Hannah Richmond
Imogen Allport

Cover design
Debbie Clement

Data and analysis
Mark Alder
Mohamed Bussuri

Editorial
Natalie Edwards
Charlotte Hegley

Copyeditor
Jane Eastgate

Proofreader
Becca Allen

Printed in Great Britain
by Amazon

51465610R00144